Million Dollar Baby

ecce

An Imprint of HarperCollins*Publishers*

Million Dollar Baby

Stories from the Corner

F. X. Toole

Previously published as *Rope Burns*

HarperCollins books may be purchased for educational, business, or
sales promotional use. For information please write: Special Markets
Department, HarperCollins Publishers Inc., 10 East 53rd Street, New
York, NY 10022.

Designed by Cassandra J. Pappas

The Library of Congress Cataloging-in-Publication Data has been
applied for.

ISBN 0-06-084657-7

For God, the Eternal Father,

and for Dub Huntley, my daddy in boxing

And with special thanks to

Howard Junker of ZYZZYVA,

the first to give me a Shot

Boxing is for men, and is about men, and *is* men. A celebration of the lost religion of masculinity all the more trenchant for being lost.

—Joyce Carol Oates
On Boxing

Contents

Million Dollar Baby

Member of the Fancy:
An Introduction

In my mid and late forties I came to boxing by choice and by chance. But I had already been there as far back as the mid thirties. I huddled with my father in front of the radio and listened eagerly to the driving voices of ring announcers like Bill Stern and Clem McCarthy as they covered the great fights of the time. Weeks later, at ten-cent matinees, I would watch grainy newsreels of the same fights. Watched in 1939 as "Two Ton" Tony Galento knocked down "the Brown Bomber," Joe Louis.

Madison Square Garden would become Camelot for me. I saw Bobo Olson fight Paddy Young there in a middleweight elimination bout in June '53. But I saw the Garden for the first time in 1952. Eighth Avenue between Forty-ninth and Fiftieth, slinky-eyed fight guys standing out front. Greek restaurants, Irish bars, four-dollar whores. The Garden was home to me as much as Shubert Alley.

My father was an ardent fight fan, and I adored him for making me a part of something he loved. Like many another Mick and Paddy who came over as indentured slaves in the bottom of boats, who saw 30 percent of their own dumped dead at sea, he took heart from stories of the great Irish fighters. Sullivan and Corbett. Tunney and "the Toy Bulldog," Mickey Walker, who fought in every division from welterweight at 147 to heavyweight. We listened to Don Dunphy give the blow-by-blow description of the Louis-Conn fight.

I remained a fight fan through the years because I was as fascinated with the science and the art of boxing as I was with the men who dared to put every ounce of body and soul on the line. I was as taken with the losers of boxing as I was with the champions, because they had risked every bit as much as the winners.

But what did the "manly art of self-defense" actually *mean*? What made it *possible*?

What intrigued me most on the physical side of fighting was how boxers could fight round after round, do it again and again, fight after fight. Taking a horn in bullfighting is always a possibility, even an inevitability, but many more times than not a bullfighter leaves the ring unmarked. But a boxer getting ready for a fight takes punches daily, and then the punches increase with murderous intensity during the fight. *Hit and don't get hit*, that is basic to boxing. But all fighters get hit, even the best ones. So what kind of men were these who could take that kind of punishment long enough to become contenders, much less champions?

And what was it, and how much exactly did it take, before some kid with a dream of glory could learn enough to climb between the ropes? And how hard is it, not only to train and to fight, but to learn the science of the game, the actual mechanics of throwing punches—throwing them again and again?

Damn hard. And underneath it all is the question *What makes a fighter?*

In my mid forties I decided to learn. I did my best for a year or so in a bust-out gym in Ocean Park, California. I didn't learn much because I didn't have a trainer, but I did manage to get my nose broken another time—because I was sparring with dummies like myself. A pro would have played with me, because pros know when it's time to "work" and when it's time to fight.

It was about that time that I had to quit my boxing education to pursue family issues. But a couple of years later I was back at it. That's when the magic of boxing caught up to me and saved my life.

I went to a gym that's a parking lot now. Gym guys spot a beginner in a New York minute. After I'd been working out a few weeks, I had reason to show up in the gym dressed well. Harris tweed jacket and tie, flannel pants, that sort of thing, a splash of paisley in my coat pocket. All sorts were in the gym, from bantam to heavyweights, black and Hispanic, but I was the only white boy—white boy is what whites are most often referred to in fight gyms, whites being in the minority. You never hear blacks, old or young, referred to as black boys—although you will hear that a black fighter was robbed of the fight because of his paint job.

After I had finished my workout, I waited at the desk to speak with the gym manager. As I stood there, a middle-aged black trainer I'd noticed in the gym came up next to me. I thought he was waiting for the manager, too. His heavyweight watched on the far side of the desk. But instead of speaking with the manager, the trainer whispered to me and held out a Buck 110 jackknife with brass fittings and a bone handle. It's the kind of knife you can shove through a car door or use to field-dress a deer. He eyeballed me like a pimp and said, "You ever see one of these?"

I looked at the knife. I reached calmly into my back pocket. I came out with my own Buck 110. Since he hadn't opened his knife, I didn't open mine, but I could have with the fingers of one hand. I held the Buck in my palm the way he held his.

I said, "You mean a knife like this?"

The trainer jumped back—*whup!*—and his heavyweight went down on his knees laughing. He stayed there as the trainer sailed out the door with his head down. The heavyweight staggered behind him, hardly able to breathe. A few people saw it. But I didn't have any more trouble because fight gyms are calm places, places of peace, despite the machine-gun racket of speed bags and the slap of leather jump ropes on hard wood floors; despite the sound of leather gloves thumping into rib cages; despite the fact that big bags would be hanging corpses if the punches they took were delivered to living flesh and bone.

Shake hands with a fighter someday. You'll see how soft his hands are from being steamed in gauze and leather and sweat, how small his hands are compared with other athletes the same size, and how his handshake is as gentle as a nun's. Many have high voices—Jack Dempsey as a young man did. Many have cartoon-character lisps. Larry Holmes does, as does Mike Tyson, who also has the high voice.

So there I was, didn't know squat from boxing. Was slapping rather than punching, on my heels instead of toes, sticky instead of slick. But I sparred with eighteen- and twenty-year-old beginners anyhow. Had teeth cracked and inlays fall out. I got hit more than I should have, because without my glasses I couldn't see the shots coming, but I did okay for an old man. The spell was cast. I would subsequently have to stop sparring because I had to wear braces to correct a jaw condition, one unrelated to boxing. But by then I was in.

I had also hooked up with a first-class trainer, Dub Huntley, the guy who would become my partner. I had gone to him to train me after three months or so, because I saw the results he got. I offered to pay him up front, but he refused. Instead, he put it on me like he was training Marciano. He'd take me through the usual four 3-minute rounds on the punch mitts, which would leave me gasping, my left shoulder hanging dead from throwing close to a hundred jabs a round. I'd lose four pounds from the workout. But sometimes he'd work me three rounds, then take me straight through the one-minute rest period between rounds three and four. And then we'd go right on into and through the next three minutes of round four. That's seven minutes, nonstop.

Jab, jab, double up. Jab. Do it again. Jab. Two of them. One-two. One-two-hook. Do it again. Two jabs, right-hand, hook, come back with a right-hand. Two jabs, right-hand, hook, come back with a right-hand, and jab out of there. Hook to the body, hook to the head, come back with a right-hand. Move. Double up. Do it again. Jab. Jab. Jab. Do it again. Double up. Do it again. Do it again. Do it.

I thought I would die. We're talking about an old man here, one with white hair who had been into the sauce for twenty-five years, someone whose drug of choice at three in the morning was female companionship till dawn.

But gym guys would stop and stare. Tourists would take photos. Pros stopped what they were doing to watch. One day, wearing one of his famous caps, the great former light-heavyweight champion Archie Moore, "the Mongoose," stood ringside, his elbows on the ring apron.

At the bell, Archie said, "Looks like I'm gonna have to make a comeback."

I knew my trainer thought I'd fade that first day, that I'd go away. But I didn't go away. I stuck and so did he. And as I began to get into shape—four rounds of warm-up and shadowboxing, four rounds on the punch mitts, four rounds on the big bag, four rounds on the speed bag, four rounds on the jump rope, and enough sit-ups to shame a contender—I began to learn and to understand what had drawn me to boxing as a boy. It was the *science* of fighting, and the *heart* it takes to be a fighter. Boxing was an exercise of the mind. I also began to realize that despite my age, I was someone who could play the game. I was spellbound. I still am. God has blessed me with the sweet science, and with three children who love me.

In 1988, without prior symptoms or warning, my arteries began to close despite the great shape I was in. I had a heart attack, and then I had angioplasty three times in six months because the arteries kept closing down. During the last angioplasty, my cardiologist said, "The faster we run, the farther we get behind. Operation is tomorrow morning." No alternative, no problem. Once they'd hopped me up the following morning, I started singing songs in Spanish. The Mexicans pushing my gurney sang along with me.

Open-heart surgery ain't no walk in the park. But three months after a triple bypass and the complications of what is called an ileus, my memory half shot from morphine and the other junk they pumped into me, I was back in the gym jumping rope. Only a minute at first, but then three minutes. And then three rounds. I couldn't do four, because I never regained the conditioning I had before surgery, and because I have pain in one foot that apparently resulted from their taking a vein in my leg to rewire my heart. So there I was, doing the same workout I'd done before but only three rounds instead of four. Except that by then I had already been training fighters, working corners, bringing my own magic, and stopping blood. In fact, the morning after one of the angioplasties, I drove to Del Mar and hung out all day at the fair so I could work a title fight that night.

I started in the amateurs, took nights off from my job so I could work three-rounders in VFW halls, recreation centers, and the back rooms of spaghetti joints. Then four-rounders, and ten, and traveling around the world to work twelve-round title fights. I've worked seven title fights of one kind or another, and I've been licensed in ten states—from Hawaii to New York, from Missouri to Florida. There are plenty of guys who have done much more in boxing than I, but there are many who've done less. And I've fought in Mexico, France, Germany, and South Africa—where, in Cape Town, by the way, they produce a champion Cabernet Sauvignon, Fleur de Cap, that will do wonders for your spirit.

About the only thing I haven't done in boxing is make money. It's the same for most fight guys. But that hasn't stopped me any more than not making money in writing has. Both are something you just do, and you feel grateful for being able to do them, even if both keep you broke, drive you crazy, and make you sick. Rational people don't think like that. But they don't have in their lives what I have in mine. Magic. The magic of going to wars I believe in. And the magic of boxing humor, the joke almost always on the teller, that marches with you every step of the way.

There's no magic in street fighting. Street fighting may be lethal, especially when one guy is bigger and stronger than the other. But boxing is designed to be lethal, designed to test lethally the male will of both fighters, designed to see who's boss, who will stake out and control the magic territory of a square piece of enchanted canvas.

The magic of the fighter is also part of the mix, the magic that attracts people from around the world to him, the magic of seeing him play Cowboys and Indians for real. The prettier the fighter—and I'm not talking pretty as in girlie-boy movie-star pretty—the harder that fighter has worked. The prettier the fighter is, the more money he'll make, too. But what you must understand is that fighting and boxing are as different from each other as hitting is from punching, as different as a wild dog from a Chihuahua. By definition, boxing and punching are lethal. So being able to box pretty and be lethal—that makes the magic that drives the whole world wild.

Ring magic is different from the magic of the theater, because the curtain never comes down—because the blood in the ring is real blood, and the broken noses and the broken hearts are real, and sometimes they are broken forever. Boxing is the magic of men in combat, the magic of will, and skill, and pain, and the risking of everything so you can respect yourself for the rest of your life. Almost sounds like writing.

Real magic, the real McCoy, imagine! To be a part of that! Whether in the gym or during a title fight. Or standing beside the canals of Picardy at five in the misty morning while your fighter is doing roadwork. It's magic to hear frogs plop into the water as your fighter jogs by, to smell apples in the air. And it's magic to see your fighter stretch himself on the rack of his lungs and legs, his goal to take his opponent's heart as mercilessly as an Aztec priest, to leave him blinking up into the lights with his will so shattered he will take the pieces to bed with him every night for the rest of his life.

It's magic to hear your boxer gagging in the dressing room after losing a title fight. It's magic because your fighter had sweated himself dry and he's drinking fluids for maybe an hour, and he's waiting for his kidneys to kick in so he can pass his piss test, because if he pisses drugs, he doesn't get paid. It's magic because this same guy had the fight won, except he tried to trade punches with a puncher he'd nearly knocked out—magic because in the split second of that mental error he got himself flattened, like Billy Conn did, but this time with an uppercut that traveled no longer than half the distance from wrist to elbow. And it's magic because his life will never be the same, magic because he would have been champion of the world, and now he will never be. This is the magic of winning and losing in a man's game, where men will battle with their minds and bodies and hearts into and beyond exhaustion, past their second wind, through cracked ribs and swollen livers, ruptured kidneys and detached retinas. They do it for the money, to be sure. But they do it for respect and for the magic, too.

And it is magic of the mind as well, because each thing they do with their whole heart and soul takes them to a new level of understanding. The higher they climb, the wider the horizon, and they begin to see and understand combinations they never dreamed of. Like the writer, the more the fighter knows of his game, the greater the magic for him and for us.

And then there's magic of stopping blood that maybe another cut man couldn't, the magic of maybe using stuff you shouldn't use, but you keep your guy in the fight so both of you can go home winners. But it's also magic to see a fight you're winning end in the time it takes to blink, when a left hook cranks your boy's jaw into the second balcony. Even though you've lost and your guts are churning, it's still magic. And to be robbed, whether in the ring or with a gun while you are tending bar, even that's magic—magic because it's all real, every bit of it, and it's happening now and lasting forever in your mind and heart. And it's magic because it's a war you'll go back to every chance you get. And I'm still looking for the gentleman who pulled that Magnum on me, who made my heart hit the roof of my mouth, who showed me disrespect. Prior to that experience, I wasn't sure if I could kill another human being. I know now.

Respect is part of the magic of boxing. Most outside the fight game expect the victors to denigrate the vanquished. That would destroy the magic. Ali was yappy before, during, and after a fight, but we always knew he was playing the fool, was a pup so full of life that he had to yip and yap, prance and dance. There are imitators, to be sure, but there's no fun to what they do.

But even if one fighter thinks he was robbed, and regardless of the trash talked before the fight, fighters will with few exceptions congratulate each other afterward, will say *Good fight* at the very least. There is a kinship between winner and loser that outsiders don't understand because boxing, after all is said and done, is about respect. When a fighter doesn't get respect, say when he's a ham-'n'-egger and someone says, "Get a job!" his skin turns to flypaper and dreadful things stick to him all the way to his grave.

Remember the humility of Mike Tyson at the press conference after his loss in the first fight with Holyfield? How he wanted to *touch* Holyfield, how Holyfield smiled and allowed him to shake his hand? When a fighter gets his ass whipped in a round, you don't tell him to go beat up the son of a bitch that did it to him. You tell him to go out and get respect. Besides, it's a small family. The members of it—the members of the fancy—need each other, not only for the money, but they need each other so they can, ultimately, test themselves against themselves.

And there's the magic that breaks your heart. You've got a kid with a bloody nose. If it's broken, forget it, it's going to keep bleeding. But just a bloody nose you can usually stop. So you wipe the boy's face clean, shove a swab soggy with adrenaline into the nostril that's bleeding. You work the swab around, and you close the other nostril with your thumb. You tell the boy to inhale, so the adrenaline will flood the broken tissue and constrict the vein and widen the blow hole. But the boy doesn't inhale. You say, "*Inhale!*" Nothing. You say it again, "*Goddamn it!*" Time is running out, and then you see the boy looking at you like you've been speaking Gaelic or Hebrew. So then you understand, and you say, "*Breathe in!*"

He breathes in through the adrenaline while you put pressure above his upper lip. The adrenaline gets to the tear, and the blood stops coming, and he's ready to fight again. Blood is pumping in your neck because you almost didn't stop the blood. But part of you has traveled to the place where the boy lives, to the place where no one uses words like *inhale*. That's magic, too, but it's the kind that hurts you, the kind that makes you better for hurting.

Today in the U.S., for the most part, the white boys of boxing are gone, though the percentage of white fighters who fight well is quite high. In fact it surprises me that more midsized white athletes don't come into the game.

White trainers, with some exceptions, are faded memories as well. Angelo Dundee, of course, still hangs with the big kids, as do a few others. My situation is unusual: 95 percent of my friends and associates are of a different color than I. I recently gave a rubdown to a 240-pound Ugandan who speaks English, Swahili, and Japanese. By the time I spread extra-virgin olive oil over him and then worked wintergreen liniment into him, he was black and shiny as a berry. He has a temperament sweet as a berry, as well. He's a polite and gentle Catholic boy—outside the ring. He lives and fights out of Japan. His regular trainer is Hawaiian Japanese.

Several years ago I was working with another heavyweight, was giving him a rubdown. He was a rubdown whore, wanted one every day. Said his wife gave good rubdowns, among other things, but hers couldn't compare with mine. Always had some little pain or pull. But he was a good guy with heart, so it was worth it. He was berry-black as well. His problem as a pro was that he only wanted one big fight so he could buy a house. He went sour along the way because he never had the drive that would take him through the pain of boxing, both in and outside the ring. He never got that house. If he had aimed for the title, even if he never won it, he would have had several houses.

Anyway, there I was, sweating my ass off on the guy, and about half looped from the alcohol fumes. It takes forty-five minutes to work the tissue in a heavyweight. Into the gym came a recently paroled featherweight two days on the street, broke and hungry and begging quarters, who had fallen in love with "that shit." He was high on it and talking about how he was framed by the muhfuh white-racist power structure, that he had been a victim of the boot of white oppression, that the pig was out to get the brothers, that white was shit. What he left out was that he had been convicted of robbing, beating, and raping a crack-head street whore from South Central.

So there he was, going on about pigs. I should mention that my heavyweight had a white wife. When he asked the featherweight if he couldn't see that I was white, and that maybe he should watch his jive-ass mouth, the featherweight didn't miss a beat.

"Yeah, I see he white, but Toole be different."

Magic. It's why I'm in it. For the voodoo.

The Monkey Look

I stop blood.

I stop it between rounds for fighters so they can stay in the fight.

Blood ruins some boys. It was that way with Sonny Liston, God rest his soul. Bad as he was, he'd see his own blood and fall apart.

I'm not the one who decides when to stop the fight, and I don't stitch up cuts once the fight's over. And it's not my job to hospitalize a boy for brain damage. My job is to stop blood so the fighter can see enough to keep on fighting. I do that, maybe I save a boy's title. I do that one little thing, and I'm worth every cent they pay me. I stop the blood and save the fight, the boy loves me more than he loves his daddy.

But you can't always stop it. Fight guys know this. If the cut's too deep or wide, or maybe you got a severed vein down in there, the blood keeps coming. Sometimes it takes two or three rounds to stop the blood, maybe more—the boy's heart is pumping so hard, or he cuts more. Once you get the coagulant in there, sometimes it takes another shot from the opponent right on the cut itself to drive the blood far enough from the area so the stuff you're using can start to work. What I'm saying is there are all kinds of combinations you come up against down in the different layers of meat. When a good cut man stays ahead of the combinations, he can stop most cuts, but not every one.

Fights can be stopped for a lot of reasons. A football eye swollen shut can stop a fight. But fights aren't stopped just because a fighter is cut. It's where he's cut. Below the eye, or alongside it, that won't usually stop a fight. Neither will a cut if it's in or above the eyebrow, or up in the forehead, or in the scalp. Broken nose? Sometimes yes, sometimes no. A cut in the eyelid, because of possible damage to the eyeball and the threat of blindness, that can stop a fight quick. So will blood pumping down into a boy's eyes. Blood can blind a fighter, maybe cost him the fight, or worse, because when he can't see he starts taking shots he wouldn't otherwise take, and now he ends up on his ass blinking through the lights and shadows of future memories.

Boy gets cut, I always crack the seal of a new, one-ounce bottle of adrenaline chloride solution 1:1000. When it's fresh, it's clear like water but has a strong chemical smell. The outdated stuff turns a light pinkish color, or a pale piss-yellow. When that happens, it couldn't stop fly blood. I might pour adrenaline into a small plastic squeeze bottle if I need to use sterile gauze pads along with a swab, but I never use adrenaline from a previous fight. I dump it, even if three quarters of it is left. This way it can't carry blood over from another fight, and none of my boys can get AIDS from contaminated coagulant. I'd give AIDS to myself before I'd give it to one of my boys.

Trainers and managers and fighters call me. They know me from when I used to train fighters. But I got too old and was walking around with my back and neck crippled up all the time from catching punches with the punch mitts. Boxing is a game of half steps and quarter inches, a game where old men belong as much as the young. Without us, there couldn't be fights. Fans think boxing is about being tough. For members of the fancy, the fight game is about getting respect.

My first fight working the corner of Hoolie Garza came after his trainer talked to me, Ike Goody. Ike was a club fighter in the fifties, but like most first-rate trainers, he was never a champ. With the exception of Floyd Patterson, I don't remember another champ who ever made a champion. Hoolie Garza is a twenty-six-pounder, a smart featherweight Mexican boy who thinks he's smarter than he is. He was born in Guaymas, a port on the Gulf of California inside Baja. He was raised illegal in East Los Angeles, where he fought with his big brothers for food. His real name is Julio César Garza, but as a kid he was nicknamed Juli—in Spanish it's pronounced "*hoo*lie." Juli was Americanized to Hoolie, the way Miguel, or Michael, is sometimes Americanized into Maikito.

After the Korean War, I went to school in Mexico City on the G.I. Bill. I wanted to learn Spanish, maybe teach it. So I hung around with Mexicans rather than other Americans. Some of my friends were bullfighters. I had a fling with the daughter of the secretary to the president of Mexico, a natural blonde who drove a car with license-plate number 32. She, God bless her, was one of the ways I learned Spanish on several levels and in different accents. I usually keep my Spanish to myself, like a lot of Latinos in the U.S. keep their English to themselves. But if they find out and ask about it, I tell them I was a student in Mexico and Spain both, and I say, "*Hablo el español sólo si me conviene*—I speak Spanish only when it's to my advantage." They always smile. Some laugh out loud and wag their finger. A lot of Latino fighters coming to fight in L.A. use me in their corner; some fly me to Vegas. I'm as loyal to them as I am to an American, or to an Irishman, which is why I never bet on a fight I'm working—not on the boy I'm working with, and not on the other fighter. This way, if I somehow screw up and cause my boy to lose, it can never be said that I did business.

Ike caught up with me at Bill Slayton's gym in South Central Los Angeles. "Hoolie's got a fight in Tijuana, Old Mexico. He wants you."

"What's he getting?"

"Short money. You know about his California suspension problem? The Mexicans know about it, too. A lousy twenty-five hundred dollars for ten rounds. It's with a tough TJ boy, Chango Pedroza. They want to make a name off us. It's Hoolie's third fight after his suspension. Two wins by kayo. Hoolie says he'll pay the regular two percent. I told him no good, you won't work ten rounds for that, but he kept after me, so I said I'd talk to you."

"He smoking dope again?"

Ike shrugged. "I know he's hurting for bread."

"I don't work that cheap, fifty lousy dollars tell him. Tell him to get someone from down there."

"He's a bleeder. That's why he wants you."

"It's a hundred fifty miles down there, Ike, so I go for a tank of gas, right? Now I don't get home until after four A.M. I don't work for fifty here in L.A., unless it's a four-rounder."

See, Ike had always told me the truth, always done square business with me, so I believed that Ike was telling me the truth about what Hoolie told him about the purse . . . but I knew some things about Hoolie, and who could tell what kind of truth he was telling Ike? Let me tell you, Hoolie was a hell of a fighter, a tough little bastard who'd meet you in the middle of the river and fight you. He had an underslung jaw and a hooked nose that pointed off at an angle. And scar tissue. At twenty-nine he was losing his hair, so he shaved his head. Tattoos from jail and from every country he'd fought in, roses and daggers, same old shit. Fought for a title his third fight out of the joint, where he did time for assault with a deadly weapon. Not his hands, he didn't want to hurt his hands, he pistol-whipped some guy who smiled at his wife. He almost won his title shot, but he got tired late, and the other guy came on in the tenth, eleventh, and twelfth. Hoolie, like always, was cut up, but the cuts didn't become a factor. After the title fight was over, Hoolie failed his piss test. They found traces of marijuana in his specimen and suspended him in California for a year, and held up his purse as well. It means Hoolie can't fight anywhere else in the States that counts because most state boxing commissions honor each other's ban.

But Hoolie was a good draw; promoters from all over wanted him because he was so tough and because of the blood. That's why Hoolie had to fight outside the States for short money—in Australia, in Latin America, in the Philippines, wherever there are little guys. And to stay busy, so he could be ready for his next shot at another belt.

So after Ike made three phone calls, I settled for a hundred. I took it because Ike was a longtime friend, and because it gave me an excuse to go down to a seafood restaurant there in TJ named La Costa, a place you can get some of the best *camarones rancheros* in the world—shrimp in a hot sauce with garlic, peppers, onions, tomatoes, and cilantro. Wash it down with a couple of Bohemias. For appetizers, they serve deep-fried freshwater smelt with fresh salsa and limes. I say an Act of Contrition every time I leave the place. Been going to La Costa thirty years.

I also took the fight because once the suspension is lifted, Hoolie's was sure to get another title fight. He uses me, I can make a little money. Ballpark, I get first cut of the purse, 2 percent. Some guys get more, some less. It's business. On a fifty-thousand-dollar fight, that means a thousand for me. But maybe my boy doesn't get cut at all, so I just sit ringside and watch. But I still get paid. Bigger fights, I try to get the same 2 percent if I can, or I charge a flat fee. But a four-round prelim boy, he needs a cut man same as a champ, right? So if I'm going to be at the arena with another boy anyway, and I like the prelim boy and his trainer, or maybe I feel sorry for a scared kid, a lot of times I don't charge—the prelim boy's only making four hundred bucks in the first place. Out of that, he's got to pay his trainer 10 percent off the top, and his manager another 33 ⅓. Ike doesn't charge his prelim boys.

But this is a game of money, right? So I got to be careful. I charge too little at the start, some boys won't respect me, and then they don't want to pay more when they make more. And some will stiff you, even after you save their careers.

Before I left Ike at Slayton's, I told him that the Tijuana Commission would look for any way to disqualify Hoolie, and he should warn Hoolie that they'd be sure to make him take a piss test if he won.

"You right, you right," said Ike. "Damn."

"Is he clean?"

"Say he is."

In TJ, Hoolie's got his wife, his mother, and two brothers he's got to feed; he's got to feed Ike and me, and Ike's backup corner man. There are two more as well: a homeboy member of Hoolie's Frogtown gang, and a black kick boxer, a kid called Tweety, who's as polite and well-spoken as a Jesuit. The weigh-in was at noon the same day of the fight, with the fights to go off at ten that night. Hoolie was staying in the same hotel where the fight's going off. He wants to eat at five, but not in the hotel, where at lunch he was pestered by people after his autograph. He's a big man in Mexico, what with him being born down there and making it in the States.

He asks me about seafood and if I know a good place to eat in town. I tout him on La Costa, but tell him it isn't cheap, and he says no big thing. So many people eating, it had to cost Hoolie a bundle. I wondered why he was paying for people who weren't family or working his corner, but he paid the tab without a bitch. No problem, until the waiter collected and counted Hoolie's money. I could tell from the waiter's face that Hoolie had stiffed him. So now I got to wonder if he'll do the same to me. I slip the waiter thirty dollars for himself. With the tank of gas I had to buy, I was working for nothing, right?, since the adrenaline I know I'll be using on Hoolie's cuts later that night has already cost me another seventeen dollars and change. But what am I going to do? I'd known these waiters for years, and I can't let them get stiffed on my call.

Some fighters cut all the time, others hardly ever. Hoolie's a bleeder, it's what you call a fighter who cuts easy. Guy like that can make for a long night. It's not something he can do anything about, being a bleeder, any more than a guy with a glass jaw can do something about not having a set of whiskers. I don't know if it's the bone structure around the eyes of a bleeder, or something to do with the elasticity or the thickness of the skin, but some of them get cut damn near every fight. It doesn't take long for a bleeder's eyes to droop from severed nerves, or before they develop a monkey look around the eyes from the buildup of scar tissue. Hoolie's got the monkey look. Nature builds up scar tissue to protect the eyes, but in boxing it's often the scar tissue that's the problem—the soft skin next to the scar will tear free from the scar because of the difference in texture between the two.

It was in the second round that Hoolie's eyes started to bleed. I kept him going, but the cuts in his eyelids got worse as the fight wore on. But as long as Ike and I could get him ready for the next round, he was standing up at the ten-second warning and waiting for the bell. Little shit, he recuperates between rounds better than anyone I ever saw. Punch by punch, he wore Pedroza down. Pedroza went after Hoolie's eyes, twisting his fists on impact to tear open the cuts even more. Hoolie stayed close, went to the body with shots to the liver, ribs, and heart. The liver shots made Pedroza gasp, the heart shots made him wobble.

Pedroza was a local boy, a good fighter with the will to win. The crowd was clearly in his corner, and so was the ref, who took a point away from Hoolie by calling a phony low blow. In Mexico, if somebody is cut, they tend to let the fights go longer than in the U.S. But if you happen to be the guy from out of town—and you're the one who's cut—and if the promoter is looking to get a win for his boy—you know you better knock him out in a hurry, because they'll stop the fight on you as soon as they figure the local boy's ahead on points. The ref kept calling time and looking at Hoolie's cuts, but I stopped the blood and the ref couldn't stop the fight.

I repaired Hoolie's eyes after the third and the fourth. After the fifth I did it again, then swabbed his nose with adrenaline to jack some energy into him through the mucus membrane. Hoolie punched himself on each side of his face and slid out to the center of the ring, his hands intentionally down low. Before Pedroza could get off on what he thought was an opening, Hoolie caught him with a sneak right-hand lead that stunned him. Then he caught him with a short left hook to the liver that paralyzed him. Pedroza went down on his face from an uppercut and then twisted into a tight ball of hurt. The timekeeper and the ref stretched the count, but they could have counted to fifty for all it mattered.

The crowd was howling and throwing beer into the ring. We got to the dressing room as fast as we could. The shower and the toilet were in the same closed cubicle within the dressing room. All of Hoolie's people crowded in while Ike and I were pumping fluids into him and trying to towel him down. We were all happy and toothy. It's always like that when you win. The press was polite, and Hoolie's fans pushed in to shake his hand. A bottle of tequila was passed around, an uncommon thing, and Hoolie took a couple of hits. Tweety positioned himself inside the crapper, turned off the light in there, and closed the door so he couldn't be seen.

Two minutes later the Commission doctor pushed through the dressing room door, followed by the promoter, whose number-one boy Hoolie had just dropped. With a smug look, the doctor held up a plastic specimen bottle. Ike glanced over at me, rolled his eyes.

"La-la-la," said the doctor, sure he'd busted Hoolie.

If Hoolie fails the test, the promoter's boy doesn't suffer the loss on his record, and the promoter doesn't have to pay Hoolie. Hoolie doesn't get paid, neither does Ike, neither do I. Hoolie took the piss bottle with a smile. He pulled open the door to the toilet so it covered half his body. It also blocked Tweety from the doctor. Hoolie dropped his trunks and cup to his knees and stood where the doctor could still see his bare ass. From my position, I watched the action. Hoolie handed the bottle inside the toilet to Tweety, who already had his dick out. Tweety pissed into the bottle while Hoolie made a piss face and jerked his arm around like he was shaking his dick. Tweety gave the bottle back to Hoolie, and after closing Tweety in, Hoolie passed the hot bottle back to the doctor. Hoolie's gangster pal stood in front of the door picking his nose.

From Hoolie's relaxed attitude, and from the heat of the specimen bottle, the doctor was no longer so sure that he'd nailed a drug offender. The promoter saw the doctor's face and began talking to himself.

The reason behind what the doctor and the promoter tried to do disgusted me, not the piss test. But the game Hoolie and Tweety ran got to me even more. I love boxing almost as much as I love the Sacraments. You play by the rules. You never throw a fight, and you never throw intentional low blows . . . unless the other guy does it first. When I realized that Hoolie was still smoking dope, I got out of there as soon as I could.

"Hoolie," I said, "I got to go. How about takin care of me."

"I'm broke until the promoter pays me, man."

"When's that?"

"Tomorrow morning when the bank opens, homes. Hey, I'm good for it, you know me, man. I don't see you around, I'll give your piece to Ike so he can take care of you, what you say?"

"It's only a hundred."

"I'm broke, man, that's why I took this shit fight, and my wife's knocked up, man."

I took off. I saved a doper's ass, and it cost me money. I knew then I'd never get my hundred. I saw Hoolie ten times in the gym in L.A., but he never once mentioned my money. It wasn't enough to shoot him for, so I let it go.

It was 1:00 A.M. when I got back to the U.S. border. Since the fight was on a Friday night, there were long lines waiting to get across. Venders selling hats and serapes and pottery stood along the Mexican side of the road. Groups of eight- and ten-year-old boys begging for change flowed like alley cats along the lines of cars; haggard women with scrawny kids sat by the roadside with their hands out. A stunted three-year-old boy stood rigidly between two lines of traffic. Tears streaked his dusty little face, snot ran down over his lips. He wailed a senseless little song and beat two small pieces of scrap wood together. Sanity had left his blue eyes.

On the way home I stopped at a Denny's for coffee and a piece of gummy lemon pie. I'm still thinking about that kid.

My brother had some income property on Bull Shoals Lake down on the Missouri-Arkansas border. He died suddenly and left it to me, and now I moved back there to fix it up and sell it. I forgot all about Hoolie when I learned that he'd dumped Ike, who'd been with him since the amateurs, and who had hopes of winning a title with Hoolie, Ike's first. So three months after I'm in Missouri, Hoolie gives me a call. He says he's got a new trainer and a manager from Mexico. The manager's positioned him into a WBC feather-weight title fight with Big Willie Little in Kansas City, Missouri.

"I want you in my corner, homes."

"Why Kansas City?"

"Big Willie's from there. It's a big deal on one of the riverboat hotel casinos, pay TV, all the shit."

"Why me?"

"The promoter only came up with four plane tickets, and I'm using one for my wife. That leaves tickets for my trainer and one more corner man from out here. Besides, I don't want to chance it with some hillbilly, white-bread mayonnaise sandwich from back there, right?"

"Like I say, why me?"

"You're the best, man, look what you done for me in TJ, man, they'da stopped it except for you, man, shit. Besides, you're already back there, homey."

"How'd you get my number?"

"From Ike."

When I heard that Ike had given him my number, I knew Ike was scheming on the punk, that Ike wanted my presence in Kansas City, and I got interested.

"You owe me a hundred dollars, forget the gas and what else it cost me in TJ."

"I know I do, man, but you gotta know how broke I been since the suspension. It's over now, but now my old lady's got cancer in the tit, *ese,* and it's costing me, but I'll give you your bread, no sweat, man."

"Is Tweety going to be there?"

"No, man, I'm squeaky clean for this one, shit."

"Here's my deal," I said. "It's something like three hundred miles from here to Kansas City. That's all day both ways and three tanks of gas. So if I do come, I don't want to waste my time, understand?"

"No doubt about it."

"How much you gettin? Level with me."

"Yeah, yeah, only fifty grand, see? I'm takin it cheap just to get a shot at that *maiate* Big Willie mothafuck." *Maiate* is a word some Mexicans use for black people. A *maiate* is a black bug that lives in dung. "I'll take his black ass easy."

I don't trust Hoolie the fight's only for fifty thousand, not with his name on the card, but if I can make a grand, it'll buy the paint I need to finish the work on my brother's buildings.

"I'll come," I say. "But up front, you send me my hundred you owe me by overnight mail. I don't get it overnight, forget it. Once I drive up to Kansas City, the day I get there you pay me one thousand up front, which is two percent. Or I turn around and come back home."

"You got it, *ese,* no problem, man."

"When's the fight?"

"A week from Saturday. We're flying in day after tomorrow."

"When you want me there?"

"Promoter says two days before the fight, to get your license and all. I already got a room in your name. Your meal tickets will be at the desk."

"I don't want to lay around that long, so I'll be there one day before. Give my name to the Commission at the weigh-in. I already got a Missouri license from a fight last month in Saint Louis."

He gave me the name of the casino and the address. I gave him my P.O. box number, and the deal was made. It took three days for my hundred to get to me, because I live way out in the hills. I cashed Hoolie's money order and drove down to Gaston's on the White River for catfish, hush puppies, and pecan pie.

The day before the fight, at six in the morning, I picked up highway #5 out of Gainesville, Missouri, and slowly headed up the climb north to Mansfield. It had snowed in the night, and the shivery landscape glowed in the high light before the Ozark dawn. Before the turnoff to Almartha, I watched a ten-point buck and three does race below a line of cedars, the snow kicking up like puffs of fog behind their white tails. Going west from Mansfield took me through the rolling hills of Amish country. Along #60, a four-lane divided highway, black horse-drawn buggies were driven by bearded men in black wearing wide-brimmed, round hats. I passed through Springfield and on up #13 and across the backwater of the Harry S. Truman Dam to Clinton. #7 took me to Harrisonville. #71 put me on #435, which brought me on into the jarring cityscape of sooty Kansas City.

The snow on the highway had been melted by pounding semis long before I got to Springfield, but there were drifts of dirty white along the road most of the way north. Up from Springfield and Humansville, there's a stretch of gas stations and a little spot called Amy Jane's Café at Collins, Missouri. Amy Jane's sign says HOME COOKIN & HOMEMADE PIES. With a gut rumble, I wheeled my brother's '64 Chevy pickup right on into Amy Jane's parking lot. Inside, I was greeted like folks. There was a billboard high on the wall with a day-glo handwritten pie menu. It offered sixteen flavors, everything from coconut cream to blueberry. I had two pieces of lemon with my coffee, which was country good. Most of the customers were good ol' boys and their buds. There were truckers and families as well. Everybody ate pie.

Pie and radio is how, in my family, we entertained ourselves during the Great Depression. Even after World War II, when not everybody had TV sets. Picking up crumbs with my fork, I sat there thinking back. I do that more and more. I've started to miss people I've never missed before, to return to scenes from my childhood that are as fresh as if I was standing there again.

After taking the wrong exit twice in Kansas City, I got to the casino at three-thirty in the afternoon. At the front desk they told me the weigh-in had been at noon and that Hoolie's fight would go off at eleven the following night. From fight guys, I also learned that Big Willie Little had been three pounds overweight and had to take them off in the steam room. Three pounds is a ton to a featherweight. It sounded good for Hoolie.

After leaving off my gear in the room, I went to the buffet, where, among other things, they prepared fresh Chinese food. I hadn't had good Chinese food since L.A. In Springfield and Branson and on down in Mountain Home, Arkansas, it was hog slop. The stuff in the casino was first-rate, and I stuffed myself. I wouldn't eat anything else that day. When I finished, I went straight up to Hoolie's room and asked for my thousand. He was playing dominoes with Policarpo Villa, a scumbag trainer living in Los Angeles who'll put a green kid in way over his head and then dump him for losing. By destroying the careers of his own boys, he helps other managers build a record for their fighters, and that's how he also picks up a couple of hundred under the table each time he sells a boy out. He sports a mandarin mustache that he grows down over his mouth to hide his bad teeth, and he wears a white Stetson indoors and out. It turned out that Policarpo was Hoolie's new trainer as well as his new manager. That saves Hoolie the 10 percent he'd have had to pay Ike, because a manager/trainer only gets 33 percent of the purse. Ike gets zip.

When Hoolie didn't answer me about my dough and instead kept right on playing dominoes, I started tipping his pieces over so Policarpo could see his numbers.

"Hey! whatchoo doin, man? I was kickin his ass!"

"We got a deal, or not?"

"I'm playin dominoes, I'm thinkin, man, I got ten bucks ridin!"

"You got my money."

"I was gonna pay you out of my trainin expenses, *ese,* but I had to pay more for sparrin partners back here than I thought, you know how that goes."

"We got a deal or not?"

"We do, we do gots one. Only, look, I can only come up with three hundred now. Sparrin partners back here tapped me, man, mother's honor, but you'll get the rest right after the fight when the promoter pays up, I promise."

"Do yourself a favor. Cross my name out of your chump-change address book," I said, and started for the door.

"Come on, come on, goddamn it! Don't be like that, you got to go with the flow."

Policarpo said, "Screw it. I'll be the cut man, save us both fuckin money, *ese.*"

I laughed in his face. "You gonna handle cuts on *this* guy, and give him the right instructions in the corner in the one minute you got, yeah? You got a kit, one that's ready to go? You got all the shit? You bring adrenaline? Missouri ain't like California, you got to have a prescription for adrenaline here. And where you goin to find a drugstore that even handles it? We're dealin with a bleeder, did you miss that? Go ahead, lose the fuckin fight for him, I don't give a rat's ass. I'm gonna hang around just to watch the fucker bleed."

"Calm down, calm down, *ese,* be cool," said Hoolie. He turned to Policarpo. "How much you got on you?"

"Two hundred, that's all I got."

Hoolie counted out his three hundred, and Policarpo added two hundred more. "Here," said Hoolie. "Take it, homes, no shit, man, it's all we got until after the fight. Gimme a break, okay? We're gonna make big money together, you and me, word of honor."

"Gimme an IOU for the five more you owe me," I said, taking the five hundred. "You stiff me, I go to the commission."

"Hey, you write it, I sign it, that's how much I respect you, homes."

I did and he did and I left. On my way out he asked, "When am I gonna see you?" all humble and small and best of friends. "We got to get together before the fight so I know you don't split, right?"

"You want your chiselin five hundred back?"

"I trust you, my brother, I didn't mean nothin."

"Your bout goes off at eleven. I'll be in your dressing room at nine."

"Hey, homes, no hard feelins, right?"

"Why would there be?"

The next day I slept late and took a walk down by the Missouri River. It was muddy and dark, and there were patches of foam in the weeds along the snow-covered bank. This was the river that the Lewis and Clark expedition took to open a way to the Pacific. I would love to have been along on that ride. Less than two hundred years ago, where I stood was uncharted Indian land. I wondered what kind of ride Hoolie planned for me.

I'd had a light breakfast, and the cold air made me hungry. I went back for more Chinese food. I was seated by the same hostess at the same table. The place wasn't crowded, and I noticed for the first time that the tables were arranged in little booths made up of dividers, with screens between the tables, for privacy. On my way back to my table from the buffet, I saw that Hoolie and Policarpo were bent over hot tea at the table next to mine. I took the long way around. They hadn't seen me, and when I sat down, I realized they were speaking Spanish. I had nothing to say to them. I'd handle the cuts, I'd collect my money, and I'd go back home and start painting. That was my deal, and I'd do it. I was kicking my own ass for showing up, but now that I was here, I was going to get my other five hundred. It was a rule.

Hungry as I was, at first I didn't pay any attention to them. When I heard them scheming on million-dollar fights, I had to smile. Then I heard something about a two-hundred-thousand-dollar fight and realized they were talking about the fight with Big Willie Little. I turned up both my hearing aids.

"I know they take taxes, but I don't get what we do with what's left of the two hundred thousand," said Hoolie. "The promoter said we could cash his check here if we want to, but then what? I mean, we don't want to pack it to L.A., right?"

Policarpo said, "Two ways. First, we could trust the promoter, and cash his check in L.A. But what if the check bounces? I say cash it here, so we got it in our hands. Then have the casino transfer the money to banks in L.A., one third to me, two thirds to you, like the big guy said."

"How much we got left over from trainin-expense money?" asked Hoolie.

"About thirty-five hundred. One thousand for me and two for you, after the cut man gets his five."

"The cut man gets it in his ass," said Hoolie, "that's what he gets for hustlin me."

"He'll be pissed, *raza*."

"*Son cosas de la vida*—that's life."

"Can we get away with that?"

"What's the old Paddy cunt gonna do?"

"You signed your name, *ese*."

"What I signed was Julio Cercenar Bauzá, not Julio César Garza." They laughed about the one word, *cercenar*—to trim, to reduce. "Dumb old fuck didn't see the difference."

It was true. Because of Hoolie's scrawl and fancy whorls, I hadn't picked up the name switch.

"What if he says you signed it phony?" said Policarpo.

"I say I never signed it at all. He's the one who wrote the IOU, not me, right?"

"What, we just split his money, one third/two thirds?"

"No," said Hoolie, "half and half. After I kick the nig's ass, we'll go buy us some black pussy on the old man, eh?"

When they gave the high five, they saw me for the first time. I turned to one side and didn't make eye contact.

"Hey, man," said Hoolie, looking through the screen, "how long you been here?"

"Couple minutes," I said, shoveling rice into my face with chopsticks. "What's up?"

"We're gonna take a little walk, it's not too cold, and then maybe I'll have me a little siesta," said Hoolie as he and Policarpo came around the divider. "How come you don't say hello or nothin, man?"

"I was eatin. Didn't see you."

"Yeah, we didn't see you, too."

They stood there while I continued to eat.

Policarpo said, "You don't speak no ehSpanish, right?"

Hoolie's eyes flicked between Policarpo and me.

I shrugged, kept eating. "About like the rest of the California *gringos*," I said. "*Cerveza*, and *puta*, and *cuánto*—beer, and whore, and how much."

That got a laugh, and they left feeling satisfied. I went back for seconds, took my time, and chewed on the fact that I should be getting four thousand dollars, not one. There were 24-by-36-inch posters of Hoolie and Big Willie in the café. More were set up throughout the hotel. This was Big Willie's fourth defense of his title, and he hadn't looked good in his last fight. With his weight problem, and with Hoolie's speed and boxing ability, it figured that Big Willie was due to lose his title. But he was a durable little battler who loved being champ, and under pressure he was mean. He was big in the back and shoulders and neck. He would have gained weight and regained his fluids since the weigh-in, and Big Willie could bang, even when he was tired. Of course Señor Julio Cercenar Bauzá was known to bleed.

When I didn't see anyone around that was connected with the fight, I went into the casino and checked the line. Big Willie was a three-to-one underdog because of his weight problem. That's when I went to the nearest ATM and pulled some cash from three banks.

I looked for someone who knew me from nothing. There were hillbillies and bikers and college boys. There were sorority girls and telephone operators and welfare mothers. Old people and young. Sporting types, squares, drunks, and junkies. All colors. None looked right, so I waited.

I got a whore, a skin-and-bones Thai whore with frizzed hair, who was all knee bones, ankles, elbow joints, and skull. No ass left on her. She was maybe thirty but looked fifty. Nobody looked at her, neither males in lust nor females in sympathy. I wondered how she could make a dime much less pay the rent. I don't know if she was a crack-head or had AIDS, but for sure she had lived hard in the night. She made me for a typical old john, someone who wanted to feel her, not fuck her. I told her what I wanted and that I'd pay two hundred. I told her that I'd be right on her tail, that if she made a run with my money, I'd stab her. She understood. What I did was slip her 15 one-hundred-dollar bills in an envelope, and had her lay it all on Big Willie Little for me at the Sports Book. I win the bet, I pick up a fast forty-five hundred. Afterward, I tailed her to a video-game room. She gave me my fifteen-hundred-dollar printout, and I gave her 4 fifties. She shoved them into her training bra.

She said, "You no wan' mo'? You no wan' bro jo'? I goo'."

I gave the poor bitch another hundred and told her to go home. She squinted at me and gave me a tight little smile, maybe the first she'd given in a year, maybe her last ever.

In my room, like I always do, I opened my aluminum attaché case and spread my goods out to make sure everything was there.

But this time, instead of reaching for a new bottle of adrenaline, I unsnapped a flap pocket and took out an old bottle I knew had gone bad, an outdated bottle I hadn't used from a couple of years before. I'd taped the lid so I wouldn't make a mistake, but kept it for when I needed a backup bottle with a rubber seal that would hold. When I twisted off the thin metal cap and poured the old stuff on a tissue, it was a pale piss-yellow. I mixed a fresh batch of salve, as I always do, using Vaseline and adrenaline. It smelled right, but the salve I prepared was from the piss-yellow stuff, not the clear. The salve's color wasn't affected. Once I made up the salve, I diluted the remaining outdated solution with water to lighten the color. Under the ring lights, no one would notice, especially since it still smelled legit.

Even though I'm no longer a trainer, I always walk off the size of the ring. I test to see how tight or loose the ropes are. I check how hard or soft the canvas is, which is to say how fast or slow it will be. I check the steps up to the ring, how solid and wide they are, and how much room there will be at ringside. This time I checked dick.

It was a twelve-round fight, and it went off on time. Hoolie and Big Willie split the first two rounds, but Hoolie came on in the third and fourth. In the fifth, each fighter knocked the other down, but neither could put the other away. Hoolie had planned to fight Big Willie from the outside, to keep him at the end of his punches, but Big Willie was a bull and wouldn't allow it, so Hoolie had to fight on Big Willie's terms. The fifth was even, but at the end of the round, Hoolie returned to the corner with a small laceration in his left eyelid. I was quick into the ring and used just enough fresh adrenaline, along with pressure, to temporarily stop the flow of blood. I also used the phony salve, which meant there would be no coagulant continually working in the wound.

Hoolie was winning the sixth easy. Near the end of the round, Big Willie countered, whacked Hoolie on the way in with a solid one-two, one-two combination to the face, the second left-right even harder than the first. Suddenly there was a deep cut above

Hoolie's right eye, and the cut in the eyelid was split wide open. The ref called time and looked at the cuts, but he let the fight continue. By the bell, Hoolie was seeing black from the blood and scraping at both eyes to clear his vision. Once he was in the corner between the sixth and the seventh, I cleaned the wounds with sterile gauze and applied pressure with both thumbs. Once the cuts were clean, I applied my outdated-piss adrenaline with a swab and went back to more pressure.

Hoolie said, "You can fix it for me, right, homes?"

"No sweat, man."

"You're the best."

Because I had cleaned the cuts properly and because of the pressure I applied along with the swab, and because of the bogus salve I packed into the holes, it appeared that I had solved the problem. Policarpo and the other corner men were so busy giving Hoolie instructions and watering him that I could have used green paint and they wouldn't have noticed.

The bell for the seventh sounded. Big Willie and Hoolie fought like bats, each turning, each twisting and bending, each moving as if suspended in light, neither stepping back, and both wanting the title, both ripping mercilessly into the other. Both were splattered with Hoolie's blood. The head of each fighter was snapping back, and the ribs of both were creaking as each unleashed his force. Big Willie suffered a flash knockdown, but he was up again by the count of two. As he took the mandatory eight-count, his eyes were focused on Hoolie like a rattler's on a rat. The ref waved the fighters on. Big Willie stepped up and delivered a left-right-left combination, the second left snapping like it had come off a springboard. It would have destroyed most welterweights, but Hoolie grabbed Big Willie and held on.

The bell ended the round, and I cleaned the wounds and applied more pressure, temporarily stanching the red flow. I used more piss-yellow.

"I thought you fixed it, *ese*," said Hoolie, his voice coming out small between bruised lips.

"I did fix it," I said. "But you let him pop you, so it opened up on me. Be cool. Go with the flow."

In the eighth, Big Willie looked exhausted, but there was no quit in him. He sucked it up and concentrated his shots on Hoolie's cuts. Blood filled Hoolie's eyes until he was punching blindly and getting hit no matter how he tried to cover up. People at ringside were shielding themselves from the flying blood. Big Willie saw the ruined flesh, and his heart jacked as his own adrenaline pounded through him. Walking through Hoolie's wild punches, he drilled more shots into Hoolie's blood-blind eyes. Two more cuts opened in Hoolie's eyebrows. Veins weren't cut, but blood pumped down, and the fans were yelling to the ref to stop it. He called time and waved in the ring doctor, who immediately stopped the fight.

Big Willie Little was declared the winner, and still featherweight champion.

In the corner the doctor checked Hoolie's eyes. By then I had used fresh adrenaline, which stopped the blood cold. The cuts were an inch and a half, two inches long, which is big-time when it's around the eyes. But like I say, no vein was cut, and with the right stuff in there, Hoolie could have fought all night. Since Big Willie was sure to have run out of gas, and since I had no trouble stopping the cuts when I wanted to, I figure Hoolie should be the new champ. Except for me. *Son cosas de la* fucking *vida*.

Hoolie's corner men were washing him down with alcohol and the doctor had stitched up three of the cuts when the promoter came in with Hoolie's check. He was a big round Afrikaner from Johannesburg, with a walrus mustache and a huge Dutch gut. He had kind, wise eyes and seemed to float rather than walk.

"Too bad about the cuts," he said. "I thought Little was ready to go, there."

"I beat Big Willie's fuckin ass my eyes don't go," said Hoolie, who was desolate from the loss.

"You've got one of the best cut men I ever saw. Cool under fire, he was. I watched him. Did everything right." He sucked on his mustache. "What was the grease from the little container?"

I pulled out the flat plastic jar containing the piss salve. I unscrewed the wide lid. "Smell."

"Ahh, yes, good lad, you mix adrenaline right into the grease, yes? Keeps working, right?, during the round."

"That's it."

"Tough break, Hoolie being a bleeder."

"Sure is. Listen," I said. "I know it's not my place, but I'm not going back to L.A. with these guys. I'm wondering if there's some way they can cash out in the casino? So they can take care of me before they take off?"

The promoter looked at Hoolie. Neither he nor Policarpo said anything.

"I've got an IOU," I said.

Hoolie saw that the promoter realized something wasn't right. He played dumb. "But once we cash the check," he asked, "we can't have the money transferred to L.A., can we?"

"Certainly can. Like I previously explained, we can arrange the transfer of funds through the casino."

"Ah, yeah, I remember now. Cool."

At the cashier's window, Policarpo counted out my money in English. "One hundred, two hundred, three hundred, four hundred, five hundred."

As he handed the bills to me, I glanced at Hoolie, whose butterflied eyes were telling me he'd never use me in his corner again. I love a guy who says he's going to fuck you because you won't let him fuck you.

As I re-counted the first two bills in English, I decided to lay rotten eggs in Hoolie's mind. Without a break, I slipped into singsong

Mexican street Spanish. "*Trescientos, cuatrocientos, quinientos. Correcto, mano*—three hundred, four hundred, five hundred. Correct, my brother."

Hoolie remembered our conversation over my Chinese food. "Hey!, you speak ehSpanish?"

Now I went into a guttural, old-man Castillian. "*Pues, coño*, but only if it's to my advantage." *Pues, coño* is what nailed it—well, of course, cunt.

Hoolie blinked six times. Policarpo's jaw flopped open. For the first time I saw fear in Hoolie's eyes. *Did I fuck him or didn't I?* they screamed.

I left him standing at attention. I showered and packed and at two in the morning went down to the casino. I saw the last of the fight guys on their way out. I pissed away a fast fifty on the quarter slots to pass time. I knew Ike had watched the fight and would know that something had gone down. We would never talk about it. I waited until three o'clock and collected my bet, plus my original fifteen. I slept for a couple of hours, had three cups of coffee in the coffee shop, and then checked out.

It was seven-fifteen when I eased the old truck into traffic. I listened to news for a while, then switched to a jazz station that was playing Jackie McLean. I headed home the way I'd come. There was more snow on the ground. When I looked into the hills, the countryside was like an old-timey Christmas card.

When I got back to Collins, I pulled into Amy Jane's. Pie was in the air. A good ol' boy in a John Deere cap recognized me from the fight.

"Buddy, you looked good on TV last night. Too bad about your boy, tough little booger."

"Real tough."

I ordered two pieces of lemon pie with my coffee, and then I found myself on the couch, sitting next to my father. He was leaning into our new radio, an inlaid, upright Philco with a magical green tuning light. It was June 18, 1941, at the Polo Grounds. Irish Billy Conn, the former light heavyweight champ, was ahead on points after twelve rounds with Joe Louis, the heavyweight champion of the world. Louis outweighed Conn by better than twenty-five pounds. In the thirteenth round Billy went for all the marbles and tried to knock out Joe Louis, the greatest puncher of them all. The Brown Bomber was hurt early on, and my father was yelling Gaelic at the radio, but Louis rallied late in the round and knocked Billy Conn out in 2:52 of the thirteenth.

At the count of ten, I watched some of my father die. As he sat with his red face in his oil driller's hands, my mother turned off the radio. We were to eat lemon meringue pie after the fight, my father's favorite. I was able to eat a little piece, but not my da, though he tried. He fell off the wagon that night.

I finished my coffee and paid the waitress at the table.

"You didn't eat your pie."

"Lost my appetite."

I fiddled with my spoon. I sat for a while looking at my knees. I counted my keys. And then I fished out an El Rey Del Mundo Robusto Suprema, a handmade maduro from Honduras that comes wrapped in white tissue. I'd fire up that spicy pup and smoke it down the highway for a good hour and a half, chew on it for more.

By the time I got up to the counter, my appetite was back. I smiled the waitress over and ordered country—a deep-fried pork tenderloin sandwich, with pickles and chips, and coffee, all to go. She didn't know *what* was going on, *whup!* And pies. Two gooseberry and two rhubarb. And two lemon, too. I like tart.

Black Jew

We was brought to Atlantic City to be the opponent. Opponent in the fight game mean the one suppose to lose. Opponent is what the promoter bring for the boy he think be good enough to be champion. Opponent be the one they use to build him a record. Promoter boy get to be a contender, he start getting big purses and maybe he get a title shot. He win a major belt, we talking money and the promoter in on the cut big-time. Things go right, promoter get the biggest cut of all, ask Don King, Bob Arum, the Duvas. It the same all over boxing.

But they's promoters out there that ain't all bad. This the fight business. It about money, so they got to watch it, too. Like there was a time when a promoter would send a plane ticket to a fighter, and the fighter then cash in the ticket and then don't show up for the fight. Promoter now send the kind of ticket you can't get no refund on. See, fighters be dogs, too. But it good when you a fighter who got a promoter working with you. See, the promoter all the time be looking for ways to move his boy up while the same time he look for a edge so to protect him. Problem in Atlantic City be that we the opponent. Casino say we down 9–5 because Dashiki Jones a big hitter who come in blowing and punching like a baby Joe Frazier. Except the odds man don't know we come to win.

Name be Earl Jeter, but my friends call me Jeet. My boy Reggie Love go to Atlantic City to fight a elimination bout with Adolf "Dashiki" Jones. Dashiki camp think Reggie washed-up, otherwise they don't take the fight. It important because the one who win the fight go on to fight "Cuba Kid Babaloo" for the USBA super-middleweight title. USBA ain't a major belt, and we ain't talking big money, but you win USBA and you ranked automatic. Reggie win it, he a contender again. His manager work with the right promoter, Reggie get a shot at the big money, and Reggie want that big money. Me and Pats want it, too. But from the git, things don't look right for us with Harvey Silvershade Promotions.

First thing fishy, they fly me and Reggie into Newark from L.A. and get us there at two in the afternoon. But they don't fly Pats in until six o'clock, on another airline. Promoter say he can't get all us on the same plane, even though they make the fight two months ago.

Right away, Pats say, "Look out, Jackie, they think this is our first time in the whorehouse."

Pats the cut man, Pats Moran, he work with me from when I be fighting. He say I hit so hard I suppose to be in jail. Pats funny, call everybody Jackie. He know the game good as anybody. Worked with a gang of champions, made good money at it, too. Pats in you corner you don't have to worry, everything be there you need. Pats and me so good together only me and him work the corner. Me and Reggie manager both like to have Pats along because Pats can talk, can handle things they get tricky. Me and Pats been with Reggie since before he go pro, since when he twenty-two. Reggie turn thirty-five in Atlantic City the day after the fight, Valentine's Day, day he born on and the day his mama name him for. Reggie Valentine Love. People's talking Reggie be too old, say he a shot fighter and suppose to retire. But Reggie a slick fighter, never been beat on, and he still fast. Reggie don't see it his end time. Reggie bad.

So after four hours when Pats get to Newark, we still sitting around the airport another hour before the promoter's driver show up. And then it three more hours before we get to the hotel because by now it snowing. That a long day. It all happen on Tuesday, and we fight on Friday. That give us little time to get some work in the gym and still rest a day before the fight.

We get to the Claridge Hotel where the fight go off, and this fine brown-skinned gal at the desk say we ain't on the list.

I say, "We got to be. We the main event."

She go in the back, then come out with some envelopes our name on them. Letter inside say we staying up the block in some Roto-Rooter motel the Claridge use for overflow. Letter say we be eating in the Claridge employee cafeteria, not in the regular hotel buffet. Give us a yellow ticket to eat with. Ticket say night after the fight the ticket be no good to eat on. Like we want to eat there, forget that.

Reggie say, "Ain't this a bitch?"

We haul our stuff on over to the motel and Pats room got no heat. Ours the TV don't work. We suppose to look at the wall while we laying around waiting to fight? Forget that, too.

Close to midnight, Pats say, "Jackie, it's time to check out the grits and greens."

When you fight in some hotel, the promoter suppose to give you tickets to eat in the regular buffet place where folks short on money go. It never bad, and sometimes it so good you got to watch you fighter he don't gain no weight. But now we got to go up some funky freight elevator to the employee cafeteria, and it old and it stink in there. Steam coming up and grease all over. Hot dogs and dried-out fish and chicken fried near to black. Cold pork chops all bone and fat. Food be dead.

We get to the table, Pats say, "Jackie, this is jail food."

Reggie start laughing, shove his tray away. He love Pats. He say, "All we lack be a boom box and we be in the joint."

Place open twenty-four hours. All kind of peoples up there who work the hotel. White and black folks, Spanish of all kinds, China-men and Arabs. Mens and womens. They know we fighters and once they know we main event, and we treat them with respect, they start coming around. Nice people. Old Irish dudes with red noses spot Pats and right away come up for tickets. They talk that Irish way and Pats slip on into it.

Pats say, "I'd give 'em to ya in a minute, lads, they give us some, but with this heretic promotion we get nothin. I don't mean to crit-icize your eats, Jackie, but I got a fighter here to feed, and this jail food's a mortal sin."

You right, the peoples say, this be jail food up here, you suppose to be treated first-class, you main event. Peoples love fighters, all kinds of peoples love fighters, rich and poor. These ones so nice they clean up our table for us, dump the trash. It all be trash because we don't eat none of it.

Next morning we check out the regular buffet. $5.95 for break-fast, $7.95 for dinner and supper. Dashiki and his corner be eating down there. Pats spit on the rug. We find the promoter in the room he using for a office. No clothes in the closet, no suitcases in the room. Waiter bring in scrambled eggs on a cart cooked all pretty with onions, ham on the side. They sliced tomatoes and bagels with cream cheese. And they tea with nice lemon. He say how he be glad we fighting for Harvey Silvershade Promotions, say is there any-thing we need, say call him Harvey. Harvey got a long face with freckles and a big ass, tie open at the neck. Wearing cowboy boots, and he got bright blond hair in a ponytail. The man be fifty years old.

Pats smile real innocent and he say, "Ah, Jackie, now ain't it nice you asked? First we got no TV and we got no heat, and why are we stayin in the shit place in the first place? No offense intended, Jackie."

"Hey, hey," say Harvey, "nothing I can do about it. I ordered thirty-three rooms, but the Claridge is booked solid, and all we could get is ten rooms out of thirty-three, and that's the best we could do. The whole town's booked solid for all the Valentine-sweetheart shit Saturday."

"Where's Dashiki stayin, Jackie, I wonder?"

"Well, here. He's been in town a week and a half, so I was able get him in. His manager's staying across at the Hilton. I'd be in Bally's and take you with me, but there's no rooms, trust me. You can see this room isn't much."

Pats say, "And where's Dashiki eatin?"

"I'm not sure. My assistant arranged it."

"Dashiki and his corner are eatin in the buffet downstairs right now," say Pats. "So why are we livin out back with the pigs, Jackie?"

"Fellas, there's nothin I can do about it. I would if I could. I will have something done about the TV and the heat. Otherwise, it's outta my control, guys."

"Surely you can do somethin about the food?, since you're the promoter and all."

"What's wrong with the food?"

"Food's crap. No offense, Jackie."

"It's what all the hotel employees eat! It's good!"

"No, Jackie, it's not good."

"The Claridge guaranteed it!"

"We want to eat downstairs with Dashiki."

"What's wrong with the cafeteria food?"

"The food's jail food, Jackie."

"Jail food! It's not! Everybody's eatin there!"

"Not everybody, Jackie, and we don't want to neither."

"Can't help you. I already made a deal with the hotel. Complain to them."

"It's jail food."

"It's not jail food!"

"Come down there and eat with us, Jackie. No offense intended."

"I got things to do right now. Look, I got fifty mouths to feed, I can't spoon-feed every one of them."

"We're the other half of the main event, Jackie. Make it right."

"There's main events and there's main events," he say. His shoulders be talking, too. They say he don't have to take shit from no bust-out old cut man who fighter soon be on his back blinking through a concussion into the overhead lights.

Looked to me like Pats be ready to slap the punk, so I touch him and nod to Reggie, whose eyes be colder than a dead Eskimo dick.

Pats see Reggie eyes and like me he remember Reggie eyes from Berlin. Pats like Reggie eyes. Me, too. Pats nod real nice to Harvey and smile like they be friends, but he don't shake hands. He say, "Thanks for handling our problems, Jackie. Us bein the main event, we knew you would."

"Anytime, fellas, anytime."

In the elevator Reggie say, "Jew think we the Indians. We the cowboys."

This happen to us once before when we fight in Germany. Pats come over three days after us. Germans have us freezing cold in some skunk hotel smell of piss and beer. Pats get there he raise hell, say we got to get some sleep, so the promoter move us into the first-class hotel where the number-one contender be staying, a blue-eyed boy with muscles like Tarzan. His brother got all kinds of long blond hair and he say they won't fight us we stay same place they stay. Promoter move us to a third place, some kind of hotel for students and traveling salesmen. It be clean and the food be different from home, but we could eat. Reggie's eyes go cold that time, too. Reggie beat on that boy so bad for ten rounds he hurt his hands. Could have knocked Tarzan out in three rounds, but Reggie want respect, so he punish that Fritzie boy. Smart-mouth brother start crying in the corner when he see what Reggie be doing to his baby brother face and ribs. Reggie retired that Tarzan boy, never fight again, fuck with Reggie.

Harvey come by noontime same day, Wednesday, when we ready to go to the gym. He with a black driver. Harvey say no good to the gym, say Reggie got to go to Philadelphia for a EEK test.

I say, "What that?"

"To check out his brain."

"Brain be good."

Harvey say, "Commission gets a EEK or no fight. Their call."

I say, "But we need the work."

"Appointment's for two-thirty. Now or never."

"Reggie manager know about this tes'?"

"I told him when we made the fight. He was supposed to send it with you, but I guess he didn't remember."

Reggie say, "Who pay?"

Harvey say, "No cash out of your pocket. I'll take it out of your purse."

"How much?"

"Two hundred fifty dollars."

"Two-fifty!" say Reggie. "I ain't goin."

But Reggie go. We find out once we back home that Harvey don't say nothing to Reggie manager about no EEK business. Reggie go with the driver and be gone six hours. Driver say he be lost and waste all kind of time. Driver don't know where to eat in Philly, so Reggie eat soul fried chicken he have to pay for, and come back mad. We check him on the scale in the hotel health spa, and he now 3 pounds over the 168-pound limit. We was going to run Reggie that night, but it snow again.

Reggie say, "Ain't this a bitch?"

So we go to the cafeteria and Reggie eat some raggedy fruit salad but that all. Pats got a loose bridge on the top left his mouth he take out and wrap in a paper napkin and put it in his shirt pocket. He eat pie and cake and drink skim milk. I eat soup that sure enough come from a can. We all be mad. Reggie eyes getting colder all the time. We know Harvey be running a game on us, be trying for that edge that come if we forget why we there. He treat us like dirt so we think we dirt. We don't talk about it, but we see what going down, and all us know we got to keep our mind focus right. Reggie train hard for this fight. Come down from 189 pounds in two months. He don't have a relationship with his wife in six weeks, and Reggie be mean.

He got three kids in Catholic school, and a wife who work checkout in a market. They got a little house over in La Puente they paying for. By now all us ready to pull out the fight, except we want that money. Reggie never make any big money in his fights, but he don't do bad, and what money he do make he smart with it. Peoples say Reggie still got his first nickel.

Reggie say, "After the weigh-in tomorrow, I'm goin down to the buffet and greeze. Cos' me money, but I can't fight on no jail food, half of it swine, hell." Reggie ain't no Muslim, but he don't eat no pork. "You don't have to come wit me, you want to eat this mess up here."

Me and Pats look around the cafeteria. It loud. Two TVs playing different channels and video games making all kind of noise along the far wall. Steam and grease up our nose. We say tomorrow we go, too, we sick of the cafeteria. Breakfast here tomorrow be all right, apples and bananas and cereal and skim milk for me and Pats. Reggie won't eat. Coffee be good. Everything else be a crying shame.

Reggie say, "By rights they suppose to pay."

Pats say, "How many times we eatin down there?"

Reggie say, "Two times for me. After the weigh-in first, and I keep goin on back till I get my money worth. And then tomorrow afternoon before the fight, when I go on after it again. Fifteen dollars ninety cent. And tax, too, damn. Ain't wastin my money. Fuck a promoter."

I say, "Some of the gamblin boys wastin they money down the casino now."

Reggie say, "Never learn, these fools, between the bitches and the gamblin and that drug shit they mess wit. Today they in the casino, next day they on the street. Biggest fools be the ones come around me for money, say I the man, say I got a wife be workin, say I got a house, say I got money, say they pay me back tomorrow. I don't give *none* of my money up. They come around again, I say I be a black Jew and don't come back. Shee."

Next morning Thursday, day before the fight. Weigh-in seven o'clock that night. Reggie drying out all day, don't eat or drink, put pennies in his mouth to make him spit. Me and Pats having cereal and milk and fruit in the cafeteria. Pats take out his loose bridge to eat, wrap it in a napkin. No pocket in his shirt this time, so he put the rolled-up teeth on his tray. We eat fast and quick, get back to Reggie so he don't go off and be eating pizza and Pepsi. Before we finish our coffee and leave, a nice Porto Rican lady pick up and dump our trays for us, say she betting on us and good luck in Spanish, say her daddy a fighter in Porto Rico in the old days. She say his name, and Pats know who he was, but what Pats don't know is his teeth be gone.

We quick get back to the room, Reggie laying up in the bed watching TV, boy's mouth dry, teeth feel like gravel down a gopher hole. You don't talk about eating or water around a man what drying out. We don't eat no lunch so Reggie not be alone. Pats sudden remember his teeth been dumped in the cafeteria.

Pats say, "It's that fookin Silvershade's fault!" and he go running back. Old man can move.

Pats come back a hour later. Still no teeth on the top left. Bridge be gone. Pats be down in the garbage wearing yellow gloves he got from the chef, up to his nose in garbage. Had to go through all kinda bags down there because the upstairs trash was throw out. He say he had to lie to the chef so's he could go downstairs, say that he lost a eight-carat gold diamond ring to get the hotel peoples to let him into the garbage place. Once the cleanup crew down there know they a diamond ring lost, they down into the mess like Arabs praying to garbage bags. Somebody from the street come by and ask what going on. One of the brothers say they looking for a twenty-carat diamond ring with rubies and emeralds. While they looking for diamonds and rubies and emeralds, Pats be looking for his teeth. Six of the brothers get in a fistfight. Street peoples be grabbing garbage bags and running off with them.

Pats say, "It was a wild affair, Jackie, better than watchin *The Price Is Right*. Never did find my bridge, fookin Harvey, but the show was high drama. Next hotel we check into I'm gonna pull the same stunt, only I'll be sayin I lost a diamond-studded gold Rolex. Imagine the bloodshed."

Reggie be laughing. That be good.

Four o'clock we go to the spa. Reggie still don't eat or drink and be dry to hurting. He get on the scale and he be two pounds over. He don't make weight, fight be off. That, or he have to give up some of his purse to Dashiki to get Dashiki to fight him overweight. Maybe Dashiki say no.

Reggie lucky. He have to go to the toilet and he get rid of one pound right there. That mean he only have to lose one in the steam room. But that steam room a bitch when you already dried out. Thank God we got another day before the fight. Thank God for Pedialyte, that baby stuff, for fluids. Pats rub Reggie with baby oil. Reggie go into the steam and it run him out of there. He bent over after five minutes and he hardly wet. He rest a minute and go in for five minutes more. This time he wet and ain't hurting so bad, getting used to it. Next time he go in for ten minutes, move around, and come out sweat pouring off him, but he still ain't standing up straight. He get on the scale and need to lose another quarter pound. He go back in and shadowbox. He do it in three minutes, but we had to help him back to the room, where he too thirsty to sleep. So weak he don't even turn TV on.

Pats say, "At least we didn't have to take shit and piss medicine."

Seven o'clock we at the weigh-in they have near the hotel pool.

Hundred peoples there, most of them fighters and corner men and hang-ons hoping to make a few dollars handing up the stool and water bucket. Me and Pats handle all that. Reggie weigh exactly 168, Dashiki 166. They got fresh fruit up there, and after making weight, Reggie eat it up while Pats pouring Pedialyte over ice like it be orange pop. Pats use a orange-juice carton he bring along so nobody know what Reggie be drinking. Reggie drink almost a quart while we doing the paperwork for the license, and he keep on eating grapes and cantaloupe and slices of orange. Pedialyte be nasty. Pats say to eat olives for the salt. New Jersey Commission man want the name of all the peoples working our corner. I give him my name and Pats's.

He say, "This is only two. Rules say you can have three. You can have four at a title fight, but this ain't a title fight, so you can have three."

I say, "Two be fine."

Commission man look at me like I don't know the business, shake his head. I been in this game all my life, and Pats in it longer than me. We know what we need. What we don't need is loud. Ain't no fighter what can win a fight by himself. He like a racehorse. Even John Henry can't win without the jockey. But you get too many mouths going in the corner and the fighter tune them out, he close down his mind and don't hear nothing. That's why me and Pats work alone.

I the chief second, the only one in the ring with Reggie for the introduction, the only one in the corner inside the ring between rounds, unless Reggie be cut. In the one minute we get, I got to grease him and tell him what he got to do. If he cut, Pats go in with his medicines to stop the blood. I work the water bucket outside the ring and talk. Otherwise Pats be outside washing the mouthpiece, catching the spit, watering the boy and cooling him down he need it. He use ice bags and stop-swell to bring down mouses and lumps. I get the stool into the ring, Pats get it out. He get the bucket up and down, unless he working a cut, then I do. All this be fast, no time to mess up. That why me and Pats work alone. Title fights same thing, we smooth like a BMW. Some corners be like a Chinese fire drill, everybody talking like they think they Eddie Futch. Between and during the rounds, I do the talking. I leave something out, then Pats say something, but most the time he quiet. Now, while the fight going on, outside the ring Pats be talking to me. I depend on it.

Reggie a fighter who have bad luck getting title fights because he too good. Everybody duck him. He 45 and 8 with 2 draws that he should have won. Eight of his KOs come from body shots. Had one title fight down South Africa but lost to the champ by a split decision. You lose on a split decision in the other boy's hometown, you know you win. America judge give it to Reggie by two, what is right, it a close fight. Italy judge only give it to South Africa by two, and Italy judge a ho', he be bought by the Africas. Nigga South Africa judge give it by ten to the Zulu. Three other times Reggie on the way to title shots, but he lose and have to start all over again. Like the last time five fights back. Now Reggie win his last four straight, two by kayo.

My boy Reggie fight so pretty they call him "Valentine" Reggie Love. He come in wearing pinky-red satin trunks with white trim and a white heart on the leg. He wear high pinky-red shoes with white laces. He wear a pinky-red satin robe almost to the floor that have a puffy white satin bow in the middle of his back two feet wide that got ribbons hanging down to the knees. Me and Pats be wearing pinky-red, too, can't miss us, 'specially Pats with his white hair and the busted, spidery red veins in his nose and his red cheeks. We something. We a *corner*.

After the weigh-in, the TV man come for the interview for before the fight. Dashiki say he in a hurry, say he want to go first. Reggie still drinking Pedialyte and bad be wanting to eat. He starting to hate Dashiki.

Dashiki a nice boy, serious and proud, he all muscle and bone and no loose skin. Twenty-six years old, and he hongry to be the champ, the way he suppose to be. Say this his big chance and he not letting it slip. He know that if he beat Reggie Love, that put him in line. Boy say he 27 and 0 with 22 kayos, say he got power in both hands he going to use to hurt the old man. Say he going right after Reggie. Say he want to take Reggie out early because he know Reggie a slick boxer, and that Reggie want the fight to go all the way so he can cop a decision. Dashiki say that he set everything up with his jab and come with his power behind that.

Dashiki say, "I hit him either hand, the old man go to sleep."

What Dashiki don't know is that we be listening behind the black curtain. What he can't see be Reggie eyes.

When the TV man talk to Reggie, he tell him Dashiki want to take him out early.

Reggie say, "Everybody want that."

TV say, "He's got that blinding right jab he knocks people down with. Does his being a southpaw mean trouble for you?"

Reggie say, "He a southpaw?"

TV say, "You mean you didn't know that? You mean you haven't studied tapes on him?"

Reggie say, "I don't watch no tapes."

TV say, "Every fighter I know watches tapes."

Reggie say, "Why I watch tapes? I watch 'em, and now I be goin over the fight. Can't sleep a lick a week before the fight because every night all night long I be fightin the fight." Reggie smile. "Sometimes it go a hundred rounds. It don't matter what I see on tape anyway, it all change when the bell ring. The boy change when he fight me, and I be different when I fight him."

TV say, "What about all that jab and knockout power?"

Reggie say, "Lef'-hander's right jab don't bother me. I got a lef' jab to bother him."

TV say, "You're saying you, as a rightie, are going out there to outjab a southpaw?, now, come on."

Reggie say, "Didn't say that. What I'm sayin is I'm goin take his jab away from him. I do that, all his power don't mean jack."

TV say, "How you going to take a left-hander's right jab from him?, they're always coming at you from the wrong side."

Reggie say, "You watch."

TV say, "What about you takin him into the late rounds?"

Reggie start talking like Muhammad Ali. He say, "Now, why I wants to go into da late rounds wit a Joe Fraaazier?"

TV laugh, shake hands. "Good luck, Reggie."

It nine-thirty by now, and we all so hungry we ready to rob a 7-Eleven. Buffet a big place, high ceiling, got bright lights and two long places where they feed. Reggie crazy by now. He have spinach salad and matzoh-ball soup. He have grilled fish and baked chicken. He have fettucini Alfredo and mash potato with veal Marsala gravy. He have two bananas for the potassium, and three big ice tea with lemon. After all that, he have two peach cobbler with ice cream, and he still be drinking Pedialyte.

Reggie say, "I get my muhfuh seven dollars and ninety-five cent, plus tax."

All us eat big, but nothing like Reggie. Next day early all of us have a bran cereal and prune breakfast in the cafeteria, eat apples and take a little walk on the boardwalk. It be cold but it feel good. Pats go find a Catholic church like he always do. At one o'clock we go back to the buffet and Reggie eat as much as he did the night before. Afterwards, he take a monster bowel movement and weigh 178 in the spa.

Reggie say, "I make Dashiki Jones pay for this seven dollars and ninety-five cent, plus tax."

Reggie rest and then go to the toilet again about six. Fight go off at nine. By seven-thirty Reggie stomach be flat as a door and he ready. Before and after the fight he call home. He tough-looking, Reggie, and he dark. But he talk so soft and sweet to his wife and babies it make you eyes water.

Our private dressing be small but warm. It be stocked with water and ice and plenty of clean, white towels. Pats wrap Reggie's hands and I warm him up good. They call us down and Reggie be sweating in his robe. Dashiki dressed like Africa, wearing a red and green and black and yellow dashiki for a robe, and a round hat same color. Trunks the same. Everybody in his corner wearing dashikis. Some fool beating a drum. Announcer make the introductions for TV and the crowd. Everybody yelling. Referee give instructions and the fighters touch gloves. Harvey be smiling on the far side. In our corner, I tell Reggie to bait Dashiki the first two rounds, see how he move, see what he do, hurt him when he can, but to stay loose and stay away from that power.

I say, "And breathe, baby, relax and breathe, hyuh?"

Reggie bob his head, he know. He know if you don't breathe like a fighter suppose to breathe, you get tired. You hold you breath when you punch, you going to wear down. You get tired, and now you in the other man's pocket. It happen to him his last loss. He don't train hard because he think it be a easy fight. Other boy put pressure on Reggie, bang him to the body, and Reggie tense up and don't breathe. The ref stop the fight when Reggie get hurt and be too tired to punch back.

Before the bell, Reggie touch hands with me and Pats. I get down ringside on the steps with Pats, and the bell ring.

Pats say, "Look out, Dashiki."

First two rounds, Reggie tease him. He make him miss and then he make him pay. Dashiki talking to himself by the end of the first round. Corner men know Dashiki got power, so they don't be worrying. They say take your time, press him behind the jab, and everything come. But Dashiki got doubt. He worrying because he never fight nobody before who know how to fight a southpaw. Reggie come to the corner feeling good, nice and relaxed. He breathing good.

Third round Dashiki move out like he chopping down a tree,

feet all dug in so he can throw power shots. He miss with six big
ones, then throw four more, only thing he hit be air. He try to move
in and go to his right, but Reggie step outside his front foot and
make him move to the left instead. To the right is where southpaws
want to go, just like to the left be natural for a right-handed fighter.
Dashiki move out to the right again, Reggie move farther out to the
left. When Dashiki start to throw his big jab, Reggie jab his jab, hit
Dashiki jab hard straight into the glove when the punch be partway
out. That enough to take Dashiki balance, and that mean he can't
punch until he set up again. That simple thing be how Reggie take
Dashiki jab. He do it all night long. Only thing Dashiki be hitting
on Reggie be the arms and elbows and gloves. Reggie taking the
boy to school. Dashiki desperate in the middle of the round. Most of
his knockouts have came in the first three, but he can't hardly hit
Reggie. He come charging in with a big hook, but Reggie duck
under. Reggie step to the left at the same time and hit the boy on
the way in with a right to the gut, and then he come back with a left
hook of his own to the jaw. Dashiki hands have came down from
the shot to the body, and Reggie drill him with three stiff jabs to the
nose and eyes that drive him back, make him blink. Dashiki never
been here before, don't know what to do.

Pats see it first.

Pats say, "Jeet, look. The boy can't fight goin backwards."

I wait and watch. Reggie do the same thing, and so do Dashiki.
Pats right about Dashiki backing up. Pats my man. Bell ring.

I say, "Boy can't fight backing up. Only time he hit you is when
he walk straight in, when he take three or four to land one. Back
him up's what you got to do in there, hyuh?"

Now Reggie got Dashiki backing up, Reggie keep him going
like that and keep on jabbing Dashiki jab. This open him up so Reggie can drop his right hand hard down the middle and come back
with the hook to the body, hook to the head, and then he quick jab
out and be clear of Dashiki power. Reggie keep it up. Sometime
Dashiki manage to get his right foot outside Reggie left foot, and

when he do he able to land a shot. But Reggie so quick Dashiki can't get combinations off.

Some places the commission let you yell up to your fighter more than others. New Jersey letting Dashiki corner yell all they want, so I be yelling, too.

I say, "Stick him, baby, stick and move, back him up! He can't fight a lick backing up!, see that? Stay on him!"

See, Dashiki can hear me just like Reggie can hear Dashiki corner. Dashiki hear me saying he can't fight backing up, that mess with his head. Now he wondering how come nobody taught him to. Now he blaming his corner for his tore-up face. Now he ain't focus on Reggie, and the old man be whipping his ass. Lumps coming up all along his left eye, what be closing from Reggie right hand. His short rib be killing him from where Reggie go to the body. Dashiki never been this deep. Reggie keep moving and pounding, then he be gone. Then he right back again, be whipping on Dashiki like he his daddy.

Pats say, "Reggie's beatin him up, Jeet. Reggie's beatin him *up*."

Ring girl come prancing by half bare-ass and holding up the round card. Now we in the fourth.

Reggie keep on putting a hurt on the boy. I yell to Reggie to relax and to have fun. Dashiki look over to me, can't help himself. He can't believe I be talking about fun. Boy never been in this water. Big strong boy, and he tough, he gain weight, like Reggie, but he tired from all that missing, from all that getting hit. He taking so many punches, he think he be fighting a drag queen with a purse. Pats and me see Dashiki be holding his breath when he load up to punch. We like that.

Pats say, "Look at those lumps, Jeet. Boy's tough, but he's never been hit. Eyes want to cry."

Pats be right. I say, "Boy look like a los' child." I yell up to Reggie, "Stick and move, Reggie! Back him up! Dass it! He can't fight backin up, baby! Stick him!"

Reggie hit the boy so hard he knock his mouthpiece out. Referee give it to one of Dashiki's corner men, who wash it. Reggie standing near the corner where the ref tell him. Corner man twice drop the mouthpiece from the ring all the way down to the floor. He do that to give his fighter more time to rest.

Reggie something, he talk straight to the corner man from up the ring. He say, "Say, bro', thanks for the res'."

Corner man jump like he been stuck, but he grin and shake his head because Reggie so cool.

See, boxing look like it a muscle thing, like it be two fools up there just beating each other upside the head. It ain't about the fighter using his strength, it about him delivering force. Boxing a mind game once you know the physical part. Now we deep into Dashiki mind, and he thinking about going home. But his pride won't let him back down. Not yet.

Bell ring, and once he in the corner I see Reggie be breathing hard.

I say, "What wrong."

Reggie say, "I throw a gang of punches. Second wind ain't kicked in." Reggie look like something on his mind.

I say, "Tell him, Pats."

Pats say, "Breathe for me, baby, take it all the way in and let it all fall out. Don't push it out, just let it *fall.* That's it, fill up like a opera singer, fill up from the belly first, and now just let it fall out. Make a sound for me, baby, that's it. Make another."

See, most trainers never talk about breathing and punching at the same time, only say take a deep breath in the corner. Pats, now, he teach breathing like it be a holy thing. He right. Breathing right save you ass. Reggie make a sound like Pats say, and right away he be looking ten years younger.

Fifth round and Dashiki make his run. He come out throwing bombs. Couple times he clip Reggie good and Reggie got to cover up.

Pats say, "Reggie's waiting, Jeet. Dashiki's trying to come on, but he's got zip in his tank. Reggie's got to come back on the boy."

Pats see it good. I yell it up to Reggie. I say, "Don't wait! Double up that right han'! He tired, Reggie, he tired!"

Reggie quick step to his left and he throw a right-hand upper-cut, a right hand over the top, and come back with a hook. One of Dashiki legs buckle, and he get old right there on TV. Harvey on the far side. His face so dark you think he got a rope around his neck. Bell ring and the card girl jump into the ring, all prancing and shaking her booty.

Sixth round and Dashiki all swole up and he be moving in slow motion. Reggie jump him, knock his ass all across the ring. Reggie see a knockout and step it up. He hit the boy with a six-punch combination so pretty it make you dick hard. Boy's legs wobbly and he ready to go. Reggie hit him with five more . . . jab, another left hand, hook to the body, double hook to the head. The boy dead on his feet and stumble back into the corner. But instead of going after him, Reggie back off. When he don't press, I think he hurt his hand.

Pats say, "No good. He held his fookin breath throwin those combinations and got tired. See his mouth open?"

Pats right again. I yell up, "Relax, baby. Breathe good like you suppose, take you time and then come back on him. Make that sound."

Reggie nod and do it, and now he only be jabbing pitty-pat jabs, but he moving good and got good color. When he move off, Dashiki try to come on. Reggie got to be careful. A lucky shot from Dashiki could end his career, Reggie no kid, and when Dashiki catch him a couple of times, he hurt Reggie. But he come back the end of the round, and ain't no doubt about who be boss.

In the corner, I work the grease and tell Reggie what to do out there, but I forget to talk about breathing.

Pats don't. He say, "See what happened? You had him ready to go. You were punching good, but you forgot to breathe. That's what made you tired."

Reggie sit up straight. He say, "You right! Yeah, dass right!"

Reggie smile big, because now he know that he not be tired because he old.

Pats say, "You got to breathe all the time, son. Now breathe for me and let it fall out, you know how, make that sound for me."

Reggie do it, he sigh big and he revive quick. But he was cut in the lower lip and spitting blood. He got hit while he breathing with his mouth open, when he locked up after putting that beating on Dashiki. We didn't see it until he came into the corner, so Pats worked on it from outside the ropes. Got most of it.

Little blond bitch come prancing by with card number seven in the air and that stringy thing up her behind. Be smiling at Reggie like he the king. Bell ring for the seventh. Reggie breathing right again and he all fresh and he moving like a pup. Stone kicked Dashiki's ass for three minutes. Cut his eye so bad that when Dashiki wipe at the blood he can't believe so much be on his glove. Reggie stay in that eye like he working on a pussy, bust it up some more every time he hit it, and he keep *on* hitting it. I call up to Reggie, say that Dashiki eyeball be showing through the cut lid, say that Dashiki ready to go blind. It ain't true, and Reggie know it, but Dashiki don't know that, understand what I'm saying? Dashiki cover his face, and now Reggie go the liver, go to the solar plex, go that short rib, cheat around to the kidney. Reggie fighting like he champion of the world.

I shout, "Git down, Reggie, have fun! Be pretty for me, baby!"

Reggie be tearing him up. Dashiki try, but he outclass and he know it. I keep yelling up to Reggie that Dashiki can't fight backing up. Dashiki hear that again and he want his mama. Bell ring and Pats go into the ring to work on that lip. But first he got to wipe all that Dashiki blood off Reggie. I be catching Reggie's bloody spit when Reggie jump straight into the air, run around the ring and whoop like a wild Indian. Pats look up, I look up.

What it is that me and Pats don't see is the referee have came across the ring. He waving his hands to signal the fight over, that

Dashiki quit in the corner and Reggie the winner. Me and Pats jump up like Reggie, all of us be shouting like kids at the day care. Harvey be lookin up at the lights like he the one with the concussion. Dashiki face all busted up, but they got the blood from the eye to stop. Dashiki a man and come over to say good fight to Reggie and me and Pats.

Pats say, "You're a good fighter, Dashiki, don't let this stop you."

Dashiki say, "I be back. Got some shit to learn."

With Reggie, we go to Dashiki corner to shake the trainers' hands. Back in the dressing room, Pats wash Reggie down with alcohol and we pack our gear and we ready to go. Harvey payday man come in with Reggie's check. He a little old Jewish dude, got that round thing on his head, nice little dude. He got laughing eyes and a voice like candy. He explain the deductions and have Reggie sign a paper say he understand. He say Reggie some kind of warrior, say he fight like he be from the ancient time. He give us roast chestnuts from a little brown bag. Reggie want to take him home. Little dude tell us Jewish jokes and leave us laughing.

Reporters next, and then Harvey come in smiling like he on top of the world. He go on about how pretty Reggie fight, how he slick and smooth, how he can box and how he can punch.

"Listen, you guys," he say. "I know you think this payday is chump change, and that you're pissed about the deductions."

Reggie cut him off. He say, "You owe me fifteen dollars and ninety cent, plus tax."

Harvey say, "For what?"

Reggie say, "For two times at the buffet."

Harvey say, "Oh, hell, no big thing." He smile big, pull a twenty-dollar bill from a roll in his pocket and give it Reggie. "Keep it."

Reggie take the twenty, pull four ones and ten pennies from his pocket, and he give them to Harvey. Reggie say, "I pay the tax. Here you change."

Harvey say, "No hard feelings about the chow, okay? Just don't forget that I'm the guy who gave you the opportunity to show the world you're not washed-up, right? Because of my faith in you, you're going to take on Babaloo. I got him signed for you already."

Now Harvey Silvershade love Reggie Love because he thinking to promote the Babaloo USBA fight. It funny. Harvey have sign Babaloo for Dashiki, and now he trying to make it look like he do it for Reggie. Reggie eyes be getting cold again.

Harvey say, "So this payday wasn't that much, okay?, but I figure after tonight you'll kayo Babaloo. Once we get the USBA, I say we defend it twice in Vegas for fifty thousand a fight. Then we go for the IBF title and a real chunk of change. I say you got another six big fights in you, Reggie. With the right opponents I get you, we're talking maybe a couple of million or more per fight. How does that sound?"

Reggie say, "It depend what my manager say."

Harvey say, "You're right, I'm not supposed to talk money if he's not here. So why don't we drop it for now?, and you and your guys come up to the penthouse. I've got some friends I think you'd like to meet, you know, like the card girls'll be there, and I've got some steaks ordered and some champagne on ice."

Reggie know the party was suppose to be for Dashiki. Reggie say, "Don't like no steak, don't drink no liquor, and don't slip around."

Harvey say, "Not a problem. I'll order up some ribs."

Reggie say, "Don't eat no swine."

Harvey say, "Yeah, well, whaddaya like?"

Reggie say, "Chicken and fish."

Harvey say, "I'll order both. How long'll it take you to get up there?"

Reggie say, "Firs', we got to get our stuff back to the other place up the street through the snow."

Harvey say, "Yeah, too bad about the snow. Hey! I can have my guys schlepp your gear over there for you. You can come upstairs right now. View of the boardwalk's pretty as a bitch at night."

Pats say, "We got the shit over here, we'll get it back, Jackie. We do our job." He still thinking about his lost teeth and want to put Harvey on his ass.

I see Harvey not happy. He say, "Fine, that's what you want. But I'll go ahead and order up the chicken and fish. When can I expect you?"

Reggie say, "Can't expec'. We goin celebrate wit our friends up the cafeteria."

Harvey go all pink in the face like he been caught playing with his dick. He say, "Okay, whatever. Maybe next time, whaddaya say?"

Reggie say, "Who know?"

Promoter back out the door smiling, but his eyes be sick. Now what go down here between Reggie and Harvey don't mean that Valentine Reggie Love won't work with Harvey Silvershade Promotions if the money be right. Reggie just want the white Jew to know he be dealing with a black Jew.

Million Dollar Baby

Boxing is an unnatural act," whispered the voice. "Understand me on this, kid. Everything in boxing is backwards to life. You want to move to the left, you don't step left, you push on the right toe, like this. To move right, you use the left toe, see?" The old white man didn't look into your eyes, he looked clear through your eyes, and straight to the inside of the back of your head. "Instead of runnin from pain, which is the natural thing in life, in boxing you step to it, get me? So now, once you've made the decision to *be* a fighter, now you gotta know *how* to fight, because no matter how tough you are, my friend, these dudes with the big dicks will knock you out."

The voice of Frankie Dunn pierced. In the same sentence it could climb high and harsh or loop sweet as a peach, like Benny Goodman playing "Body and Soul," or go on down deep as a grizzly's grunt. It could move sideways on you and then curl back on itself, but always the voice pierced the mind with images that stuck, because the sound out of the old man painted pictures that became part of you, made you hear his voice when he wasn't even there. When Frankie Dunn told a fighter how to move and why, the fighter could see it through Frankie's eyes, and feel it slip on into his own flesh and down into his bones, and he'd flush with the magic of understanding and the feeling of power. Some called the old man Doc, some called him Uncle Frank. Old-time black fighters and trainers called him Frankie Dunn Frankie Dunn, repeating his name with a nod or a smile. Frankie loved warriors.

It was close to one hundred degrees in the Hit Pit, a gym located down a flight of twenty crumbly brick steps on Fifth near Maple—smack in the middle of the Nickel, Skid Row in downtown Los Angeles. It was summertime and steamy, packed with fighters of every color, some of them eight and ten years old, some of them thirty and more, vets who'd fought anyone anywhere.

Two of the fighters sparring, one black and one Chicano, had title fights coming up in different weight divisions. It was nothing for fighters to sweat off six pounds in a workout, often more. Nearly all of the fighters were men, but there were three who were women as well.

Trainers, swaying like cobras, worked with their fighters, isolated in the noise and the heat and the steam. Some hunched close to whisper, others yelled out loud. Sweat poured off of everyone, even the dozen or so onlookers who sat in the short stretch of low bleachers facing the two rings. Boom boxes blared different music from four corners and along the walls, making the place sound like a cell block.

Frankie toweled off a promising 130-pounder, a sixteen-year-old Chicano kid from Boyle Heights. The way he was going, the boy looked like he had a shot on the Olympic team. The next boy scheduled to work with Frankie was a black professional, a ten-round heavyweight with a record of 19, 1 and 1, with 17 kayos. Despite Frankie's age, he hung with his fighters on the punch mitts, regardless of their size. Frankie had slopey shoulders, and the veins in his forearms stuck out purple and dark against his fair skin. His brows were thick with waxy scar tissue. He was blind in his left eye, and the eyelid drooped. When he slept, it stayed open. He'd been a freckle-face as a kid, had curly black hair. Now his nose was a lump and his face was weathered, a pink map against his full head of wavy white hair. Except for the white girl sitting in the stands, he was the only Caucasian in the gym. But race had never mattered to Frankie, and since he wasn't afraid of color, never had been, he was respected by everyone in the gym, including the Muslim trainers and fighters. Africans especially delighted in him.

Moving pictures play in the heads of old people that young people don't know about. Sometimes a whole day from fifty years ago will play between two winks. For no reason, Frankie remembered when retired fighter Houston "Stone" Stokes came through the gym one day. He had his two youngest children—a six- and a seven-year-old, a boy and a girl. Frankie had trained Houston, and they'd made money together, traveled all over. But Houston couldn't get the kids to stay out of the rings, so he hollered out to scare them.

"Any y'all wanta buy these two? Sell 'em bof cheap!"

That got the kids' attention, especially when Frankie said, "I might buy 'em, Stone. Will they work?"

"Hell, yeah, dey'll work!"

"But will they pick cotton?"

At the checkers table, old Earl McClure, tubercular and looking like a mummy, slapped his thigh and liked to fell out of his chair laughing. Earl was gone to God now, and was in Frankie's prayers. But in a lick, the kids crawled up their daddy's leg and Stone winked at Frankie and whispered, "Man, you still da bes' in da game."

Frankie was old enough to have such memories, and often they tugged at his sleeve. But he had some goals as well, dreams that still thumped through him. His heavyweight might just be the one—on a two-million-dollar purse, two hundred thousand would go to Frankie. As he stood thinking how he'd split the money with his children, someone tapped him on the shoulder from behind and said, "Sir?"

Frankie turned to see the white girl from the stands.

"Yeah?"

"Yessir, your name's Frankie Dunn, ain't that rat?"

The way she said it, it was more a statement than a question, and she spoke with a hillbilly accent. Two thick braids of deep auburn hair hung down behind each ear, framing a freckled face and a pair of agate eyes, like Frankie's daughter's. She was maybe five feet nine and weighed a fit 140. She was relaxed and stood gracefully, her weight balanced on both feet, and despite a broken nose, she was a looker. Frankie had seen her hanging around the gym for a week or so, had seen other trainers buzz her. He had the feeling he'd seen her someplace before.

"Frankie Dunn's the name," he said, expecting the worst. "What, I owe you money?"

"No, sir," she said, serious as a pregnant girlfriend, "but we got us a problem bigger'n a tranny in a Peterbilt."

"We, did you say? *We* do?"

"D'I stutter?"

Frankie said, "What's this great big problem we're supposed to have?"

"Problem's about me gittin you to start trainin me."

He laughed out loud. "Tranny in a Peterbilt's right! See, I don't train girls."

"You don't remember me? Couple a winters ago, up Kansas City? My first fight?"

Frankie's eyes wandered off, then squinted as they swung back into focus. "Now I do."

"Got my nose broke good, 'member? Almost knocked down, too, but went ahead on and won anyway. In the dressin room everyone was whoopin like it was Jack Daniels night at the auction, but you kept out of it. 'Member that?"

"I was in K.C. with my heavyweight for a eight-rounder. Yeah, saw your fight on the monitor in the dressing room."

"'Member what you said?"

"Well, didn't you ask me?"

"You said, 'Girlie, tough ain't enough.'"

"I did," said Frankie.

"And then you said, 'This game's about money, not tough.' Right?"

"Right."

"Well, sir, that's why I come to L.A."

"Wait, now, no way did I say I'd train you," said Frankie.

"Don't I know it?"

"Then what's the problem?"

"Problem's still the same," she said. "Me gittin you to train me, boss."

"I ain't your boss."

"If I don't call you boss, will you train me?"

"No."

"Then I might jus' well call you boss, right?"

"Wrong," he said. "Come on over here."

Frankie led her to the weight room, where the only noise was grunts and clanging weights. On the way, he thought of all the reasons against training a female fighter. Most important, he simply didn't like seeing women getting hit. Regardless, there were now girls in the amateurs, and soon they'd be going to the Olympics. There would be more and more of them, so they would get better and better. That meant they'd be better than the ones currently fighting, and people said that would be good for the game. He didn't care how good they got. Girls getting busted up went against everything he believed in.

Okay, he thought, times have changed. Dames are doing what guys is doing, but that don't make it right. And then there were the practical reasons. Scheduling fights around periods. And bruised tits. And what if one was pregnant and had a miscarriage because of a fight? That, and he couldn't cuss. Not that he cussed that much. But sometimes cussing was the best way to say what you had to say. Like, *Keep your fookin hands up!*

"Yeah," he said to her, continuing his thoughts aloud, "and half of them are degenerates wearing purple jockey shorts and talking feminist bullshit, know what I mean? And when you train broads, you can't cuss because you get sued."

"Not by me, boss, I'm from the Ozarks."

"And then there are the ones who swagger in braggin about what their tongues had been up to the night before at the Puss 'n' Boots or the Yellow Brick Road."

"I ain't no lezzie, if that's what's you're sayin," she said. "I can lay a little pipe with the best of 'em."

"That's none of my business either way, and that's the point . . . whatever the hell you are, leave it outside the gym."

"So does that mean you're gonna train me?"

"No, damn it." Then he softened. "It's nothin personal, see? But I'd have to change too much. And I only got so much gas in my tank, see? Besides, you're too old, too."

"I'm only thirty-two."

"See what I mean? Guys start young, you have to, because this stuff takes time, like ballet. You wouldn't start ballet thinkin you could get to the top at your age, but people seem to think they can come to this game late as they want. It takes four years to make a fighter, like college. And that's besides the time it takes to get and win fights, forget about the setbacks."

"I been at it almost three. And it ain't as if I ain't been a athlete."

"A ton of gals come from karate, which is another thing entirely, startin with balance. The women also come from softball, or basketball, or volleyball, or soccer. Which one is you?"

"All of the above."

"Or they're out to make some kind of social statement in a game that's about kickin the shit outta the other guy for money. I tried to train a couple of gals, I know what I'm talkin about. One old bull come in wearin a deerstalker with her BILLYBLUEs for Chri'sakes. Besides, women poundin on women, that just don't make no sense to me, not when so many of them are pushed into the ring before they know anything. Sure, there are some who can fight. And when you have two in there who can, you get a good show and usually nobody gets hurt. But a lot of the time you get girls in there who can't fight, or one is so overmatched it's a cryin shame."

"Ain't it up to the fighters to do what they want, no matter their sex?"

"To a degree, sure it is, but what about fights that are freak shows?, more like dog fights? I saw two little hunred-ten-pounders, and all they did was stand toe-to-toe and wing punches like they were out behind a liquor store fightin on broken glass. Got their eyes all tore up. One got a broken jaw, and the winner went to the hospital with a ruptured spleen. What the hell is that? And then, what if a gal up and dies on you? Nah, get one of the other guys."

"I don't wont one'a them." She smiled, and it almost broke his heart.

"Why are you so set on me?"

"'Cause with you, I know I can make money."

"That's the first smart thing you've said. But most of the girls don't make money. Yeah, right now they're makin double a round in the prelims what the preliminary boys are makin, but girls're only fighting two-minute rounds, so we're back to the freak show again. And what's this crap about some of the girls gettin title shots after only six or eight fights, maybe less? The titles ain't real, see? No big gates. That's why it's a long way off before girls get big dough, understand?"

"I'd fight three-minute rounds if they'd let me."

"But they won't. See?, it ain't the same."

"Look at me, Mr. Frankie Dunn. Let's say you're right about girl fighters. But I'm thirty-two, and if I can't slop my trough boxin, where in hail is this ol' hillbilly gal gonna?"

"Let's say you get hurt."

"It's on my shoulders, not yours. You won't regret it, boss, I promise."

"No deal."

She hung her head, then looked up at him and left the gym.

"Good," said Frankie.

She was born and raised in southwestern Missouri, in the hills outside the scratch-ass Ozark town of Theodosia. Many of the towns strung along two-lane Highway 160 were little more than a gas station and a post office set into the cedars and the oak trees somewhere between nowhere and good-bye. She was trailer trash, like so many of the people in the region, and grew up being looked down on. Before her daddy died, things had been different.

Her oldest sister, Mardell, ran off when she was fifteen. Her brother Eustace was in jail. The other one, J.D., was a corporal in the army. J.D. had four kids and a pregnant wife and was collecting welfare just to get by. Her other sister still lived with her mother, both of them weighing over three hundred pounds. Welfare and food stamps got them month to month. Aside from fried catfish or fried chicken, they lived on biscuits and gravy, Oreos, and Always Save cola.

She got to the gym every day before Frankie. She wore shorts, two T-shirts, and a sweatshirt cut off at the elbows. She wrapped her hands and worked nonstop, mostly jumping rope and belting away at the big bag, the body bag. She didn't know how to work it properly, and knew it, so when she finished one day she went straight to Frankie, who was pulling gear from his bag.

"Sorry to pester, but I ain't got it right, right?"

He nodded.

"Gotta be a trick to it."

He spat in the ring bucket. "Okay, I'll show you, but just this once."

He went to the big bag and gave it a shove. Then he began to move with it, maintaining the same distance as he slid toward it or back, whether he pivoted to the side or moved around it.

"Stalk, don't walk," he said. "You gonna work the big bag, first you got to think of it as a man, not a bag. Once you understand that, you don't start punchin until the bag swings away from you." He demonstrated as he spoke. "It's dead weight, see? So if you hit it when it swings toward you, it knocks you back, smothers your punches, takes your balance—it don't allow you full extension on your shots, no follow-through. Joe Louis said you don't punch your opponent, you punch *through* your opponent."

She did as Frankie had instructed. She was awkward at first, but once she found her balance, she began to move as Frankie had, rotating first one shoulder forward, then the other, which kept her head moving without her having to think about it.

"That's it, rotate. That way your head's always movin and you always have one shoulder back ready to fire a power shot—so you don't have to do somethin before you do somethin, say if you got a openin. Don't stop, move with the bag, circle it," he said, giving it a shove. "It will tell you when to punch, just like an opponent."

Frankie walked away and forgot about her as he focused on his boys.

"Dang thing does tell you when to punch," she muttered, a world of angles and planes opening up to her. She stayed with it until well after Frankie left the gym. By the time he got there the next day, she had it down, was throwing punches to the body and to the head—hooks off the jab, uppercuts, stinging jabs, and right-hand leads followed by double hooks, and moving off to the side behind double and triple jabs.

"How's 'at?"

"Not bad, but you're throwin arm punches still. They're good shots, because you're strong, but you got to work too hard. First, you got to line up at a forty-five-degree angle, understand? And then you got to turn your waist as you punch. When you throw a right-hand, you got to step out to the left six inches as you move half a step in with both feet. That frees your right hip and leg and foot, like this, so you can *snap* your ass into your shots. I mean your back-side."

"You got it the first time. Got one on me like a forty-dollar mule."

Do you ever, Frankie thought, and long legs with calves like a ballerina. Long arms and a short body, perfect for a fighter. Because of her sweatshirt and T-shirts, he couldn't be sure about her bust-line, but she didn't seem to be top-heavy, which was good for a girl fighter.

Next day she was still throwing arm punches. The next as well, and the next—no knockouts that way. Frankie watched her while he worked his fighters, watched as other trainers tried to hook up with her. She smiled politely, sometimes nodded, but mostly shook her head.

She sat down beside Frankie on a low blue bench. "Keep on tryin, but I just ain't gittin it. How come?"

"No balance," said Frankie. "Don't know how to switch your weight."

"How'm I gonna learn, boss?"

"Any of these trainers can teach you."

"Not hardly."

"Why not?"

"'Cause even I can see that most a their fighters got the same problem I got."

He smiled. "You know how to hit the speed bag?"

"Arm punches, like they do in the movies." She smiled, confessing her ignorance. "It's all I know."

"Where's your speed bag?"

"Ain't got one."

"Christ."

Frankie reached for his speed bag, pumped it firm with a bicycle pump, and screwed the swivel into an adjustable round platform overhead that was the right height for both of them.

"In the movies," he said, "you're right, all flash and no ass." He caught himself. "I mean no backside. But there's more to it than that. There's rhythm and hand-eye coordination. But most of all it's balance. Remember that word, balance. I'm talkin about bein able to switch it from one foot to the other quick as you can blink."

"I thought it was about hittin the dang thing hard."

"You don't hit hard in boxing, you hit right. Watch," Frankie said. "And count with me, one, two, three, four. I drive my left fist straight through on the count of *one*. As I do, my weight is on my right foot. Then I rock over and put my weight on my left foot and leave it there while on *two* I punch the bag with the butt of my left fist like I was stickin it with an ice pick from the side, like this. While my weight is still on my left foot, I drive through the bag on *three* with my right. Now I drop my weight back over to my right foot again, and on *four* I do the ice-pick move with my right."

Frankie sped up slightly, and she could see how the bag moved in a figure eight. Frankie said, "Watch my hips turn as I go from foot to foot. Ass is where the power comes from, understand? Sorry about *ass*, but I don't know what else to call it."

Frankie shifted into high gear, banging the bag in a steady one, two, three, four count that had the bag smacking the platform three times for every time Frankie punched the bag—*bip*-bip-bip, *bip*-bip-bip, *bip*-bip-bip, *bip*-bip-bip. His waist turned with every punch, and because it did, the punches were delivered effortlessly. Tickled by the show, Maggie watched as the old man also moved his feet in a half circle beneath the platform and then back again—balance, leverage, speed, power. He continued until the bell rang, the bag a blur. Breathing easily, he stepped back for her to try.

"Wait," she said. "You did something with your breathing, too."

"You noticed."

"How'm I supposed to breathe?"

"We'll get to that when"—he caught himself. "No, we won't. I don't have time, honey, honest."

"I told you we had a problem," she said.

"Go on," he said. "Show me how good you are."

"I can't do all that. I know I can't."

"You want balance, you will," he said, taking his bag down and walking away.

"Dang!" she said.

The next day she bought a speed bag just like Frankie's. She'd be on short rations for a few days, but she didn't care. She waited until Frankie left late in the afternoon, and then she went after the speed bag, in absolute slow motion at first, and then, as her switch in balance became fluid, she was able to speed up. She worked until the gym closed at eight. *Bip*-bip-bip, *bip*-bip-bip, *bip*-bip-bip, *bip*-bip-bip.

She was ready for him in a week and was so good he had to grin.

"Okay," he said, "now show me what you can do on the big bag."

She tore it up, moved, bobbed, and weaved, rotated her shoulders and fired her shots without having to do something before she did something. Stepped to her left and in when she threw her right, and drove with her ass, her balance on her front knee.

"Not bad, *macushla*. Keep movin that behind."

"You won't regret trainin me," she said. "I promise."

"*No,* I said."

She worked on both bags, getting better each day, her punches so quick and sure that fighters and trainers stopped to watch her bang.

On the following Monday she was ready for Frankie again. She handed him a dated document, handprinted on lined paper ripped from a spiral notebook.

> To who it may concern Mr. Frankie Dunn has my OK. to use any word he sees fit. That means all 3 letter words and 4 letter words and 5 letter words and 6 letter words and 7 letter words and 8 letter words and even 10 and 12 letter words too and any other words he sees fit. I am in sound mind and body and these are my true wishes that come from my heart and my mind and my soul.
>
> > Signed,

Her signature was a scrawl he could not decipher. He stared at her, and she stared right back.

He said, "Who trained you for the fight in K.C.?"

"Me."

"You got a manager?"

"You."

"You got a job?" He didn't want somebody looking for a Santa Claus.

She said, "Waitressin breakfast six to noon on out by the beach."

He said, "What's your record?"

"Nine and three, but only one knockout."

"You never had a trainer?"

"I tried workin with some at first, but what they wanted was to bed me, men and women both. Hail, I wanted to learn how to fight, not the dirty leg."

He said, "What's your name, anyway?"

"Margaret Mary."

"Margaret Mary what?"

"Margaret Mary Fitzgerald. But my daddy called me Maggie."

Fightin Maggie Fitzgerald, thought Frankie, turning away. "Ah, Jaysus."

"Here's my deal," said Frankie. "You do what I say. I don't do what you say."

"I do."

"I show you moves and you can't do them, that's okay. But I give you moves you can do but don't want to do, that ain't okay."

"I do."

"You don't like workin with me, quit me at any time, no hard feelins," he went on. "I don't like workin with you, I quit you anytime, no hard feelins."

"I do."

So it began, Frankie stripping her down to the bare wood. She worked so hard he wished his boys worked the same way. He tested her power and stamina by taking her round after round on the punch mitts. He went with her to make sure she ran right. He taught her the correct stance, how to keep her legs under her the width of her shoulders, instead of spread wide and dug in.

"Why?"

"Balance—with balance you're free, and because your reach is longer when your legs are under you than spread wide apart." He proved it to her.

He showed her how to move in and out, and side to side. He taught her how to fight backing up. For her legs, he randomly tossed the punch mitts to the canvas one at a time and had her scramble to pick them up. She lasted a minute before her legs gave out the first day. In two weeks she was going three 3-minute rounds and learned how to use her thighs, glutes, and leg biceps the way fighters use them.

He taught her how to stay on the balls of her feet, how to generate momentum off her right toe; how to keep her weight over her left knee, to flex on it when she fired her jab; how to double up and triple the jab, which would keep the opponent backing up on her heels. He taught her how to cut off the ring, how to slip punches and counter off lefts and rights. No matter how hard he drove her, she was always ready for more. His heart went out to her, *macushla—mo cuishle* in Gaelic: darling, my blood.

"You got a bad habit of dropping your left hand, like so," he told her. "Joe Louis had that problem, even though he had won twenty-seven fights in a row, twenty-three by knockouts. That was before Max Schmeling came over the top of Louis's lazy left and knocked Joe out."

"Louis beat him the second fight."

"Yeah, but they're one and one in the record book," Frankie said. "It's okay if you're baitin someone, gettin her to throw a lead right so you can slip or counter—it's okay because you're ready for the froggy to jump. Sugar Ray Robinson would do it, then he'd take a short step back and *yop!*, fire a good-night hook. But you ain't there yet."

"Protect myself at all times."

"It's a rule."

He had her spar with the other girls in the gym. As he suspected, she held her breath under pressure and got tired. So he taught her how to breathe. Breathing correctly allowed her to shoot quicker shots at will, and she whacked the punch mitts relentlessly. When he had her spar with the girls again, she ran them out of the ring.

"How'm I doin, boss?"

"Better."

"I'm down to one-thirty."

Just right, Frankie thought, tall and rangy for her weight, with reach and power. He smiled to himself as he turned away—and she's getting so slick she can fight in the rain and not get wet.

When Frankie couldn't get sparring for her with the girls, he put her in with boys to toughen her up, to get her system used to shock. The boys weighed the same and had the same experience, and usually she'd take a pounding. But sometimes it went the other way, and one day she knocked a boy down with an uppercut off a jab, followed by a straight right-hand, picture-book stuff. A gym rat called up to the boy. "Hey, man! You gonna let a girl beat you?"

Frankie said, "That ain't a girl, that's a fighter."

The rat put his hands up and backed away.

In the beginning, given Maggie's mediocre record and apparent lack of power, it was easy to get her fights, especially since promoters were eager to put on fights with girls—club fights in Reseda and Sacramento, casinos on remote Indian reservations. Maggie was to fight four 2-minute rounds at two hundred dollars a round. Frankie dressed her in traditional kelly-green, a big gold shamrock on the back of her robe beneath MAGGIE in white, and she kicked ass. Four fights and four kayos, two coming in the first minute of the first round.

A week after her last fight, with her record now at 13 and 3 with 5 kayos, Maggie was offered a shot in the 130-pound Junior Lightweight Division in Hamburg against Billy Astrakhov, "the Blue Bear," for twenty thousand dollars. Frankie turned it down, though he had to cash in some savings bonds.

Maggie asked, "Why, boss? I coulda bought a car."

"We ain't ready."

In her last fight, Maggie had dropped her left hand and got a black eye off a lead right-hand.

"You got Irish skin. What I say about keepin your mitts up?"

"I didn't even feel it," she said.

"Wait till you start playin with the big kids," Frankie said. "Tell me when you're ready for six rounds."

"Yesterdee."

Going up in class, Maggie won her first and second six-rounders by decision but knocked out her next three opponents, all in the third, sending one of them to the hospital with a broken eardrum and a concussion.

"Welcome to boxing," Frankie said.

"Will she be all right?" Maggie said.

"Probably. But what if she ain't?"

"Guess she'll hafta git herself a ol' hairy leg and have a batch of kids," she answered. Having said it, she saw herself at thirteen standing barefoot in the dirt in a faded little dress, impetigo spreading across her face. "Naw, I don't mean that."

Now her record was 18 and 3, with 8 knockouts, and Frankie was getting her eighteen hundred a fight. She was beginning to get attention in the media, and several articles about her had appeared in the fight magazines. But other managers became afraid to put their girls in with Maggie, not wanting to risk their fighter's record for the short money the small-time promoters could afford to pay. So Frankie sweetened the pot on his own, pulling cash from his savings account to pay as much as three thousand dollars extra to the other girl through the promoter. Maggie's record became 19 and 3, with 9 knockouts, which was less than a 50 percent kayo ratio. But her record with Frankie was 10 and 0, with eight opponents being counted out, a knockout ratio of 80 percent.

"Let me pay at least half of what you gotta pay," she said.

"Nah, I'll get mine back. Quit your job."

They took an eight-round fight in London for eight thousand dollars, and two thousand in training expenses. They were on the undercard of a featherweight title fight, and for the event Frankie had a new outfit made for Maggie, the green so pale it was almost white and would sparkle under the lights. On her shorts, in kelly-green Celtic lettering, was MAGGIE. On the back of her robe was a gold Irish harp. Above the harp, in kelly-green Celtic lettering trimmed in gold, was the Gaelic MO CUISHLE. Frankie had her wear the robe at the weigh-in, and when the Irish press saw it, news of her immediately went on Irish TV and into the newspapers. The

English media followed, and the Irish living in England filled the stadium. Frankie had pipers in kilts escort her to the ring at fight time, and the crowd was chanting *Ma-cush-la! Ma-cush-la!*

The fight was shown in the States on Wide World of Sports, and Maggie stopped her opponent—a tough Jamaican girl in dreadlocks with a record of fourteen straight knockouts—on cuts in the sixth. When Maggie got back to Los Angeles, all the TV stations wanted her for interviews. Her price went up, and Frankie got her fights in Vegas and Atlantic City for fifty thousand dollars, which was more than most top male contenders were getting. Now all the promoters had pipers march Maggie to the ring. The Irish, who had laid low for so long, began to strut. Based on her last two wins, one of them by knockout, Frankie signed a conditional contract with a New York promoter for two 10-round fights in Madison Square Garden. For the first fight Maggie would get an unprecedented seventy-five thousand. If she won that fight, the purse would be a hundred thousand for the second. Irish fight fans from Boston filled chartered trains down to New York.

Maggie's first New York opponent hit the canvas in the fourth. The other quit in her corner after eight. The headlines on the sports page of *The New York Times* read MACUSHLA FIRST MILLION $$$ BABY?

Another offer for the title came from Atlantic City, but Frankie turned it down because of the money split.

"No way we're takin less than the champ," said Frankie. "We're the draw, not that Russian kraut, whatever she is."

Frankie and Maggie were putting money in the bank. And now all the managers of all girl fighters everywhere, because of the big money Maggie generated, wanted to fight her. Frankie knew she could beat them. But by then they'd been working together almost three years, and he also knew that time was running out for Maggie, that her body could only take so much punishment. Her brothers and sisters were writing and calling for money. She began sending five hundred dollars a month to her mother, Earline. Between fights, Frankie went with her back to Missouri, where she bought and furnished a comfortable, two-bedroom brick house for her mother as a surprise.

"But how'll I get welfare and my food stamps?" said Earline.

"Can't you and Roxanne git a job?"

"Your sis and me watch late movies and sleep too late for that."

"Then sell the damn house."

"Can you spare a little cash, honey?"

"Here's two hundred," said Maggie.

"When you come home next time, leave your boyfriend behind."

"Mama, what have you become?"

She fought in Johannesburg and Paris. Frankie had taught her to stick and move, to rip and tear, to keep her opponents out at the end of her punches, instead of letting them get in close. Both girls quit in the corner. From Paris, she went to Dublin, where she sparred with three girls—two rounds each—in an exhibition to raise money for Ireland's amateur boxing program. The lord mayor proclaimed it Maggie Macushla Day and gave her the key to the city. The streets were packed with cheering fans.

"Money in the bank," said Frankie.

Though Frankie now devoted much of his time to Maggie, he never shorted his other fighters, working with them daily and traveling with them when they had fights out of town. Jet lag killed him, but he was always back at the gym the next day. His fighters, eager as baby birds, never knew how tired he was. Girls from as far as Brazil showed up wanting Frankie to train and manage them.

"I'll split the money fifty-fifty," they'd offer. One of them offered a seventy-thirty split and showed him nude photos of herself, the implication clear.

"I know you won't understand," Frankie would tell them, "but I don't train girl fighters."

More than one called him a male chauvinist pig.

When Maggie's ten-round title fight with Astrakhov was finally made, it was to be held at the Mirage Hotel in Las Vegas, and to be shown on HBO. Frankie negotiated a two-fight deal that gave $225,000 to Maggie. If Maggie won that fight, the contract for the second title fight, against an unnamed opponent, stipulated that she'd get $500,000.

For the Mirage fight, the champ Astrakhov would get $125,000, or $75,000 more than she'd ever got before. The champ was outraged that she got the short end and vowed revenge for the insult.

Frankie knew that Maggie only had two, maybe three more title fights in her. For sure he wanted her to be the first Million Dollar Baby, wanted her to be somebody before she hung up her gloves, so she'd always be somebody afterward.

"You'll be quittin, too, won't you, boss?" Maggie asked.

"Nah. I'd miss the stink."

Billy "the Blue Bear" Astrakhov was a big-busted, masculine-looking Russian girl living in Hamburg, who grew a faint mustache and dated fashion models. A former Moscow prostitute, she paraded herself in white tuxedos and lavender ties. She was a banger who waded in winging shots from all angles, and she'd been easily beating girls from Berlin to Australia. Considered the dirtiest fighter in the female ranks, she was known to head-butt and throw elbows. She was a big draw in Germany. Her favorite trick was to get inside and jam the palm of her glove into her opponent's nose, breaking it. That she might kill them didn't worry her. She promised to knock Maggie out.

"After I vip her," she said at the weigh-in, grinning and winking at Maggie, "I take her to my room. On a leash."

Maggie was asked to comment.

"I'll break her down like a Winchester and clean both her barrels."

■ ■ ■

Billy wore a Russian fur hat and was dressed in an electric-blue outfit with bright bolts of red-and-purple lightning down each sleeve. She took the hat off to reveal a polished shaved head and clowned confidently around the ring, flexing her arms and smiling to the crowd. Maggie, in her pale green, was iridescent under the colored lights. Slightly flushed, she had broken a sweat in the dressing room and stood in the corner serious and hard.

The Irish were everywhere, different groups of them breaking out in Irish songs. The haunting sound of bagpipes filled the indoor arena.

"Box her," Frankie said. "Stick that jab straight into her big tits till they turn blue and fall off."

The way Frankie sang his war song made Maggie smile. "Now you ain't sorry you saved this ol' hillbilly gal, are you, boss?"

Frankie kissed her on the cheek and whispered, "Macushla, you're my blood. Now go out there and kick the shit out of her."

The bell rang, and the Bear charged across the ring throwing a right-lead haymaker. Maggie slipped under it and, stepping to her left, drilled the Bear with her own right hand to the gut. It was a little low for the sweet spot of the solar plexus, but the Bear still went down gasping for air. The crowd was standing up and cheering, but at the count of nine the Bear got up, too.

"Tough bitch," Frankie said to one of the seconds he'd brought in from Los Angeles.

"Bulldaggers *be* tough."

Maggie hurt Billy twice more with combinations, but the Bear grabbed and held and made it through the round.

Because of the metal legs, Frankie had trouble shoving the heavy corner stool beneath the lowest strand of ropes but had it ready when Maggie got to the corner. He watered and greased her and admonished her to fight from the outside. When the bell rang, the cut man took the stool from Frankie and set it where Frankie could sit on it to watch the fight from ringside.

The bell for the second round rang, and Maggie fired her jabs. Billy continued to grab and hold, in an attempt to turn the match into a brawl and thereby switch the momentum of the fight back to herself. But Maggie was too slick for her, and kept drilling her with jabs and left uppercuts that kept Billy back on her heels. Billy missed so often that she was gasping as much from missing as from the punches Maggie landed. Billy caught Maggie with an elbow but missed when she tried to jam her palm into Maggie's nose. Maggie continued to work on her from the outside, shooting her jab to Billy's breasts like she was ramming her with the end of a two-by-four. The Blue Bear caved at the waist and grunted in pain.

In the third round Maggie's jab had Billy off-balance and stumbling, allowing Maggie to dart in with combinations to the head and body. Billy went down from a one-two-hook combination. Frankie thought Billy had been hurt badly enough to stay down. Since it was a title fight, there was no mandatory eight-count, and after five she was right back in Maggie's face.

Billy grabbed Maggie and tried to throw her to the canvas. The referee warned her that he'd start taking points away if she kept it up, but Billy didn't give a shit and cursed him in Russian. She stepped on Maggie's foot and tried to shove Maggie down again. When Maggie was still off-balance, Billy caught her with an elbow the ref didn't see and cut Maggie's left eye slightly. The real damage was to the tissue around the eye, which caused it to puff up. Frankie's cut man had no trouble stopping the blood, but his ice packs and his ice-cold metal stop-swell did nothing to keep the swelling down, and the eye threatened to close completely.

Frankie told Maggie to go out in the fourth firing, to try for a knockout, because he was afraid the eye would close and the ref would stop the fight. She nailed Billy repeatedly, but Billy stayed up and continued to head-butt. The ref took points away and warned her. Billy would give a fake apology and then go right back to her dirty ways. Between rounds, Maggie complained of blurry vision. She also told Frankie she didn't know how to counter Billy's dirty tactics. Frankie illegally flooded her eye with Visine, and when she said she still couldn't see, he told her she only needed one eye to fight.

"Okay, but what I do about the Bear?" said Maggie.

"You know how to step outside her right hand, and go to the liver with a left hook, right?"

"Been doin that. She's made of steel."

"Not for fookin long," said Frankie. "This time, instead of goin for the liver, I want you to go to the right cheek of her big dyke ass with your left hook, stick it into her sciatic nerve like a dagger, and keep on stickin it."

"What if the ref sees me?"

"Keep the bull bitch between you and him, and he won't. And keep on stickin into that degenerate ass. Got it?"

"You betcha."

Near the end of the fifth, Billy's right leg was dragging and white with pain. Exhausted, she went to one knee for a voluntary eight-count in an attempt to regain her strength and to relieve the pain. It was a good sign, but Frankie was still worried about Maggie's eye, afraid it might close like a clamshell and cost her the title shot.

By the time Billy got up, Maggie's vision still hadn't cleared completely, but she kept the pressure on. She jumped the Russian with combinations that had her head wobbling and the crowd on its feet. The ref was about to stop the fight, when the bell rang.

Maggie had thrown four solid shots in the middle of the ring, all of them landing, and was about to finish Billy off with a left hook to the jaw, but on hearing the bell, she was able to catch herself. Instead of letting the shot go, in an instant she turned to her right, looked with her good eye to see Frankie pushing the ring stool under the rope, and dropped both her hands.

Billy had been ready to throw a righthand at the bell. But instead of holding back like Maggie had, and knowing that Maggie couldn't see properly out of her left eye, she stepped in and ripped a right that caught Maggie on the left ear.

Since Maggie was moving away, the force of the blow was lessened. But it was hard enough, landing where it did, to affect Maggie's inner ear. Suddenly, her equilibrium gone, the ring was a roller-coaster, and she felt like she was stepping into post holes. Though she was fully conscious, her legs began to snap and buckle. She'd never been knocked off her feet, and her mind and body rebelled at the idea of hitting the canvas.

Frankie, busy with the stool, hadn't seen what happened and looked over just as Maggie had begun to stumble toward him, her legs like rubber bands.

"Jaysus!"

He took a step, but Maggie's legs gave out before he could catch her. Falling like deadweight, she plunged past his outstretched arms. Trying to prevent her damaged eye from hitting the canvas, Maggie wrenched her body in an attempt to break the fall by taking it on her side and shoulders. But she twisted too hard, and the back of her neck came down full force on the metal band of the ring stool, her neck breaking at the first and second vertebrae, the sound of it like a boot squashing a snail.

"No!" Frankie cried, watching as she slumped to her side.

Ring doctors rushed to her as Frankie stretched her flat on the canvas. She had stopped breathing.

At all fights in the major boxing states, a fully equipped ambulance and crew stand ready. The doctors immediately called for a stretcher, and Maggie was carried out at a run. The crowd was silent, the pipers numb. Billy stood stock-still, the sweat on her going cold as her pale eyes.

At the ambulance, Maggie was hooked to an Ambu-bag and air was squeezed into her flat lungs just before the four-minute time limit that would have meant brain damage.

As oxygen reached her brain, she mumbled, "I love you, Daddy," but remained unconscious.

Several hours later, specialists at the hospital announced that Maggie was in ICU and had not regained consciousness.

Frankie lied, said he was her grandfather. "Can she breathe on her own yet?"

"No."

"Is there damage to her spinal cord?" Frankie asked, pressing.

"It's too soon."

"I'm a C-1 and C-2 complete, boss," Maggie said. She was gaunt and sallow and the spunk in her was gone. The flesh around her sunken eyes was dark and lifeless. "That means my spinal cord's so bad they never can fix me."

She'd been nine days in a coma. They'd kept her doped-up to keep her head immobile for two weeks after that. Because of her MRI and other tests, her neurologists determined that she was a permanent, vent-dependent quadriplegic unable to breathe without a respirator. As a C-1 and C-2, she was injured at the first and second cervical vertebrae, which meant she could talk and slightly move her head, but that was all. She had lost the ability to breathe on her own, to move her limbs. She could not control her bladder or her bowel movements. She'd be frozen the rest of her life.

It took several hours every day to get her ready for the wheelchair, to check the tubes into her bladder, her stomach, and through the front of her neck. After stretching and manipulating her arms and legs, her attendants would lift her into the wheelchair, where she'd be strapped in. Her bed respirator would be switched for the one built into the wheelchair. Since she couldn't breathe on her own, her bed and wheelchair respirators would always be on Control rather than on Assist—Control meant oxygen was pumped into her twenty-four hours a day.

Because of complications, she remained in Las Vegas two months. She had no appetite but maintained her weight because of the calories they fed her through the stomach tube. She developed skin ulcers because she couldn't change positions and the skin broke down. Her lungs filled with fluid and had to be pumped out when pneumonia struck. There were blood clots in her legs and problems with hemoglobin. To induce a daily bowel movement, she was placed on her side and pressure was applied to her lower abdomen until her waste was pushed out of her. She was humiliated every day of her life.

It was late afternoon. Frankie was sitting by her bed when she woke up. "You okay, darlin?" he asked.

She was still groggy. "Well, you know, they got tubes stickin up me in places I'druther not think about. You ever heard of dysreflexia?"

"Can't say I have."

"It's somethin that happens real quick, like when you git a kink in your pee tube? Gits your heartbeat all to rushin." Embarrassed, she looked away. "I didn't tell you, but a couple a times I liked to have a heart attack in the night. Awful as it is when your heart's fixin to explode, it made me happy, boss, 'cause I thought I'd be free of this mess. Almost made it once. But then I was brought back to bein this same old snowman in January, same old twisted-up snowman sittin here wishin to God it was July."

"Ah, Jaysus," Frankie said. "I knew I was wrong to train you."

"Don't say that, " Maggie said. "Hail, workin with you was the only time since Daddy passed I had respect. Hey!, and we almost did her, too, didn't we, boss?, huh? almost made me the world's first Million Dollar Baby!, ain't that rat?" She smiled but then had to look away, her lips quivering. "Daddy'd a been proud."

. . .

The Boxing Commission would pay for Maggie's hospitalization and rehab. Frankie remained in Vegas for the time Maggie was there. He bunked with a trainer friend and spent all the time with Maggie her doctors would allow. He read newspapers and magazines to her. He brought in a small TV set with a VCR so she could watch movies. He wheeled her around the hospital grounds when it was cool enough.

He arranged for trainers in Los Angeles to work with his fighters and called his boys once a week. They were devastated by what happened to Maggie. All were proud to say they knew her. They called her Macushla.

Maggie could have gone to a rehab clinic in Las Vegas or Missouri but chose to return to Los Angeles for treatment to be close to Frankie. They made the six-hour trip by ambulance. Twice she spasmed into a grotesque caricature of herself, and the attending pulmonologist had to ask Maggie how to untwist her.

"Worse part is the dang bedsores, when they git to stinkin."

At the Evergreen Rehabilitation Center near Third and Alvarado, there was a wide expanse of landscaped lawn, California sycamores, and palms. Maggie was given first-class treatment with genuine concern for her well-being. She was one of ten quadriplegics there, but there were many more paraplegics, and amputees of all kinds. Most of the patients were cheerful. Maggie was one of the ones who wasn't, as each day the dread of a frozen life engulfed her.

Frankie tried to tell her that there was always hope, that new medical miracles were developed every day, but she would turn away and bite her tongue to keep from screaming.

"And even if they don't, now that you're off the heart monitor, you'll be able to move around on your own. They got wheelchairs you can use by blowin into a straw, and TV sets and computers you can operate by your voice. You could go to school. I'd drive you."

Maggie would nod. "I know you would, boss. But somewhere down the line I'll finish up here like ever'body else. I surely can't go home, and there's nowhere else I can go."

"You can stay with me."

"Bein a burden ain't somethin I could handle."

"You're same as my daughter to me," Frankie said, pain and tenderness washing across his Irish moosh. "You'd be no burden, not to me."

"You have no idea," she said. "And all the money I made'd be gone quicker than a whitetail over barb wire."

"I got money."

When Frankie wasn't there, and once her daily care had been administered, Maggie was wheeled from her room at the end of the wing out onto the second-floor balcony. On cold or windy days she sat before the domed window of her room. She never complained, never asked for anything, except for stronger sleep medication. She wished to God she'd get dysreflexia again, get it so bad her heart would squirt right out her ears. If she felt it coming on, she'd keep it to herself next time.

Someone from Maggie's family called every day at first, then once a week. When her brother J.D. learned she was being moved to Los Angeles, he said the family would be out. Maggie told him not to bother.

"Naw, naw, big sister," he said. "Mama wonts to make sure our bidness matters is bein tended to."

The family had been in town a week, spending more time at Universal Studios and Disneyland than with Maggie. On what was to be their last day in Los Angeles, they arrived in Maggie's room with a notary public and a lawyer, who had drawn up papers giving power of attorney to Earline. Maggie told them all to get their hillbilly asses back to the Ozarks. Frankie had watched in silence.

"Did I do wrong?" Maggie asked, when everyone had left.

"Whatever you want is right by me."

"What I want is to donate my money to the American Paralysis Association, so no one else has to live like this."

"Check with your doctor and do it."

"Already did," she said. "Family made that trip out here for nothin."

"Not nothin," said Frankie. "Saw Donald Duck and Mickey."

A day later Maggie's family confronted Frankie in the parking lot. Maggie watched from her balcony. J.D. was six feet three and weighed 260. He was a big-boned man with beefy arms and legs. His hair was a pale blond, and his belly strained the shirt of his uniform. Frankie was five-eight and weighed 160.

"Hey there, bud," said J.D. "We wont you to stay away from our kin."

"Tell you what," said Frankie. "Let's go see Maggie. She tells me to stay away, I stay away."

"Ain't gonna be like that," said J.D. "You're suckin up to Sis just to git her money, an' that dog don't hunt."

"You're wrong, bubba. Just knowin her's been enough."

"If I gotta hurt you, I'll hurt you, old man," said J.D.

"You couldn't hurt a ant with a hammer."

"How old are you, bud?"

"Pick a number," Frankie said.

J.D. slammed Frankie into a car and tried to get him in a choke hold. Frankie dropped his chin to his chest, kneed J.D. in the balls, and spun free when J.D. involuntarily grabbed to protect himself. Frankie faked a left, then threw a right-hand lead, and J.D. raised his hands to cover his face. As Frankie threw the right, he'd also stepped to his right and drilled a left hook to J.D.'s big gut, popping the buttons off his shirt. J.D. grunted and bent over in pain as Frankie slipped to his right again, which placed him behind J.D. Frankie put everything into a right hand and a hook that were designed to rupture J.D.'s left kidney. J.D. screamed and rolled into a gasping ball on the asphalt.

Frankie took two quick steps to the mother and daughter and slapped both of them full force in the face. The sister sat flat down, and Earline yelled at J.D. for not protecting her.

Frankie was on fire. "Git!" he shouted, treating them like dogs. "Go on, git!"

Maggie's mother struck a pose. "Take us back home, J.D., where folks is decent."

Maggie had seen the beef and was proud of Frankie when he climbed the back steps to her balcony.

"Dang if you still ain't got some of the moves, Mr. Dunn," she said, smiling.

"Sorry about what happened, it bein your family," said Frankie, sitting down.

Maggie said, "You remind me of my daddy, I ever tell you that?"

"No."

"Same slopey shoulders, same veiny arms," she said, watching as her family drove out of the parking lot. "See, he was a over-the-road trucker, Daddy was, and he kept that rig of his lookin like a Easter egg. Had this big ol' dog Axel, a German shepherd that traveled ever'where with him. Daddy was gone a lot, but whenever he come home it was like Christmas, and we'd have us a high old time. Clothes and toys for us kids, dresses and silky things for Mama, and store-bought pie, if he'd come through Collins.

"Only thing Daddy spent money on for himself, besides work clothes, was chew, and he was a dude about chew. Back then there was this tobacco shop out here in Santa Monica someplace where he'd drive outta his way to stop in and buy ten pounds at a time 'cause it was so far from home. It was tasty stuff, flavored and sweet like candy. He'd buy licorish, and lime- and rum-flavored stuff called *dakree*, and the thick, dark natural stuff, and peach-flavored.

His favorite was peach-flavored, and it was my favorite, too. You ever chew, boss?"

"Not me," said Frankie, smiling and shaking his head. He was delighted that Maggie was talking. It was the first spark he'd seen in her since the accident.

"Chew got a hail of a kick to her, yessir."

"You used to chew?"

"Dip, too. Hail, when I was ten I could shift gears from compound low all the way up and on back down again, double-clutchin all the way. Daddy promised to take me on a run with him soon's I finished sixth grade. I was a all-A student, too. And I could outrun, out-hit, and outfling a football farther than any of the boys my age, and a lot of them older. Daddy said I was a pistol."

"How old were you when your daddy passed on?"

"Almost twelve. It was April, and I was due to make that run in June. Daddy said he'd try for a load out here so we could buy peach chew together, and eat lobster out Santa Monica Pier, and ride the merry-go-round till we caught the brass ring. We had a house, and Mama had a new pickup, and there was money in the bank. Then Daddy come down with cancer of the tongue and throat, and you don't wont to hear more 'bout what that's like. But Mama stuck it out.

"See, Mama wasn't born bad, but what she needed was a keeper. She was the prettiest little ol' thing you ever did see, and afterwards I saw after the kids, and she went to waitressin to keep the house. Lost it, a course, and we become standard trailer trash.

"When Daddy got sick, old Axel didn't know what to do with hisself. He'd come and stand with his chin on the side of Daddy's bed. Daddy couldn't talk, but all he had to do was to look at that dog, and ol' Axel'd start yippin and his tail'd start to waggin. It wasn't long before Axel's hindquarters started to give out on him. Happens a lot to shepherds, comes from inbreedin. Pretty soon ol' Axel couldn't barely walk from the pain. Daddy was so sick he couldn't hardly stand, but one day he got Axel into his rig by hisself, and both of 'em sat there half a hour while Daddy got his truck warmed up. Daddy took a shovel and a forty-five with him. Axel thought he was a goin on a run and was actin like a pup. Then Daddy drove up into the hills so's he could put his best friend down. Mama and us kids sat close on the floor waitin. Near sundown the shot come through the trees. It took Daddy a long time to git back home. His eyes was all burny when he come in, and he never got into his Easter egg again.

"Somethin died in me, too. When I was sixteen, I quit school and went to waitressin myself. Then I was a box girl at Shop 'n' Save and part-time cashier. Only thing I was ever gonna git was burger-flippin jobs, I knew that.

"I got a little stake together and moved around. I took karate for a time when I worked up Springfield, and I was good at it. I played baseball and basketball in the night leagues up Kansas City, where I was a security guard in a mall. And then I saw the gal fighters on TV, and I figured my luck had changed. Luck has a lot to do with things."

"It does."

"Frankie, I was wonderin," Maggie said, her eyes squinting against the glare, "would you do me a favor?"

"Anything at all, you know that."

"Favor bigger'n a tranny in a Peterbilt?"

"Bigger than that, if you want it."

"Frankie," she said, now looking him straight in the eye. "I want you to put me down like Daddy did Axel."

Frankie bent forward in his chair, felt like he'd been kicked in the stomach. "I'd die if I did that."

"I'ma dyin ever' day. Now they're talkin 'bout cuttin off my ulcerated leg. I know you can smell it."

Frankie nodded.

"I'm gettin worse, boss," she said, speaking in what seemed slow motion to Frankie. "I don't wont to live on like this."

"Don't ask me this. I love you."

"That's why I'ma askin."

The next day she asked him again. "You'd do it for a dog."

"You're not a dog. You're my blood."

They remained silent for twenty-eight minutes.

Frankie said, "You can't give up hope. Even the doctors say— "

She cut him off. "Ain't no hope. I'm deadweight, can't you see? Ain't no insides to this body you're lookin at. The bird in me can't fly."

Frankie's heart began to race, and he felt his face flush with blood and his mouth go dry. He had no answer for her. He'd die for Maggie, but he couldn't kill her. He felt like a coward for the first time in his life. He tried to breathe normally but couldn't. After a deep breath he heard her voice again, still in slow motion.

"Night nurse makes her rounds at midnight, at two, at four, and at six. Quads like me is the first on her list. Takes her forty minutes, and then she's back doin paperwork at her desk. You could come in while she's busy. You could stick a Buck knife into my heart. I wouldn't even feel it."

"Ah, God."

"I ain't one to beg, Mr. Dunn," she said, a little smile at the corner of her mouth. "But I'ma beggin."

Frankie covered his face with his hands and shook his head.

"I understand," she said.

When Frankie returned the next day, the nurse told him he couldn't visit Maggie.

"Why?"

"I'll get the doctor."

The doctor hurried in. "She's been transferred to Cedars-Sinai in West Hollywood. She's in Intensive Care."

"Why?"

"She tried to commit suicide," said the doctor.

"How could she do that?, she can't move!"

"She bit off her tongue in an effort to bleed to death."

At Cedars Frankie was allowed to look in on her. What remained of her tongue was sutured and so swollen it protruded from her mouth. Frankie camped in the waiting room at Cedars, though Maggie was sedated most of the two weeks she was there.

She was returned to Evergreen alert, but she was unable to speak. The nurses taught her to communicate with her eyes. To say *Yes* to a question, she was to blink her eyes twice slowly, then look away. To answer *No*, she learned to close her eyes and count to three before looking back at the person who was speaking.

On the second day after she returned to rehab, Frankie asked if she was feeling better. She closed her eyes and counted to three. *No.*

She opened her eyes and Frankie said, "Fightin Maggie Fitzgerald. God, I'm sorry. It's my fault."

She closed her eyes for a three-count. *No.*

"'Tis," said Frankie. "If only it had been me."

She closed her eyes for another three-count.

"Ah, Christ," said Frankie, swallowing hard to keep from losing control. "Isn't there anything I can do at all, at all?"

She blinked twice and looked away.

Yes.

She looked back at him and blinked twice again.

Yes.

Then she blinked nonstop, *Yes-Yes-Yes-Yes-Yes-Yes!*

Frankie placed his hand over her eyes. He felt the flutter of her eyelashes as she continued to blink.

Frankie squinted against the slanting sunlight as he climbed the steps of St. Brendan's Roman Catholic Church like an old man. It was October 28, the Feast Day of St. Jude. Though it had been a typically hot autumn day for Southern California, a chill was now coming in off the nearby Pacific, where distant passing tankers, shrouded in fog, wailed. In his heart, Frankie Dunn was already doomed.

In a few days it would be All Saints' Day, a Holy Day of Obligation. Frankie hadn't received the Eucharist since Maggie's injury. He felt gut-shot for staying away, his rage at God having ruined his faith like a drop of Monsell's solution in an eyeball. He yearned for the sacred host, to taste its unleavened blandness, was not whole without it—feared he would never be whole again. He dreaded going to confession like this, a half confession, something he'd never done and something he knew would do him no good, not in his eyes and not in the eyes of God, not with God knowing what was in his heart. He hoped that Father Tim O'Gorman wouldn't be the one hearing his confession; then he reversed himself and wished it would be Tim. Whoever the priest was, Frankie ached for absolution of all his sins, venial and mortal, but especially this mortal sin slithering through his soul.

Flies bobbed and weaved in the heavy, open doorway that separated the outside light from the inside shadows. Frankie pushed through the flies, dipped his fingers into the cold marble basin containing holy water, and made the Sign of the Cross. His fingers trembled.

He made his way down a side aisle to the tiered rows of votive candles in front of the shrine of St. Jude, patron saint of hopeless cases, of things almost despaired of. He lit five candles—one for his wife, whom he missed terribly; one for his parents, brothers, and sisters; one for his sons and daughters and grandchildren; one for his friends, dead and alive, though most were dead. And he lit one candle for his girl. He knelt, made the Sign of the Cross again, and prayed.

"Intercede for me, Jude Thaddeus. Though I hate God, I ask for one impossible thing. That if it pleases God, I may be allowed to sleep again. I ask this, and only this, in the name of the Father, and of the Son, and of the Holy Ghost. As it was in the beginning, is now, and ever shall be, world without end. Amen." The incongruity of his hate for God and his kneeling in church was not lost on Frankie.

It hurt his knees and back to stand. By now his eyes had adjusted to the diffused light, which filtered through the stained glass and swirled like tails of cats around the statues of the tortured Jesus, the agonized Mother, and the suffering saints. St. Brendan's was an old church, one in which the smells of burning candles and incense were ever present. For Frankie it was a holy place, and he took solace from it, knowing that his torture was mirrored in the broken body of the crucified Christ.

"Oh, my God, I am heartily sorry for having offended thee . . . "

Father O'Gorman was the same age as Frankie. Still spry, shaped like a grape, he walked down the aisle as if he were wearing a derby.

"Ah, Frank, lad, have you any stalwarts for me on the television?"

"No, Father Tim. None."

Two penitents preceded Frankie—an old Italian gardener in his work clothes and a pregnant young black woman. Both were finished in minutes.

Frankie entered one side of the confessional, closed the door behind him, and knelt. Father Tim, seated on the other side of the partition, slid the solid grating aside and prepared to listen. He knew Frankie from childhood in Ireland. Both had been schooled by the hard Christian Brothers, both had played at the enormous Neolithic Proleek Dolmen near Dundalk. At nine Frankie had come to the States with his parents, in 1938. Father Tim arrived as a young priest in the early fifties. He had never lost his brogue. Frankie had lost his, having finished school in California. But when he was around the Micks, and hearing them talk, the brogue came back on him.

Frankie could barely make out the dark figure of the round priest beyond the screen that separated them. "Bless me, Father, for I have sinned," he said. "It's been a while since my last confession."

"Maybe more than a while, Frank?"

"Yah, you're right, Father. More." He wondered if the priest could smell the drink on his breath.

Frankie wanted to continue but couldn't. The priest heard him choking on his words.

"Nothin to say to me, at all, at all?" asked the priest.

"I do, Tim. But only because a jar I have lifted."

"Ah," said the priest, who himself was known to lift a jar. He waited the eternity of one whole minute before he spoke. "Go on, lad."

"I can't."

"So terrible, is it?"

"What I'm thinkin 'tis," said Frankie, falling even deeper into the old way of talking.

"So terrible you can't talk at all?"

"Ah, Tim, I murthered a girleen."

"Jaysus!" whispered O'Gorman, making the Sign of the Cross. "Jaysus, Mary, and St. Joseph, Frank, say you didn't."

"I did. In me mind."

"Sure and we're not speakin of a wee lass, are we now?"

"Nah, Tim, nothin like that. You saw this one on the television with me."

"The one who fell?"

"Aye . . . the one who fell."

"Are you tellin me she's already dead, Frank?"

"Not yet."

"Then what?"

"Tim, I don't know. But I think I do, only I can't say."

"Not even here?" asked the priest, gently, gently, feeling the doom Frankie felt. "You know you can't do that, Frank."

"I know it, Father."

Frankie sat beside Maggie on the balcony. After his whispered hello, and Maggie's double blink, he remained silent the whole of the afternoon, watching trees. He wanted to tell her that he'd do it, but he couldn't tell her, because he wasn't sure he could.

She wanted to say that she had asked too much of him, and would have told him, but she had no tongue.

At his one-room apartment off Venice Boulevard in Culver City, Frankie tossed off another shot of Jameson. He removed a fresh, one-ounce bottle of adrenaline chloride solution 1:1000 from the refrigerator, where he stored it to maintain its effectiveness. He twisted off the metal cap, the metal tearing with a snap, but he sat there awhile before doing anything else. On the Formica-topped table was an old-style, glass-and-metal army-surplus hypodermic needle he'd taken from his gear bag. He'd used it maybe a dozen times to inject procaine into the crushed knuckles and fractured metacarpals of fighters so they could make a fight. He'd also used adrenaline more than a hundred times to stop blood from cut eyes, saving fights and even careers of bleeding fighters. And he knew what else adrenaline chloride could do.

He placed the syringe and detachable needle into a clean nine-inch Pyrex pie plate and was about to pour alcohol over them. He would light the alcohol afire to sterilize the instruments. He caught himself, then set the bottle of alcohol aside. There was no need to sterilize.

He drew the entire contents of the little brown bottle of adrenaline into the calibrated barrel of the syringe. Once it was loaded, he placed it back in its polished, stainless steel case. He put the case into the inside pocket of his navy-blue windbreaker in an upright position, so the adrenaline wouldn't leak. Dressed in dark clothes, he drove his old Ford to Evergreen, arriving in the parking lot with his headlights out at 1:50 A.M.

Frankie prayed he wouldn't be noticed. When he saw the night nurse move along the long hallway at two o'clock, going first to Maggie's room at the end of the wing, then working her way back toward the desk, he crept into the building and up the front stairs. He hid in a broom closet, leaving the door slightly ajar. When he saw the nurse move past on her way to the other wing, Frankie took off his shoes and tiptoed down the hall and into Maggie's room.

A pale night-light was on. Frankie moved to the table next to Maggie's bed and put his shoes on the floor. Maggie's ventilator was on, but she wasn't hooked to a monitor. Frankie took his works from his pocket and saw that none of the adrenaline had leaked. He looked finally over to Maggie, whom he expected to be asleep. He was met by two eyes staring at him.

Maggie blinked twice. Frankie nodded and blinked twice as well.

He moved as quickly and as deftly as a surgeon, knowing that if he stopped to consider what he was doing he might not be able to do it at all, at all. He leaned close to Maggie, whose eyes were now closed.

"*Mo cuishle.*"

Maggie looked up and smiled, then frowned as they both heard the nurse approaching in her sensible shoes. Frankie held his breath and stood behind the door as the nurse looked in. Maggie looked at the nurse, who didn't find it unusual that Maggie was awake.

"Are you alone?" asked the nurse in a whisper.

Yes.

"Do you smell whiskey?"

No.

"Funny, thought I smelled it in the hall. Did you hear anything?"

No.

"Oh, well," said the nurse, who returned to her station, which was some forty paces from Maggie's room.

Maggie looked to Frankie, who bent to kiss her on the cheek.

"I won't hurt you," he whispered in her ear. "First I'm going to put you to sleep. Then I'll give you a shot."

Yes.

Frankie stood behind her so he wouldn't have to see her face. He firmly pressed his thumbs to both sides of Maggie's neck, cutting off the blood flow to her brain at the carotid arteries. In a few seconds, Maggie's eyes closed and her mouth came open. Oxygen from the vent escaped and became part of the whirlwind inside Frankie's head. He stood pressing for three minutes, long enough to give himself the time he needed.

Frankie looked at her, had to choke back a howl. But he still pried her mouth open the width of three fingers, and injected the contents of the hypodermic needle beneath the stub of Maggie's tongue. The adrenaline, all thirty milliliters of it, was enough to kill a dragon, but Frankie knew it would dissipate in Maggie's system shortly after being injected. Should there be an autopsy, the tiny spot where the needle had entered would not to be noticed. But even if it were, the adrenaline would never be detected.

Frankie quickly placed the syringe back in its case and returned it to his inside pocket. Now he was calm, the same calm he'd felt in his toughest fights. He checked Maggie's pulse. It raced faster than a speed bag. Then the stroke hit her and her face contorted, one eye sagging open.

The brief shadow of a bird's wing sped high across the far wall and passed through the glass of the domed window. Frankie closed the eye with the tip of his finger, made sure Maggie's pulse was still with his thumb. With his shoes in his hand but without his soul, he moved silently down the rear stairs and was gone, his eyes as dry as a burning leaf.

Fightin in Philly

We gotta turn this African to his left," the cut man repeated to himself on the plane into Philadelphia. "We fix him so he can't set, big S.O.B. can't punch."

Stick and move and turn him, that was their strategy. The African could hit, so make him go opposite to what he was used to; fight him low and from the side, angles; turn him, make him miss, and tire him. Take his power away and then you take his belt.

The cut man was a slick old white man, was Con Flutey. He had white hair and wore trifocals. He was in the fight game because of the beauty of it, a game where old men could still go to war. It was in his bones, the fight game. He'd been in it a long time. He'd been in the game of living a long time, too, and there were parts of himself that were so different from the other parts that he could not understand how they could all be in his one self. But there they were, and though the disparate parts often surprised him, he'd come to enjoy the merry-go-round that was his soul. What else was he to do?

Besides, the older he got, the more things made sense, the more they connected, even though in recent years he wasn't able to train fighters the way he used to—couldn't work with them on how to move because of his legs, couldn't catch their punches with the mitts because of what it did to his back. Now he taught young ones theory, and some seasoned pros, too—angles and distance; how to shove off their back foot to move forward, how to shove off the front to go back; balance and how to pivot off their front foot, off the back, and why, and how to fight moving backward; how the ass moves before the hands when you punch and how the hook to the body looks like it comes off the front foot, but like the hook to the head, it comes off the back; and breathing, always breathing. And thinking, always.

So there he was. He stood on the lovely Ben Franklin Parkway and delighted in all the international flags fluttering against the green of early spring. After Old Glory, the South African flag was his favorite. He didn't like the orange in the tricolor of Ireland— orange had no space in his Irish heart. Up the way was the Philadelphia Museum of Art and the steps Sylvester Stallone as "Rocky" ran up, the music of the soundtrack pushing him on, ennobling him. The trouble was that Stallone couldn't spell fight.

Con had flown in from another flight, coming in on an earlier flight from Vegas. His partner and his fighter were due to arrive in an hour and a half from Los Angeles. They would all be on the same flight going home. Their faction was from L.A. and they flew into Philly for a twelve-round fight at the Blue Horizon for one of the alphabet titles—not a major belt, but if they beat the African, the cut man's kid was sure to get another shot at one of the majors. Members of a faction always said *my* and *we: we* fought; *we're* gonna fight; *we* won; *we* got beat; *my* kid. They say *we* because they fight when their fighter fights and when their fighter gets hit, they get hit. When the fighter wins or loses, they win or lose, and together they feel what that's like. That's why he thought of Mookie as *his* kid and why he said that *we* were fighting the main event on Tuesday night. And that's why he knew you had to learn how to win and you had to learn how to lose, and why you had to learn to always do your best. Not *try* to do. *Do*. Because these kids put their lives in your hands.

Con Flutey had never won a major belt; neither had his partner, Odell Blue. Odell trained their kid and as his trainer he would be the chief second, the only one going into the ring between rounds. If there was a bad cut, the cut man would go in and Odell would handle the water and the ice and the grease from outside. Odell had been a ranked fighter with a big left-hand. He had a slight stutter from being hit. If someone wronged him, the stutter took control; it was best not to have wronged him because when Odell couldn't talk he began to punch. But between rounds during a fight, he spoke to his fighters with no trace of the stutter, and he still had a physique that made women look.

Odell had suffered a detached retina back when there were only eight weight divisions, starting with flyweights at 112 pounds, and when there was only one champion to each division. He'd been ranked number five as a middleweight when you had to have fifty or sixty fights to get a title shot. He was due for his shot, but then he began to get hit with the right. Unable to slip right-hands, he was also unable to get his big left-hand off, and the nights got longer. When he realized he had to hang up his gloves, he worked the docks in L.A. Harbor fifteen years before he could come back to the gym and start all over as a trainer in a game he'd been at since he was eleven—when the only meat his family ate in Cairo, Georgia, was the rabbit or the coon his daddy brought down with a single-shot .22. Odell was respected by everyone in the game, and people who knew him figured he would have had a champ already. He'd been disappointed more times than an old priest. The cut man knew Odell hated to lose as much as he did, but Odell never quit and neither did the cut man.

"If I could only get me a white heavyweight," Odell would say. "We'd be rich, you and me, old man."

Con believed him, Odell was that good. He knew how badly

white people wanted a white heavyweight champ, how much they'd pay. He wished they had a white boy, too. He would be able to help his own kids that way, help them get a leg up in a world that cared less and less about the things that he cared about more and more.

So now they were in Philly and Mookie Bodeen was leaving the gym at 157 and 158 and would make the 160-pound middleweight limit easy. Middleweight was Con's favorite division. Mookie was from South Central in L.A. and raised by his mother, who also had four girls by two other fathers. Mookie hated his father, whoever he was, and loved his mother and his sisters, whom he was sending to beauty school so they could be somebody. He'd promised his mama a house, too, but she was still renting. He was 42 and 3, a left-handed boxer-puncher with 24 kayos. He'd been knocked out twice, once in his second title fight and once in an eight-rounder after he'd lost his first title fight by a split decision in Paris. Dejected, he quit fighting altogether. But then he went broke, tried to manage himself and switched to a different trainer, thinking to blame Odell for his Paris loss. Out of shape, he took an eight-round fight in Tijuana for eight hundred—a buck a round. With strangers in his corner who were trying to earn enough to buy a new tire, he got clocked in five by a 170-pound marine moonlighting out of Camp Pendleton. He quit again.

But what else was he to do? The fight game is a damning game, but Odell was a forgiving trainer, and Mookie came back to his black daddy and his white grandpa. Yeah, he got stopped in the first round of his second title shot, but now he'd won five in a row, three by kayos. The African's faction took this fight because they'd seen the tape of Mookie going to sleep in the first round—but they forgot that the first round for any fighter is the most dangerous round in boxing, that everyone is vulnerable in the first.

Despite being in great shape and the cut man thinking of him as his kid, Mookie wasn't a kid anymore. He was thirty-two, and

God only knew what would happen to him and his sisters and his mama's house if he didn't beat the African. But he was a young thirty-two, and he had a young body and young eyes because he didn't drink or use drugs. How he escaped those habits, especially after his title losses, the cut man didn't know. Many didn't. Well, Mookie did have one habit, pussy, but that didn't make him a bad guy.

And now they were fighting a six-foot-two African monster from Uganda, one with a big head and no nose and skinny long arms and legs, arms as long as a heavyweight's. And he had that big back and rocks for shoulders, and he could crack—twenty-six wins, nineteen by knockout, and no losses. Con loved the Africans, loved their heart, their discipline; and he loved them because they weren't afraid to love their dream. He loved their courtesy as well, and how in their modesty they cupped their private parts with their hands when coming out of a shower. And he loved how they could fight, and would fight, how they put everything on the line.

Mookie had two managers, one white and one black, both good guys who'd had him for ten years except for the foolish time he managed himself, foolish because you can't be the horse and the jockey and win. They'd brought Mookie along, picking the right fights, and though he'd been knocked out, he'd never been beat up, and getting Mookie his title shots was some kind of slick because most managers of champions avoid southpaws like they've got AIDS. But the African's faction wanted to see the African against a name fighter, a boxer who would test him but who was getting old, someone they thought they could knock out with the African's big right-hand. The African wanted to fight Mookie because Mookie was ranked number five; he was ranked number seven, and by beating Mookie he would move closer to his own shot at a title. The African wanted to win, but so did Mookie, and Mookie was so slick and quick and pretty that people in the gym watching him train would hold their breath or whine or say, "Dayamn."

But when Mookie got to Philly, he could hardly walk. Con was unaware of it, but that morning, Saturday, Mookie's last day of running before the fight, while wrapping up his workout with wind sprints, ten strides into the seventh and last set he felt something go in his left leg, the leg he pushed off on when he jabbed, the leg that generated speed and power. Since Con had arrived in Philly first, he took his walk along the parkway and then returned to his room. He was watching the news when Odell called him from their room down the hall.

"You better come down, old man. Room 645."

From Odell's voice Con knew something was wrong. When he got to 645, Mookie had his face in his hands. It was like a wake in the room. "What's up?" Con asked.

Mookie told him about the leg, how it was killing him, and he showed how he could hardly walk, dragging the left leg like a cannonball was chained to it. Con had Mookie describe in detail what had happened. Mookie added that he'd thought of pulling out of the fight, but that he had come on anyway, hoping Con could fix him.

Con started with the big question first. "When it went, did you feel it go *pop?*"

"No, it just felt like it kind of came apart, or pulled or something behind my knee, and it hurt like a bitch right away."

"Well, we've got four days. Three, really."

"I feel it, but I can't believe it," Mookie said, his face long as a casket. "I worked so hard, two months, man. I'm in the best shape of my life. Better than for my title fights. They got me a nutritioniss this time. I came down from one-eighty, but what I lost was fat and water and not muscle. Look at my eight-pack," he said, lifting his T-shirt so Con could see his abdominals.

"You got no ass, either," said Con, referring to how Mookie always put on weight in his high behind. It made Mookie smile, and some of the tension left the room.

Mookie, as if to validate himself, began pulling bottles from his suitcase. "Look, look," he said, lining up a display of pills and powders and liquids, explaining the function of each and how he'd maintained muscle mass as he'd taken off fat. "I been runnin my drawers off, Con, this ain't right, I can't believe my leg was what went, not my leg, my legs is stronger than anything on me, you understan what I'm sayin?, this ain't right."

Con had him strip to his underwear, the little Frenchie kind. Mookie had the body of a twenty-two-year-old, with jackrabbit legs and a series of deep indentations from his solar plexus down to below his belly button. But his face was so sad that Con touched it, patted it like the face of a hurt child, and not knowing whether he was lying or not, said, "Don't worry. I can fix it."

"You really can?"

"Damn straight," he said, but this time he knew he lied. "Now, tell me. You sure it didn't go *pop*?"

"If it did, I didn't hear it or feel it."

"Did it make you flip?"

"No, man, it made me sad."

"I mean did it knock your dick in the dirt."

"No, I just grabbed my leg and limped down to still. It ain't my handspring, is it?"

"If it was your hamstring, your dick is already in the dirt. Have you told anyone?"

"Just you and Odell."

"Good. Did anyone see you limping into the hotel?"

"No," said Odell. "I told him to walk right."

Con had the kid lie on the low bed and asked more questions, lightly touching the leg and watching Mookie wince. What he liked was that there were no bunched-up knots in the muscle or the tendon. He went to his room for the medical kit that was his private emergency room. It had everything from cough drops to diaper pins, from adrenaline chloride solution 1:1000 for cuts to Nupercainal ointment, ass medicine that he used to soothe scraped faces and rope burns after a fight.

"I'm going to give you codeine," Con said, returning to room 645. "It won't show up in your piss test this far from the fight, so don't worry. I want your leg to stop hurting so I can get down into it, okay?, like a dentist into a tooth."

"You the doctor."

Odell watched it all, his face and good eye expressing nothing.

Con got his alcohol-based lineament and the extra-virgin olive oil he used to lay down a slippery base. It made the skin supple when he gave a massage, and it made the black kids glow and feel happy with their pretty selves. Now he'd use the olive oil only from below Mookie's ass to his Achilles tendon. Trainers were usually careful not to massage a fighter too close to a fight because they wanted him hard, physically and mentally, didn't want to cut off the flow of adrenaline to the mind and tissue, didn't want to siphon off the warrior's edge. But Con had to go after Mookie's leg, had to soften it up, or there wouldn't be a fight.

"Ice?" asked Odell, not waiting for an answer, going out the door to the ice machine with one of Con's 11-by-12½-inch lock-top plastic bags.

By then Mookie had given himself over to Con in the complete trust fighters will give to their handlers. It always touched Con, whether something went wrong with their hands in the gym or when he was in the corner working to stop the flow of blood in less than the one minute he had between rounds. It made him love his fighters close to the way he loved his own children. He worked very slowly on Mookie, reaching into the wounded tissue an eighth of an inch at a time until the back of his kid's leg was like pudding and Mookie could walk around the room free from pain.

"You fixed the muhfuh!" shouted Mookie. "You the king!"

"Maybe it'll tighten up," said Con, "but we'll go back at it. I think we got a shot."

"But you said you could fix it," said Mookie, doubt in his voice.

"I did fix it. Now let's see if I can keep on fixing it."

"What about my weight? I got to sweat."

"We'll be okay if we eat right and go light on liquids. Then we go to the gym two days before the fight, stretch like I show you, shadowbox, punch the mitts, and see what happens."

"It feels fixed now," Mookie protested.

"Let's hit it with more ice and some more hurt juice and walk it."

"It fixed, man."

"Wait. Wait and see."

They napped, Odell and Mookie keeping their room so hot Con could hardly breathe, especially with the fumes he was eating. Con kept the window open in his room.

"You bloods got no blood," Con would always say.

"We cold, you crazy," Mookie or Odell would always answer.

Much of the pain had been relieved and Mookie was able to nap, but the leg did tighten up some while he was sleeping. Con worked on it until it was loose again, inhaling alcohol and winter-green fumes because he had to bend down so low to work on the leg. After two days he was half sick from the fumes, but the leg appeared to be a hundred percent and each hour Mookie was more sure of himself.

"You a witch doctor, old man, a voodoo-hoodoo man."

"Old but pretty."

"Prettiest white man I seen."

So that's the way it went, and when it was time they went to the gym in good spirits. The gym was in West Philly, at the very bottom of the 'hood, and after stretching like Con showed him, and after a complete workout, including eight hard rounds on the punch mitts, Mookie was wringing wet. He weighed out at 157, still three pounds under the 160 limit. The leg held.

"You did it, old man," said Mookie.

"Wait."

The leg was fixed. Con knew it would be when it didn't tighten up after the gym work. They didn't have to pull out of the fight, and Mookie would get his shot. Except for the managers, with whom Odell and Con were always square, the leg injury never happened as far as the promoter, the Boxing Commission, and the African ever knew.

Mookie was in the shower. Odell smiled his shy smile and looked down the way he always did when he had something to say from his heart. "You didn't believe," Odell said to Con. "I believe, but not you."

"Yeah, I believed."

"No good."

"I believed, but I didn't know until now," said Con.

"Once I see you wif him, you talkin wif him the way you talk an' all, and once you start workin on the boy, I knew."

"I'm glad you did." Con nodded to the shower. "Anyway, Mookie's in shape, and that helped a ton, and we were lucky."

"Yeah, he in shape, but you the man."

Odell had stuttered a little, and Con knew how hard it was for him to say what he felt. Con was always surprised at how many ways he'd found to love Odell, so different in color and features and in so many other ways, and yet so much the same.

"You think about it," Odell had once told him. "We got the same daddy. He love us bof."

Factions travel around the world sometimes, and people often say that they wish they could see the places fight guys get to see. But fight guys get to see airports, fly in tight seats, and mostly stay in second-class hotels, eat in second-class joints. Time zones turn them upside down, and sometimes the seasons are in reverse. When the fighter works, the fight guys work with him; when he rests, so do they. In Paris or Tokyo or Philly they will take walks after eating, but then they go back to their dark rooms and watch bimbo TV shows to keep their minds off the fight, even when the language is one they don't understand.

It wasn't exactly the same with Con—he liked his mind to be working, not numb. On Sunday he was able to go to mass in the Chapel of Saint Peter and Saint Paul's domed cathedral at Eighteenth and Parkway. Walking back to the hotel, he saw the Free Library. He had read all his life, educated himself that way, and hoped he'd be able to go back on Monday. Being in the library would fill him with peace. But on Monday Mookie's managers flew in, and what with Mookie's TV interview, there was no time to go back to the library.

He and Odell got to take a walk downtown for breakfast because Mookie didn't eat and stayed in his room—it would have been too painful to tag along and have to look at food he couldn't eat. But he was so happy about his leg he didn't mind being alone. When asked by other blacks why he had a white man in his corner instead of a brother, Mookie would repeat what Odell always said about Con. "He a hell of a man."

The next day, Tuesday, the day of the fight, the weigh-in was at 9:00 A.M. Between the weigh-in and their eleven o'clock meeting with the boxing commissioner, Odell, Con, and Mookie's managers took Mookie in a cab downtown, where they fed him Irish oatmeal and a stack of pancakes. Before his breakfast, though Mookie hated it, he drank a big glass of grapefruit juice for the potassium in it and to help regain fluids in his system. Walking back to the hotel with the others, Con noticed a poster advertising an exhibit at the Philadelphia Museum of Art, one featuring Michelangelo and Rodin together. Short of going to the Casa Buonarroti in Florence, or maybe to the Metropolitan Museum of Art on an if-come trip to New York, Con had come to believe that at his age he would never stand before a Michelangelo. But here he was, just half a mile away. He hoped he could get there, but on the day of the fight, time would be tight.

Mookie returned to his room, but his faction met with the commissioner and the African's faction in a meeting room at their hotel. All manner of fouls were discussed, including head butts, low blows, and knockdowns, but low blows were stressed. In the list of rules that were handed out, it was written that after two low-blow warnings, a point would automatically be deducted for the third infraction. The commissioner was a little guy, handsome, and Con saw him for either Italian or maybe Jewish. The guy was proud of his job and crazy for boxing, particularly the fights in Philly, and let everyone know that a first-class fight was expected, adding that he didn't care whether it was a four-rounder or a twelve-round title-fight main event. Everyone understood.

Back in his room Con tried to nap, but he couldn't, even though he had slept fitfully the night before. He got nervous lying there, and hungry for something sweet. He went down to the busy convenience store across from the hotel for a small container of skim milk, an apple and a coconut Tastykake. Part of one ear had been bitten off in a street fight when he caught someone trying to break into his car, and he didn't hear well on that side. So as he stood in line to pay, he didn't hear the up-tempo soul music that was piped into the store—Patti LaBelle high and jamming above the bass and drums, improvising lyrics and playing hide-and-seek with the melody. Con noticed the music when someone standing somewhere behind him began singing along, matching Patti's black sound word for word and inflection for inflection. Con looked back expecting to see a black teenaged boy but instead saw what looked like a Jewish college boy, his yarmulke pinned to his curly brown hair with bobby pins. He was accompanied by three gum-chewing coeds, their arms full of books, and as he hit the high notes, snapping his fingers and matching the singer's style exactly, Con decided he was showing off in hopes of getting laid. The way the girls eyed each other, Con thought the guy might nail at least one of them if he kept working at it. Con's mind went back to his kid resting in his hot, dark room, to his baby boy, to his fighting man.

"Excuse me, sir. Sir? What is that?" Con only half heard the question, his mind now on his Tastykake. "Sir, excuse me? You with the tattoo?"

Con turned and saw the yarmulke guy, noticed that the girls had vacant eyes. "That's a tattoo on your wrist, isn't it?" the guy asked rhetorically.

Con looked down. As usual, his heavy Timex wristwatch had slipped down to reveal a blurred tattoo that resembled jailhouse art. Close to fifty years before, in the throes of his second steady piece of tail, and just before signing himself into the navy during the Korean War, it had been legible. It wasn't anymore.

"You did it yourself, right?" the singing guy asked excitedly.

There was wonder rather than disrespect in his voice, so Con answered him. "No, I had it done."

"Where?"

"On Skid Row in L.A., if it matters."

The boy looked disappointed; Con could see that he'd hoped to hear the tattoo was from Sing Sing or Alcatraz, or maybe Devil's Island. "What, were a bunch of you out drunk or something?"

"It was two in the afternoon," said Con, but what came to mind, as they often did, were lines from García Lorca:

> At five in the afternoon.
> It was exactly five in the afternoon.

"You got it so early, the tattoo? Really?"

"I was sober, alone, and it cost me my last two dollars."

"What does it say, the tattoo?" the guy asked, and one of the girls giggled. The guy squeezed her shoulders, and she leaned back into him.

"Well," said Con. He waited a moment and wondered if he

should go ahead and tell. "It says, *Rubáiyát of Omar Khayyám.*"

"Says what?" the singing guy asked, thinking he was familiar with the sound of *Rubáiyát,* but he wasn't sure. "You mean the, what?, is it a book or something?"

"Something like that."

"What, that book inspired you or something?"

"It did when I was twenty."

"What was it got to you?"

"Got what to me?"

By now the girls were staring at Con, and the rest of the people in line were interested, too. The girls' heads were tilted, and the guy wasn't as sure of himself as he was when he was doing his soul sing-along. "You know. What about this *Rooba*-thing was what inspired you?"

Con looked at him dead on. He spoke slowly and the girls began to nod.

> Come, fill the Cup, and in the Fire of Spring
> The Winter garment of Repentance fling:
> The Bird of Time has but a little way
> To fly—and Lo! the Bird is on the Wing.

The girls and the yarmulke guy's mouths were wide open.

"Ask a question," said Con, paying for his stuff, "you get an answer."

"The answer was vast!" the guy said, twisting and jerking and shaking his head. "Man, that's the best answer in the history of questions!"

Con collected his change, nodded to the cashier, and headed back to his room. He slowly ate his Tastykake and drank his milk before peeling and eating his apple. At 3:00 P.M. they were to meet and feed Mookie the last time before the scheduled ten o'clock fight. After that he could drink water, but that was all. In the

interim, he'd gain three to five pounds. If or when fighters starve
themselves or take piss pills and laxatives to make weight, they will
gain more. When the weigh-in is held on the day before the fight,
many will gain eight to ten pounds, sometimes more.

Con had an hour, so he went over all the gear he would need
before, during, and after the fight. It was in his gear bag just where
he'd stowed it before leaving Vegas—the sponges, the stop-swell,
the ice bags. He had backups for everything, including the adrenaline, cocoa butter, Vaseline, swabs and sterile pads, and even Murray's pomade, the thick yellow gunk some blacks used in their hair
but that he would sometimes use to lay down a slippery base in the
eyebrows or across the nose or to plug up a wound over a cheekbone.
Some blacks were offended by the Murray's, but white and Hispanic fighters didn't give a damn as long as it worked. His medicine
kit was as organized as an operating room. Having rechecked it, he
set aside two rolls of gauze and rolls of one-inch and half-inch tape,
the half-inch to use between the fingers to keep the layers of gauze
protecting the knuckles in place. Then he placed his kit back into
his gear bag, including the fanny pack he wore into the ring. He
used the same care here in the quiet of his room that he would use
in the clang and clamor of the dressing room before the fight.

Using the tapes and rolls of gauze he'd set aside, he wrapped his
left hand just as if he were preparing it for battle. It was rare that
one of Con's fighter's hurt his hand during a fight. By now, wrapping hands was an instinct with Con, having wrapped hundreds of
them. But he had to be sure for these kids who put their flesh and
bone and futures in his hands. So to best protect them from any
mistake or oversight, he always took time to wrap his own left hand,
to practice before going to the arena. He would often wrap his hand
while watching fights at home on television. He figured his left
hand was the most wrapped hand in boxing. When the inspector
from the Boxing Commission wrote his initials on Mookie's wraps
just before the fight, he said, "Yeah, these is real."

At three o'clock Con went with the faction to an Irish pub a few blocks from the hotel. Mookie had broiled breast of chicken, seafood chowder, and several pieces of chewy rye bread. He drank two glasses of grapefruit juice, wincing after each swallow. Con had chowder as well but didn't feel much like eating. Nobody did except for Mookie, whose body was yelling at him for nourishment and fluid, a baby bird piping for bugs and worms.

"After the fight I want me a whole pizza and a gallon a Coke."

There's always some choke in everyone before a fight, especially one on which so much was riding, and as they walked back to the hotel, nobody was talking. It was ten after four when they got to the hotel.

"Meet down here at six forty-five," said Mookie's black manager. "A driver'll be here to take us to the fight at seven sharp."

As the others went up to their rooms, Con told the manager that he wanted to check on something personal but that he'd be back no later than six. "I'm set."

The manager nodded, knowing that Con would be on time and ready. As the manager went to check for messages at the desk, Con went out to the front of the hotel, where he climbed into a cab driven by a courtly black man with long white chin whiskers.

"The art museum, please."

"It will be my pleasure, sir," the driver said in a singsong accent that Con figured for West Indian.

The cabby left him off at the base of the stairs. The fare for the short ride was $2.30. Con handed the driver a five and said, "Keep it."

"You are kind, sir."

The sky was blue, and young lovers strolled hand in hand in the bright sunlight. A couple of winos hustled change. Con ran up the same stairs Rocky had, but Con was running to see the stuff of Michelangelo Buonarroti.

The long hallway leading to the exhibition was to the left and just inside the main entrance. A sign indicated the exhibition closed at five o'clock. As Con started down the hallway, he was intercepted by one of the guards, all of whom were black.

"Excuse me, sir," said the guard. "The exhibition is closed."

"But the sign says five."

"I know," said the guard. "But everyone has to be out by five, so we stop admitting at four. You'd only have another thirty minutes, anyway."

"That's okay with me," said Con, reaching for his money clip. "How much is it?"

The guard smiled politely. "The cashier goes off at four, I'm sorry, because to charge for less than an hour wouldn't be fair." The guard saw Con's face go from young to sad and was touched by the sadness. "We'll be open tomorrow, though. You could stay all day."

"I won't be here tomorrow." Con sighed, and his mind went back to the fight. "Oh, well, I did my best."

"Wait," said the guard. Like the others, he wore a navy blazer and gray pants. He stood six feet six inches and weighed close to 320 pounds. He had a shaved head and the face of a kindly genie. He had a gold eyetooth, but he spoke with no trace of a black accent. "Come with me." He led Con a third of the way down the hall. "See the lady guard down at the end? Tell her the lieutenant said it's okay to let you in."

"Thank you. Damn. Thank you."

"Not at all."

Inside the exhibit, Con was touched by the works of Rodin, the oversized studies of hands and feet, the tortured dark forms. But it was Michelangelo that stunned him, even though several of the works were plaster casts or small sketches done in pen and ink and colored chalk. He walked from piece to piece, sketch to sketch, and he was transported to Italy in the fifteenth and sixteenth centuries and his breath began to catch. He clasped a hand over his mouth so no one could hear. A short, thin guard noticed and silently crossed to Con.

"You like these?" he asked, suspicion in his voice.

"They are miracles."

The guard smiled, nodded, and slipped back into the shadows.

Con gulped in as much beauty as he could before the guards quietly informed people individually that the exhibition was closing. Con photographed the exhibit with his heart, then headed down the long hallway. On the way, he palmed a five-dollar bill and then approached the lieutenant, who stood near the exit.

Con held out his hand to the lieutenant's, who extended his to shake hands. His hand swallowed Con's, but when he felt the palmed bill, he said, "Oh, no, sir, I can't. I wouldn't, anyway."

"It's my only way to thank you. Because of you I saw God's hand."

"Your eyes thank me plenty."

"God bless you, my friend."

The lieutenant blinked, stepped slightly back. "And may God bless you."

Leaving the museum feeling refreshed and alert, Con took the pathway that curved along the turn in the parkway. Traffic was heavy, and Con was curious about what was on the side streets. Walking beneath a wide stretch of trees, he breathed deeply of the cool air and wondered if he'd ever feel old. Beyond a wide stretch of grass and up a small rise, he saw what appeared to be the shingled steeple of an old Catholic church, its weathered cross high and unashamed in the air. Con had time, so he strolled up Green Street and found the Church of Saint Francis Xavier, the Apostle of the Indies. The great Christian missionary of the midsixteenth century, Francis Xavier was one of the original members of the Society of Jesus, the *Jesuitas*, and though he died in his early forties, Con recalled that it was he who had brought Catholicism to India and Japan. His church in Philly was old and rather spare, but it was traditionally Catholic, and Con felt at peace.

Near the altar, Con went to his knees. "I am not worthy to receive you, Lord," he prayed, as if he were about to receive Communion, "but only say the word and I shall be healed."

He prayed for those he loved, living and dead, and for those who had no one to pray for them. He prayed that he might always do his best, especially when serving God, but now he prayed for strength in the corner during Mookie's fight, that he would function with grace under pressure. He also prayed for Mr. Ernest Hemingway. There on his knees he remembered what Spanish existentialist philosopher Miguel de Unamuno wrote about boxers. To make a point about believing in God with one's whole being, Unamuno described fighters as being capable of throwing punches with such economy of effort that they are able to focus the force they unleash and thereby knock out their opponent by using only those muscles necessary. Unamuno was right about fighters: instead of using strength to win, they deliver force. Unamuno added that a blow delivered by a nonprofessional may not have as much effect on an opponent as would a blow by a professional, but that it would have more effect on the nonpro who *threw* the punch, since it caused him to bring into play almost his entire body and energy. Con smiled at the insight of the austere Spaniard and remembered that Unamuno's point was that one blow was that of a professional, the other of a man of flesh and bone—and that when a man of flesh and bone believed, he did so with his whole being. Since the pro only uses what he needs when he needs it, this explains how one fighter will run out of gas in the second or the sixth round, while another can fight all night. As Con loved the Africans, he also loved the Spaniards—men like Cortéz, Bernal Díaz del Castillo, Manolete, and Pedro Romero; men such as Loyola and Francis Xavier, Unamuno and Federico García Lorca—and he loved Santa Teresa de Avila, that mystical lady doctor of the church, that powerhouse little Catholic nun whose grandfather on her father's side was a *converso* Jew from Córdoba.

All of this ran through Con's mind, a tapestry before which Mookie's fight at the Blue Horizon would be played, and again he prayed that he and Odell would be able to help their fighter to prevail.

"We go to win, not just to fight, Lord," Con reminded God. "And we ask your blessing that we might be victorious. We know that only one corner can win, and that you love both, so if it is your will that the African wins . . ." Con hated to lose, despised it, but he also knew that how you lost was as important as how you won. He whispered Christ's words in the garden of Gethsemane: *But let be as You would have it, not as I.*

Con crossed himself at the end of his prayers and then again with holy water when he backed out of the church. He walked up Green Street to Twenty-second, crossed himself again in front of the Roman Catholic Chapel of Divine Love, and then turned down the hill toward the hotel. While crossing the street at Spring Garden, Con and several other pedestrians had to pull up short because of a car that illegally pulled through the intersection. They had the green light, but the driver yelled at them to hurry up. A female pedestrian yelled back, "Asshole! I got the right of way, you colon breath!"

The car continued on, and the yeller strutted across the street on dumpy legs, a bitter woman with a face like a lawn dart, who acted as if she had just done something grand. Con wondered how she'd handle a broken nose, or maybe a few shots to the liver.

They were driven through parched neighborhoods to get to the Blue Horizon, which was already packed to standing room only.

"You got pizza in Philly?" Mookie asked the driver.

"You want pizza before the fight?"

"No, but after I'm buyin everybody a big pizza, the whole-thang special. You one, too."

"You like anchovies, too?"

"Hell no!"

Parking was forget it, and cars were jammed along North Broad Street, parked down the middle of the street. The crowd was milling out front of the old building, boxing's remora feeding on what was available—a free ticket, a pocket to be picked, lies. Mookie and his corner ran up the stairs of what appeared to have been a theater or maybe a dance hall. Fights were already in progress, and Con noticed how small the arena was, that there were balconies on three sides of the ring. The ring was lit brightly for the TV cameras, and the light carried out into the crowd, which was packed in closely to the ring. The crowd was eight out of ten white. Almost all of the fighters and their fight guys were black or Puerto Rican.

The arena reminded Con of New York's old St. Nick's Arena before TV took over the fights, there where Lincoln Center is now, when neighborhoods had their heroes and backed them with money they earned with their hands. In those days, most of St. Nick's fighters were Italian, and there were hard-eyed Italian guys in bib overalls carrying lunch pails—men who paid to see fights, Irish guys, too, who stopped on the way to work or on their way home from work, wearing caps and with cigar stubs stuck in their teeth. The Irish and Italian fighters were the tough ones, fighters who would take shots to land shots, the bangers who could take you out with one shot from either hand. The black fighters were quick and slick and pretty and didn't like getting hit, but would hurt you like the Inquisition. The Puerto Ricans were still coming up, but the great Jewish fighters like Benny Leonard and Barney Ross were from another day and time.

That night at the Blue Horizon there were two white fighters, one Irish and one Italian. The rest were Puerto Rican or black, and except for the semimain and the main event, Con's fight, they weren't that good—they were tough, but they weren't smart fighters, not tactical fighters who fought like Hannibal or Rommel or Robert E. Lee, who thought in terms of hitting but not getting hit, fighters who made you miss and then made you pay with shots to the solar plexus that made your eyes bug out, made you think you were going to die.

Most fighters fought cleanly, others not. Refs were mostly right guys, but others could be got to, like some of the zebras in football. And who knew what would be going on in the heads or the pockets of the judges. Money was the name of the game, any game, and that made for corruption somewhere along the way. Most thought the game was corrupt because of the money. Con saw it otherwise, that there was money because of the corruption.

Half the fighters were sent to the blue dressing room, the area designated for fighters fighting out of the blue corner. The rest were sent to the red dressing room. In the old days, there was the white corner and the black corner. It was changed so no one would be offended by the color of the corner. Con had snorted, wondering how anyone white or black could be pissed because of the color of a corner.

Mookie was assigned to the red dressing room. All the chairs were already taken, either by prelim fighters getting ready or by others just finishing up. Gear bags were everywhere, as were factions with as many as six guys, some half drunk and rootin and tootin for their boy. These were four-round fighters and many didn't last that long; the room was mostly cleared by eight-thirty. Mookie would go on at ten.

Con liked to set up early. But he had to wait for the other factions to clear out. There were tables lined end to end along one side of the long room, but he couldn't set up there because they were covered in plastic sheets and crusted with fallen plaster that had mixed with drippings from the plumbing or the roof. Sound echoed harshly in the dimly lit room, and people squinted without realizing it. A gummy shower held a hundred-pound plastic bag of chipped ice that corner men like Con would draw from while setting up. One toilet was allotted. It had a sprung wooden door, the design of its geometric woodwork blurred over the years from rainbow layers of paint. The one shower didn't matter because most fighters didn't shower after a fight unless it was held in an upscale arena that housed pampered basketball players and such. Con had fought in worse than the Blue Horizon. Pissing could be a problem. There was lots of pissing.

Con filled his ice bucket and bags from the shower, and he filled his water bottles with distilled water and enough ice to chill it. He always had two bottles of water to make sure he and Odell could cool Mookie down if they needed to. As soon as some chairs cleared, he set up at one of the free tables, where he laid out his gauze and tapes. He tore six 9-inch strips of half-inch tape. He stuck one end of each strip to the side of the table, allowing the strips to hang free. The crowd was either booing or cheering, and after Mookie got his fighting shoes on, he began to stretch and move. There was no pain in the leg, and it wouldn't bother him during the fight— but at that point they still didn't know. Before Mookie began to sweat, Con wrapped his hands, hands never made by God to support the terrible force fighters could deliver. Con was always careful to support and protect the eight bones in the wrist, the fragile bones across the back of the hand, the thumbs and the knuckles. The wraps had to be tight, but not so tight as to cut off circulation. Con had seen blue hands, had seen fighters miss punches because they couldn't feel their hands. He'd seen fighters shatter bones for the same reason.

Once Mookie's hands were wrapped, he began to move with purpose, to get his legs moving, to sweat, to prepare his body for shock. He stepped up the pace and began to shadowbox, shooting punches like bullets. As his time came near, the Commission guy came in with Mookie's gloves, which Mookie had chosen at the weigh-in and which his white manager had signed to guarantee Mookie got the right gloves at fight time. Con helped get them on Mookie. He wrapped Mookie's hands, but Odell had a killer way of taping the outside of the gloves at the wrists, wrapping the tape as far below the wrist toward the thumb as the inspector would allow. Both Odell and the African's trainer had gone too far, and the inspector made them force the tape back up. Both trainers had tried for an edge, to compact the stuffing in the gloves. You tried for every edge, tried to tip things for your guy.

They heard the crowd go native, signaling a kayo ending to the semimain. They'd be up soon. Mookie put on his cup and his fighting shorts. Odell put on the punch mitts, slapped them together, made them crack like a bull whip. Mookie took his stance, moved to his right as southpaws are supposed to, but he was trying too hard to be too fast and Con talked to him like in the gym, low and easy.

"Slow down, get your balance first. Get your balance and the speed will come."

Mookie nodded once. He tucked his chin next to his shoulder by lowering it, not by raising his shoulder, and laid back a fraction on speed until he had his feet under him right. With balance came his timing and speed, and then he was punching in combinations an untrained eye could never follow. He did it for a solid five minutes, sweat streaking his oiled body, his movements liquid.

"Yeah, that's it, you got it, that's pretty!" shouted Con. "Yeah, it's pretty fighters what make that money!, and my Mookie's a pretty fighter!"

Mookie's eyes were set deeply behind his lowered brows, his eyes focused like the eyes of a big cat on a gang of hyenas. "He can't stay wif me, no good, uh-uh!, gonna teyh 'im up!"

The TV sound guys came in and wired Odell for sound. The TV announcers would be able to pick up what Odell's instructions were between rounds. They'd wired the African's trainer as well. What went on in the corner would be on record for the Boxing Commission as well.

Mookie was dazzling under the hot lights, all tassels and sequins and shine. The African wore white, which was incandescent against his ebony skin. His face showed no emotion. He was a good 172 by fight time, outweighing Mookie by at least 7 pounds. The weight differential was bad enough, but it was the height and reach of the African that also worried Con. What troubled him even more was the size of the ring—seventeen feet square, if it was that, and Con wondered if it had been scaled down by the promoter to allow the African, the promotion's fighter, to make use of his size and reach to bulldoze Mookie into the ropes and the corners, where the African could bang away. Con worried that Mookie would have to kayo the African in order to win.

In the audience was a large contingent of Ugandans, some in African garb. All were chanting, some in haunting counterpoint, and Con wondered if it was in one of the Bantu languages, or in another of the many tribal languages of Uganda, even though English is Uganda's official language.

The action moved swiftly once the fighters were in the ring. Con watered Mookie, removed his mouthpiece from the ice bucket, and slid it into his mouth. To the crowd, Mookie, Odell, and Con looked peaceful enough, but inside they were on fire. The ref had phony hair, weighed maybe 145, and stammered as he gave his instructions. The fighters touched gloves, the chief seconds left the ring, and the bell rang for round one.

The African came out swinging, thinking Mookie would be easy to stop in the first round, but Mookie wasn't there and the African stumbled. The African looked to his corner and Mookie hit him six times, all power shots. Then it was stick and move and Mookie danced the African to death, slipping punches and sliding away like a mist in the wind. The African managed to clip Mookie from time to time, but Mookie was moving side to side or backward and at an angle and the glancing blows had no effect. The Ugandans chanted from the crowd for the first round or so but then grew silent as Mookie continued to score. The African's corner was screaming at him.

"Get off first, goddamn it! Don't wait! Get off, get off!"

But since he couldn't set, he couldn't punch, and Mookie ate him up. In the corner, the African's trainer slapped him between the third and fourth rounds, but it did little good. Near the end of the fourth, Mookie unloaded a nine-punch combination that had the crowd on its feet. It nearly dropped the African, who looked like a lost child. Between rounds, while dousing him with ice water, his trainer leaned close to his ear. Too close.

The bell rang for the fifth, and the African came out with his legs spread unnaturally wide. It looked like he was trying to get into a crouch so he could punch straight into Mookie instead of down, which would ordinarily be to the taller man's advantage. Getting low didn't work, and it didn't make sense to Odell or Con, unless it was maybe an act of desperation. Mookie pivoted, turned, spun, all the while staying even lower than the African and sticking his jab into his face and gut. When the African tried to straight-arm Mookie and force him back into a corner, Mookie nailed him with a right uppercut to the left elbow that made the African stop that shit. Mookie won the fifth round as easily as the first four. But when the timekeeper banged on the canvas to signal the last ten seconds of round five, the African skipped twice and charged directly into Mookie, his left forearm jammed up under Mookie's chin, forcing him against the ropes. As Mookie struggled to slide free, the African dropped even lower, his legs spread wider still. Con saw it coming, so did Odell. The African hit Mookie with two uppercuts below the belt. He cranked both with all his might, the punches connecting at the very bottom of the cup and driving it upward and directly into Mookie's nuts. One shot landed at the bell, the second shot landed after the bell. Now Con and Odell knew why the tall African had gone to a crouch. Not only do low blows hurt a fighter, they sap his strength and can tire him in later rounds.

The ref jumped in and warned him. The African's face showed no shame. Bent over and wincing, Mookie limped to his corner and sank to his stool. Odell pulled the protective belt away from Mookie's waist, and Con scooped ice down to Mookie's balls.

The ref angled over. "You got up to five minutes if you need 'em."

It was a rule that was aimed to compensate for any immediate pain and to forestall a possible delayed reaction that might force an end to the fight.

"What we need is points deducted for low blows," Con snapped. "There were two of 'em, for Chrissakes, one after the fuckin bell, ref, come on!"

The ref acted like he was the injured party. "I already warned 'im, okay?"

If Mookie was to get another shot at a big title, there was no way he could quit, so they were between a rock and a hard place. If they toss in the towel, they lose and all their work and dreams were for nothing; if they hang and Mookie weakens from the foul, they lose anyway, and a bad hurt could be put on Mookie besides. Con understood that his kid now had pain for a second opponent in the ring and fretted that Mookie's age would let him down—it was a matter of heart and what kind of condition Mookie was in. So maybe, if they could fight one more round, or two or more, who could tell? Angie Dundee had said it best: Anything can happen in boxing.

"How you feel?" said Con.

"Sick."

"Shall I stop it?" asked Odell.

"Naw!" said Mookie, almost shouting.

"Tell him, Odell," said Con, ripping loose the sound unit from Odell's belt and tossing it outside the ring. Soundmen in the booth grabbed their ears and started cussing.

Odell was serious as a heart attack as he spoke to Mookie. "Hit the nigga in the nuts so hard his dick'll die."

They sponged Mookie down and watered him, and he appeared to have regained some of his strength. The ref came back at the ten-second warning, telling Odell to leave the ring and to pick up the ice that had fallen from Mookie's cup. Odell kicked the ice from the corner. As the bell rang, the ref turned to Mookie.

"You need more time?"

Mookie saw himself as a warrior and shook his head, surprising Con, who thought either Mookie or Odell would have called for more time at that point. The business with the mike and the ice had distracted Odell, and now it was too late. The ref looked away, and Con tossed more ice onto the canvas. As the ref looked back to wave Mookie on, he spotted the ice, called a time-out, and ordered Con to clear it. The ref was pissed, but Con didn't give a rat's ass. He took his time, and what it got was his boy another twelve seconds' rest.

"The ref be mad," said Odell.

"He ain't my daddy."

The sixth round began, and the African clipped Mookie low again, but Mookie saw it coming and took the shot on his hip. It was better there than to the family jewels, but had it landed on the soft side of his ass, it could have damaged the sciatic nerve and Mookie would be staggering. The ref gestured to the African to keep his punches up, but he gave no warning. Mookie aimed his next punch below the African's belt, but it was a glancing blow and didn't faze him.

"No retaliation," said the ref. "This is your first warning."

The African jabbed and then faked another low blow. When Mookie lowered his gloves to protect himself, he got popped over the top hard enough to make him blink. The African could crack, all right.

"Do what you gotta do!" Odell shouted from the corner.

Once again, Mookie angled in low to bang the African below the belt, but the African grabbed Mookie behind the neck and pulled him forward. Leaning his weight across Mookie's back, he banged Mookie to the kidney as he used his weight to force him to one knee. The sixth round had been even, but because Mookie was still sick, and because he was now forced to protect himself above the belt and below, the African had caught him several times with power shots to the face. The swelling had begun.

Between rounds, Con dropped the mouthpiece into the ice bucket to chill it down. "Breathe, Mookie. Deep and through your nose. Make a sigh and let it just fall out." After three breaths, Con gave him water and had him spit. Then he gave him more water and told him to keep breathing. Odell greased Mookie's nose, face, and lips.

"You okay?" Odell asked.

"I'm okay," said Mookie.

"You not," said Odell. "I know you."

"Still sick a little bit," muttered Mookie.

"A lot or a little bit?" Con asked, giving him a little more water to swallow.

Mookie shrugged, but they could see he wasn't the same. It went that way in the seventh, the African occasionally popping Mookie just low enough to keep his guard down, and beginning to land regularly with his big right. No warnings from the ref. Mookie's legs weren't the same. He was gulping air as he punched, and though he scored well, the African's mouth was closed tightly and he was coming on. He hit Mookie low again, and Mookie banged him right back.

"Second warning," said the ref, pointing at Mookie.

"Warn that muhfuh," answered Mookie.

"I'll do the reffing."

The whites booed the warning, but the Ugandans applauded and began to chant and hoot. Mookie's mouth was ripped and bleeding inside because he was getting hit while his mouth was open to breathe. Between rounds, Con would stop the flow, but the African was raining punches on Mookie that reopened the lacerations, and he swallowed blood for the remaining four hellacious rounds. The African began fighting upright again in the eighth round, marching at Mookie and firing salvos of jabs, rights, hooks, and uppercuts. At midround he broke Mookie's nose, blood catching in Mookie's thin mustache, dripping from his chin. Though

Mookie's legs were fading, he continued to move and to make the African miss. But he was too weak to fire back with evil intentions, and the African was able to keep pulling Mookie's head forward and to pound him with shots to the kidneys. Con knew Mookie's piss would be the color of port wine as he went to work on the broken nose between rounds, pressing on pressure points and swabbing up inside with liquid adrenaline and then swabbing it again with the adrenaline salve he had prepared. There was no time to ice it.

"I can't keep him back, can't keep him off," Mookie gasped. "He strong."

In the ninth the African hit Mookie with a dozen of his best shots, but Mookie wouldn't go. He sagged twice, and his face ballooned, but his legs held and Con's heart began to break. His ice bags hadn't contained the lumps on Mookie's face, and his brows now protruded like a Neanderthal's. The African swooped in again and doubled Mookie over with another low blow. The crowd was yelling at the referee. At the end of the round, Odell met Mookie midring and helped him to the corner, where he slumped forward. Con doused Mookie with ice water. Mookie had been gagging, but when the ice water hit him he stood straight up.

"I'll kill the nigga," said Mookie. "I'll kill everyone he love."

Con yelled at the ref. "Hey, come on! He keeps hitting us low!"

"I didn't see it."

"You didn't see it?" yelled Odell. "Ray Charles could see it!"

The ref made a show of going to the African's corner, but he'd only given one warning, so he wasn't obliged to take away a point.

Con temporarily stopped the nosebleed and the blood from Mookie's mouth, but after a few jabs from the African in the tenth, blood started to flow again. The African flung Mookie into his corner, where he held him and hit him and nearly closed his left eye. That's when Mookie hit the African with two left uppercuts right in his nuts. The African's legs went in different directions, and he went down like a horse shot in a slaughterhouse. The referee marched to Mookie and held up a finger. He turned to each of the three judges, in the signal to penalize Mookie one point. The African's trainer hauled him up onto his stool and began to yell for disqualification. The referee was tempted, but a chair sailed into the ring, and then another. The commissioner looked the other way. When the African was offered up to five minutes, he took all five of them. Mookie stood with his arms on the top ropes of a neutral corner and nodded to Odell and Con.

"Mookie tough," said Odell. "Africa get to res', we res'."

Mookie kicked the shit out of the African for the rest of the tenth, making him wonder what he was doing in Philly that night.

"We winnin?" Mookie said after the bell.

While Con worked on blood, he talked. "We got the first five, no question about it. The sixth was even. We won the tenth, too, but they took away a point, so that makes the tenth an even round, but it still gives us five, with two even the way I see it. The African won the seventh, the eighth, and the ninth, and maybe one of the push rounds. With the point from us, that makes it even."

"So we need bof these rounds, eleven and twelve, bof to win," said Odell. "Look at 'im over there, Africa, he tired."

"I ain't tired," said Mookie, his roadwork paying off.

"Box 'im, Mookie, jus' like the gym. He droppin his left hand, so let you left hand go!, let it go and then you git, hyuh? An' then you jab, baby, bip, bip, bip, and then bang, come back wif the hook!"

Mookie boxed the African silly in the eleventh, sticking, moving. Acting like he was going to throw low blows, he scared the shit out of the African. Then he nailed him with big left hands and combinations to his head, which began to swell and made him look like a zombie. There was pandemonium in the arena. Over it all came the Ugandan chant.

At the bell, the ref strutted over to Mookie's corner. "That's enough of this movin-movin," he said. "Work, hear me?, or I'll stop it."

"We workin," said Odell.

"He's movin too much."

"Who say?" said Odell, challenging him.

"I say," said the ref.

"You say th-th-they a r-r-rule h-he g-g-got to stand an' get h-h-hit?"

Con saw that Odell was ready to deck the ref. If he did, they'd lose the fight and Odell could be banned from boxing in most states, so Con jumped in the ref's face. Besides, Mookie needed Odell right then more than he needed Cornelius Flutey. "We can fight any fuckin way we want to fight!"

"You watch your mouth, old man. I have the power to throw you outta here!"

"Yeah?, well, this old man will shoot you in the face eighteen times!, so you figure what kind of nine-millimeter I'm packin, you cocksucker, and we'll see who's got the fuckin power here!"

The ref turned away, wishing to God he hadn't taken the money. His mouth was still slack as the bell for the twelfth rang. Con was glad the ref hadn't called him on the gun, because he'd been selling wolf tickets on the nine-millimeter from the git. He grinned at Odell, who grinned back and shook his head.

"You a baaad man, Flute."

Con shrugged. "I could always hit him with the water bucket."

Mookie fought like a tommy gun, his shots coming from all angles. The ref flat kept out of it. Mookie busted up the African's lips and cut both eyes. The African fought back with all his might, connecting several times big-time, and once nearly knocked Mookie through the ropes. The Ugandans exploded. But by far Mookie landed the most clean punches in eleven and twelve, and Con was positive Mookie had won. The Ugandan's chant was swallowed up in the rest of the crowd's *"USA! USA! USA!"* The bell rang, and both Mookie and the African raised their hands in victory. Usually fighters embrace after the bell, smile like kids playing in water. But not this time.

The rest was a formality, both corners removing gloves and cutting off the wraps. Both wiped their boys down. Both crossed to the opposite corner or met in the middle of the ring and shook hands.

"You're a good trainer," Con said to the African's chief second, a former light-heavyweight contender. "And that boy of yours can bang."

"I appreciate that. And that Bodeen, he somethin else."

The African shook Con's hand, smiled down at him. "Very elusive, your fightah."

"I didn't like you much during the fight," Con said. "But I like you fine now."

"Thank you, suh."

The announcer read the results from the scorecards. "Ladies and gentlemen, we have a unanimous decision. I'll read the totals. All three judges had it the same, 118 to 110, all for the *still*—"

The Ugandans went manic, howling and waving their flags and prancing like they'd just driven another tribe into Lake Victoria. Con, Mookie's managers, Odell, and Mookie stared at one other in disbelief, as did members of the crowd, black, Puerto Rican, and white.

"Judges be smokin hunna-dolla' bills," said Odell.

Con hung his head. The TV announcers climbed into the ring as Mookie and Odell tried to climb out. The crowd was yelling and shouting. "Fix! Fix!"

The commissioner and the promoter jumped into the ring. Both rushed to Odell. "Bodeen can fight in Philly anytime, anytime!"

"Bodeen don't want to fight in Philly," said Odell, turning away and leaving the ring with Mookie.

"What's wrong with Philly?" the commissioner asked Con.

"What's wrong is that 118 to 110 means with the round they took that we only won two rounds," said Con. "And you know what that means?

"What?"

"It means that for judges you brought in the Three fuckin Stooges."

Con slipped through the ropes and grabbed his bucket and gear bag, but he was unable to follow behind Odell and Mookie because the Ugandans were dancing and chanting up the aisle. Several looked at Con and grinned smugly, and the leader in his African outfit danced up into Con's face.

"Uganda was victorious!"

They looked into each other's eyes, the Ugandan's black, Con's green. Neither blinked. One face was the face of the slaves that were captured from East Africa and taken to the Muslim market. The other face was the face of the Irish warriors of the British Empire that once ruled the world, including Uganda. The Ugandans crowded in close, twenty to one, daring Con to push them aside. Con set his stuff on the floor. It was time to teach.

"Understand that I admire your fighter and I admire you." He extended his hand to the leader. "Your Joshua is a great warrior, a lion."

The Ugandans went silent; their grins faded and their eyes slid to each other. From the back came a voice that chided the others.

"He is a sportsmahn."

The leader shook Con's hand. "Suh," he said.

Then all of them offered their hands in the soft, African manner, and Con shook each one. As he picked up his stuff and walked alone toward the dressing room, he heard the same voice he heard before.

"He is a sportsmahn."

Racket from the departing fight fans was banging off the walls of the dressing room. The TV crew was hauling cables and packing its gear in silence. Members of Mookie's faction were quiet, but down deep inside they were loud. A guard at the door kept the crowd out, but some got through and stood silently in disgust. Some yelled through the door that Mookie got jobbed, that what happened wasn't supposed to happen in Philly. Others hollered for a formal hearing before the Commission, but the faction knew if they filed a complaint, that nothing would come of it.

Outside, the Ugandans were chanting. One had wrapped himself in the multistriped black, yellow, and red of their homeland, a flag that had some kind of bird against a white circle in the middle of it. The smell of reefer edged itself into the dressing room. Mookie's managers stood looking at nothing. Odell sat next to Mookie, who slumped in his chair holding an ice bag to his lumping face, and adjusting the ice cubes Con had stuffed down his cup. Sweat continued to pour from Mookie, and Con kept after him with a towel that was stained with dark red blotches. Con mixed equal parts of water with a small can of pineapple-orange-banana juice and gave it to Mookie to replenish the potassium he'd lost sweating. Blood no longer flowed. The ring doctor came in to check Mookie: his ribs, kidneys, his liver, his nuts, his eyes, his mouth. He shrugged when he looked up Mookie's nose and told him to see a doctor once he got back to L.A.

"It's not the first time, right?"

"I get it fix when I hang 'em up."

A reporter wanted an interview, but Mookie waved him off with a water bottle. Slipping in with the reporter was a raggedy little brother wearing a dusty black cowboy hat with a long feather. He began to move and throw punches. He had scar tissue for eyebrows and wine for breath. His pants were too big and too long, but he continued to stick and move, to slip imaginary punches. He was five-four and had probably been a bantamweight, but now he weighed 160. Mookie closed his eyes and leaned forward, his face deep in the ice bag.

The little dude hiked up his pants and continued to punch.

"You like me, bro', you like me," he called to Mookie, who kept his face in the ice. "Dig," the little guy said, bobbing and weaving and throwing combinations. "Bip, bip, *bang!* Can you dig it? Slip an' then you stick, stick, roll to the lef side and hook, *whip!* to the body, man, *whip!* to the head! Bang, bang, stick and move, bip, bip, *bang!* See dat shit?, see what I'm sayin, can you dig it? Bap, bap, bap, and *bang!*, and *bing!*, and *boom!*" He raised his hands in victory and then pranced around the room like a rooster who'd just set a record with the hens. "Yeah, you like me, baby, you like *me!*"

Odell took him by the back of his pants and gently eased him out of the room. A moment later he stuck his head through the door. "Any y'all got twenty-five cent?" The guard threw him out.

Odell said, "Mookie got a fan."

Despite themselves they all smiled, and Mookie was able to dress after Con sponged him down with alcohol, and he stopped sweating. But the ride back to the hotel was awful.

"You want to go for pizza?" the driver asked.

Mookie shook his head and put a towel over his face.

In the hotel he came out of the shower holding his ribs and all stooped over. "I be hurtin . . . be pissin red, too."

Con iced the kid's face and his ribs and kidneys. Mookie was too sore for a massage, so Con gave him a codeine pill that would allow him to sleep.

"Your flight's at eight-thirty," said one of the managers. "They'll pick you up at seven downstairs." The managers went down to the bar. The white manager had Chivas on the rocks. The black had Hennessey and Coke.

"What time is it now?" asked Mookie.

"Fifteen pass one," said Odell.

The codeine kicked in and Mookie was able to pack. "I can't believe they did that to me, all the years I been fightin."

"Money," said Odell.

Mookie sat down in disgust.

"In time," Con said, "you'll be prouder of this fight than all your other fights put together."

Con finished packing at two-thirty. He felt old when he fell into bed and knew he'd be tired for days. But his mind kept sifting through what happened, what should have been.

"Lord," he prayed, "we won but we didn't win. We drank from your cup, Lord, but I want you to know that I'm mad at you. I know I was ready to stab the judges and that I jumped on that crook referee, forgive me, Lord, but I figure someone's gonna shoot the boy he don't ref right, so maybe I did the puke a favor. Help us all through this night, Lord, 'specially Mookie, help him on the plane and help him with his face so his mama won't feel so bad. Lord, I'm not mad at you anymore."

Most of the swelling in Mookie's face had gone down, but he kept it in ice in the hotel room before they left. He wore dark glasses in the airport and on the plane. He was spitting and pissing clear, but he was still stooped over from pain in his ribs, and the white in his left eye was scarlet from a broken blood vessel.

"Africa hurtin', too," said Odell.

Con gave him more codeine, and the kid slept most of the way to Los Angeles, Mookie next to the window, Odell in the middle, and Con on the aisle. Odell slept, too. Odell always slept in the air. Con never did, though this was a soft ride. The pilot's voice came over the snapping and popping loudspeaker from time to time, and somewhere over Arizona it woke Mookie, who stared out the window. As they came across the low desert of California, the pilot spoke again.

"Ladies and gentlemen, we will be landing in Los Angeles in a few minutes. Over on our left is the famous resort city of Palm Springs. In a moment, on our right, high in the mountains, you will see Big Bear Lake."

Mookie thought about the champions that trained in Big Bear. Despite his will, his eyes began to leak. The announcement woke Odell, who always sat up smiling after a sleep. "All right," he said.

Mookie kept looking out at the scorched desert below. He put a hand over his bruised mouth to muffle the sounds coming from him, but he couldn't control the spasms in his gut. Odell looked at Con, who signaled for Odell to talk to Mookie.

"What this business?" Odell said to the kid.

Mookie couldn't look at him, ashamed of the water coming down from his dark glasses. "You know."

"You lose a eye, you go blind?"

"My mama don't get no house," said Mookie, turning to Odell.

"You quittin?"

"Hell no!"

"Then wipe you face, boy. We got no dog in us."

Frozen Water

Nobody know how Dangerous Dillard Fightin Flippo Bam-Bam Barch first come around Hope Street Gym, but for maybe two years the boy show up every month for two weeks at a stretch and then he be gone for two weeks. Dangerous Dillard Fightin Flippo Bam-Bam Barch, that be the fightin name he give hissef, but he never have a fight, except one, if that what you call it. Around the gym they cut his name down to Deedee, or Flippy or Orbit. But Danger always talk about hissef the long way, by his fightin name.

"My name's Dangerous Dillard Fightin Flippo Bam-Bam Barch outta Polk County, Missouri," he say, squinting one eye, "an' my dream is to fight the Motor City Cobra Thomas Hit Man Hearns for the WBA Welterweight Championship of the whole world."

I done some fighting back before TV, lightweight, course I weigh more now. I wasn't a contender, nothing like that, but I was a scrapper and I put on a good show every time I lace them up in the local arenas around L.A.—Wrigley Field, Ocean Park, Wilmington, Jeffries' Barn, and sometimes up in Stockton or Frisco, and down Tijuana Old Mexico. I fight at Hollywood Legion, too, right there off Sunset and Vine, but I had to say I was a Ayrab because they don't fight coloreds in Hollywood Legion in those days. Prince Hakim the Sheik. I fight there ten times as a Ayrab because I had light skin and could fool the Hollywood movie crowd, main events some of them I fight when I filled the joint *up!* Promoter know, so the sportswriters know, they don't care about colored, neither do the white boys I fight—it be a game. Posters other places say Willie "Scrap Iron" DuPree. Friends call me Scrap.

I never get a title shot, but I make me some money in my fifty-five fights, and that's when times be tough and you got to fight hard, but I never got busted-up bad or nothing. Nose be broke enough so I don't hardly have a nose, and one eye droop because of cuts and the dead nerve in the lid, but nothing serious, not like some of the boys end up stuttering and talking through they nose. I never did business or bet on the other boy, only on mysef, money I made be straight money. And because I give it my best, I always have a place to stay once I hang them up, have a room in the back of a gym for keeping it clean, for dumping the spit buckets and keeping the blood mopped up, and for keeping the place smelling good, things like that. And keeping my nose clean and my eyes peeled the wrong element start hanging around. And once I get old and stop training my own fighters, I handle the stool and ice bucket for a few dollars if some out-of-town faction be short a corner guy. They want a cut man, I charge more. Rubdown? Rubdown cost two dollars, heavyweight cost three. I know a fighter body better than they girlfriends.

These days, the old gyms be gone, like Main Street and Hope Street, but now I'm out at Hymns Gym 108th and Broadway, run by boy I used to train, Curtis "Hymn" Odom. Call him Hymn he fight so pretty and always serious as a shroud, Curtis Odom, I teach him, teach him to crack. Curtis a contender in his prime. He hit so hard you start lookin for a tittie to suck. But he got a eye detach and can't see right and that be it, but good God how the boy could punch, he slip outside on you and hook to body *yop*, hook to the head *bing!* and put you raggedy ass to sleep. Nice man, too, he decent, people respect Hymn, wouldn't say shit he have a mouthful, why people from around the world come to Hymn Gym for Curtis to train they boys and he make a gang a money, that and with what the boys he train and manage hissef make for him.

But Hope Street, where Hope Street Gym used to be, it wasn't but a block long where it runs from Eighteenth and the freeway off-ramp down to Washington and Trade Tech College. The orange brick building be a old Masonic Hall some kind, have six floors and go back to 1910. Most of it wasn't used except for storage, but the gym be up two and a half flights of stairs and be built inside the ballroom part of the hall that have high ceilings and windows and lots of air, not that you leave the windows open. Building tore down to make even more parking, but before that it sit across the parking lot behind the Olympic Auditorium where they have the fights in L.A.'s 1932 Olympics.

They a few contenders outta Hope, but no champs. There be amateurs and a lot of Latino boys come through for fights at the Olympic and the nickel-dime gym bums looking to hustle a two-dollar loan. Gym be in a neighborhood where you car ain't safe. South of Washington and east of Figueroa be mostly black. West of Fig all directions was Latino. Any white boy come through better look like he can fight.

Dillard didn't have no trouble with anyone, never did, not even ones who couldn't talk American. He tell anybody listen he a Missouri hillbilly, tell people he go to Kansas City one time and the Missouri River be too thick to drink and too thin to plow. Last time he leave Hope Street he don't come back.

Danger a farmer white boy with pale hair and eyes and skin, and when he work out he turn red as a burnt finger. Hymn train the boy free of charge knowing Danger couldn't fight a lick and never would. Danger try so hard and mess up so bad you laugh at first.

Then you watch awhile, see his set jaw, and you think on that dream of his and you end up in the boy's corner same way Hymn did.

Hymn work with anybody tap him on the shoulder. They young enough, you work with them for free, even the fatties because you never know what's inside a boy until the boy get hit. Joe Frazier a fat boy. Well, Hymn know from the git Danger never go nowhere, know that even if he could learn a few moves, he never pass the noodle exam to get licensed. Still, he never turn his back on the boy, never charge him a dime.

"My name's Dangerous Dillard Fightin Flippo Bam-Bam Barch outta Polk County, Missouri!" Danger yell out between rounds, try to be like Muhammad Ali, "and I challenge the Motor City Cobra Thomas Hit Man Hearns to fight me for the WBA Welterweight Championship of the whole world!"

"But you ain't ranked, Deedee," Shawrelle would tease. "Champs gotta fight someone in the top ten, man."

"I'll fight him anyway, anytime, anyplace!"

"But then it wouldn't be a title fight, and if you won, you wouldn't be champ," say Shawrelle, walk away say this be one dumb white boy. Shawrelle a amateur and be stone black.

Danger don't understand rankings, but when he show up for two weeks in the gym he be there working out twice a day, sixteen 3-minute rounds at noon when the pros train, and another sixteen in the evening with the amateurs, and that ain't counting his five miles every morning at six at the Trade Tech track. It be pitiful to watch, but he keep on, and after a while the boy get strong.

"Say, Orbit, why don't you go a few rounds wif me?" say Shawrelle.

I say, "Don't be talkin that mess."

Danger say, "I'll do it, Mist Scrap, do it right now."

I say, "No, you ain't goin in wif Shawrelle, forget it."

"You scared, right Flippy?, you a little white rabbit?"

"I ain't scared a no man!"

"Scrap he be scared," say Shawrelle. "Scrap got the blood of the slave master in him, see that skin? Scrap talk like a brother, but Scrap be runnin a game."

"Cut that shit, Shawrelle," I say.

Shawrelle say, "You still be lickin the boot of the oppressor, old man."

I tap the pocket where I keep my shit, say, "Till you know how it was when it was, watch you mouf."

Shawrelle walk away grinning like a shit-eating dog, like he be jokin, Shawrelle don't joke, Shawrelle ain't smart enough to be funny. Think he be tough. Tough ain't enough.

Danger loosen up with leg exercises and stretches like a fighter do. And he shadowbox four rounds and Hymn treat him like a contender, never tease or laugh at him, and always find time to work four rounds with him on the punch mitts, not that Danger can punch worth a damn. Danger don't know how to breathe like a fighter and can hardly stand up after four on the mitts, but he go on to work in his own way on the big bag for four rounds, slap at the speed bag for four, stumble around with the jump rope four more, and then do 120 sit-ups—four different sets of thirty reps each. He be so red you think he cut, but he got no quit in him and Hymn never lose patience when Danger can't remember things Hymn told him two minutes before, or a thousand times before that. Danger call Curtis Mist Hymn, picked "Mist" up from the brothers. Call me Mist Scrap.

Curtis Odom, see, he find his church early on and peoples respect him because he never run a game on nobody and because when he a contender he knock out top fighters all over the country, and in France and Japan, and in South Africa. Take me with him every fight he have except South Africa because there was no ticket but one. Joburg what he call Johannesburg, what the South Africans call it. Fought there twice and won both times and was treated white because he was a fighter. Said if he couldn't live in America he'd choose South Africa. Said he take me there next time, make sure they be two tickets. No next time. Still good-looking, Hymn, too bad about his dead eye, but his weight still same as his fighting weight, 160 pounds. Hymn be bad.

Now, Danger, he another thing. Beside being blood simple, boy have this big head on him and this big neck, head and neck like a heavyweight on this small body. He about five-six, five-seven and good-looking for a white boy, weigh forty-five, maybe fifty tops, natural welterweight. First off, you don't know he simple. It when he talk you know.

"A lotta white boys died 'cause a you niggers in Lincoln's War up around home. Fought and died all the way through them Ozarks. Lotta my kin died under Old Pap Price at Wilson's Creek, and folks still talk about it up in them hills and talk about hangin a nigger in a minute. Me, I got nothin against niggers 'cause my mama taught me that, said not to cause hurt."

I had to smile. "Is that like the Golden Rule, Dange?"

"I don't rightly know."

See, you ax him something he can't answer, he walk off and start messing with shoelaces, or fuss with his fingernails, or just stand there squeezing his mind trying to understand what you ax him. In hot weather, some trainers freeze water in plastic bottles and then add more water to the bottle in the gym so they boys can have ice water. Danger would study the ice in those bottles, squinting at it ten minutes and more. Come over to me one day like he worried sick. I be sweeping up and he ax me how they get that ice down through the small hole in the top of the bottle.

"What you do is fill the bottle partway wif water and then put the bottle in the freezer. Water change to ice and then you bring it on to the gym next day in the bottle."

Boy understand and jump around like a family dog. Next day he come in wif his own bottle wif ice in it, and his face be so proud he make you think he invent frozen water.

After Danger been coming around like I say, he stop by me in his simple please-and-thank-you way he have and we get to talking. Most times he bring me some Twinkies to go wif my coffee. I try to give him one back.

"No, sir, Mist Scrap," he say. "I'm in trainin."

"Talk to me, Danger, where you go when you don't show up 'round here?, you ain't cheatin on us now?, be goin 'round to other gym?"

"No, sir, Mist Scrap, no siree. You my friends, you'n Mist Hymn."

"So where you go?"

"I go home." Say it like a little boy.

"You go to Missouri?, boy, that be halfway to New York an' mo'."

"It is?"

"Yeah, it is, hail."

"Don't seem real far."

"Far? Damn! You from Kansas City, St. Louis?"

"No, sir, Bolivar." He say it like it was wrote *Ball*-ivar. "It's a small town like most back there."

"Bolivar, huh?"

"Yes, sir, like that Simon Bolivar freedom fighter there from south a the border? We got a statue a him was give to President Truman?, who's a Missouri boy like me. Course he ain't no hillbilly."

"Where is this Bolivar?"

"We're just a spell up from Springfield where all the fightin was? See, from Bolivar you come on down 13 to 44 West outta Springfield and keep headin west till you take up 40 West outta Oklahoma City to Barstow here in California where you get 15 down to 10 West and you wait for Main Street in Los Angeles and you get off there and walk over to Hope Street ain't but five blocks easy as that."

Danger proud he can remember all that, go on to say that he

collect some kind of welfare check back home and soon as he cash it and pick up his medicine he head on back to Hope Street.

"An' once I'm all outta money here, see, then I get to hitch back home and get some more? Easy as pie."

"So you say it take you a week to git home and a week to git back here once a mont?"

"Ain't it great?"

"How you eat you got no money?"

"Truckers. An' families when they eat I get to. Sometimes I don't for a couple a three days, but that keeps me lean and mean for the Hit Man."

"How'd you come to L.A. in the first place?"

"Come with Ervel, my mama's boyfriend?"

"Come wif you mama on vacation like?"

"Uh-unh, just me an' Ervel come in his pickup. I don't rightly know why we come, just one day we did. An' right away on the first day?, we was over on East Fifth Street there on Skid Row there in the middle of the Nickel?, an' he bought me a soda, an' next thing I know I look around an' poor Ervel was lost. Lordy, I looked for a week for Ervel, and when I couldn't find him a policeman took me to the wino shelter."

"What happen to Ervel?"

Danger smile all big and sweet. "He made it home all by himself!"

I'm thinking that jive-ass honky white-trash hillbilly Ervel. "He got there ahead a you, did he?"

"How'd you know?"

"How you get home, Danger?"

"Wino-shelter lady got a map and wrote it all down for me and then rode me in her van out Highway 10 a ways and dropped me off. When I come home my mama was spittin mad at Ervel. Started kissin on me and cryin, and then pointin her finger at Ervel and laughin. He went away an' never come back."

"But Dange, what I don't unnerstan' is why you come all the way back here?, that hitchhikin half the country, man."

"It's on account of the guidance I get under Mist Hymn for my title fight?"

"They other gyms closer, ain't they?"

That's one of the times Danger walk away because he don't have a answer. He always keep hissef clean, which is more than some with good sense do, but I don't know how he do it, or where he flop. Except for his fall-apart gym clothes he don't look but to own one set of clothes and they be secondhand army-navy. But when he come back, he always come back with Twinkies for me and with a hopeful little smile.

"Hey, Flippy!" Shawrelle call from the ring. "You got to bring ass to kick ass, ain't that right?"

"Yeah!" Danger say, hop around throwing his pitty-pat jab all pleased somebody talk to him. "You got to bring ass!"

"When you fightin the title?" ax Shawrelle.

That when Danger go stand by a wall.

Shawrelle call hissef Shawrelle Muhammad, but his real name Shawrelle Berry, and Shawrelle he eat swine in a minute. He have a hook that move a tank, I'm telling you, but he have a heart like a split pea. Right hand on him and a left hook, bof would knock you out you think you dead, knock you down with a jab. Hymn teach him to punch the way I teach Hymn. But Shawrelle think he smarter than he was, and he spend all his time telling his little lies and acting uppity like he already be somebody. He a punk, Shawrelle, but he can hit, I give him that. But he can't fight, what it is, hitting and fighting be different. All the time he talk about he so bad and what he suppose to get because he so bad, what somebody suppose to give him, but he never do what it take. Hymn be first one to train Shawrelle, think the boy would change, but one day in the gym he walk away from the boy's corner during a round when Shawrelle start yelling about the other boy hitting him too hard after it was Shawrelle hissef who tried to knock the other boy out.

"Hey, man, come back man, what I do?" Shawrelle be whining.

Hymn call off the session and explain it to him, that in the gym you be there to work, not to knock somebody out, that you work a boy too hard one day the boy ain't gonna come back tomorrow, and that it be natural for the boy he crack today to crack him back to get respect.

"Yeah, man, yeah, I can dig it."

So once Shawrelle got Hymn to give him another chance, Shawrelle think Hymn be his bitch, and next trick Shawrelle try to pull be to tell Hymn to carry his gym bag down to the street.

"Eight, nine, ten, you out," was all Hymn said.

But the look he give Shawrelle, Shawrelle don't say jack, but his eyes be mean and you know he want some git-back. Yeah, that be Shawrelle, and next day he easy get hissef a new trainer good as Shawrelle look in the gym, tall boy Shawrelle, like Sugar Ray Robinson, six feet and 160 pounds of thump, say 15 pounds bigger than Danger, but for all his talk, he want *out*, not *in*, spend all his time making sure he on the outside so he can cry about *being* on the outside. He a ho what he was, a ho looking for Santa Claus to rob, a little gangsta punk looking for a sugar daddy. Scared of white boys, too, Shawrelle. Get to amateur tournaments and come up against a white boy?, say he have a toothache, can't fight. Why he was always on Danger and want to get Danger in the ring and why me and Hymn say no good. Shawrelle mean but he got no left titty.

Maybe my fault what happen to Danger. I ain't suppose to leave a gym unless the owner or somebody like Hymn be there to cover. Well, owner of Hope Street be in Vegas and then Hymn get a call on a ten-round fighter he have, call come from the promoter over at the Olympic who want Hymn's boy in the next show, so Hymn go. Gym full of amateurs and Danger there shadowboxing. Shawrelle there too, working like everybody else. Hymn's boys be waiting for Hymn to come back from the Olympic. Somebody say that the drain in the shower be broke, and I go to fix it. Well, I'm gone from the floor maybe half hour. Not like I leave the building, but I be in the back so I can't watch.

Once I fix the drain and mop up, I hear all this yelling from the ring. I get back about the same time Hymn come on in from the Olympic. Somehow Shawrelle hustle Danger to get in the ring with him. Danger wearing some old sixteen-ounce sparring gloves, but he got no head gear and no cup and no mouthpiece. Shawrelle wearing everything, and he got himself some ten-ounce fighting gloves on instead of sixteen. His trainer know better than that, young boy for a trainer, but he think he slick like Shawrelle. Whole thing don't last but a few seconds, but Shawrelle jump on Danger like he putting out a fire. He hit Danger all upside his head, and Danger be looking around for someone tell him what to do. Shawrelle hit him with twenty, thirty shots, all combinations, *bip-bip* bang!, bip-*bing!*, but he can't knock Danger out, what he want. Both Danger's eyes bust open by the time me and Hymn get there and his face be swelling up bad, but he won't go down, and the more Shawrelle hit him the more Danger walk straight to him until Danger's hands be hanging at his side and his face look like he in a wreck and he stand there like a dumb animal so sick he ready to die. It all happen quick like a stabbing, and there be no ref to stop it, and bloody slobber be coming from Danger mouth where he bite his tongue. Shawrelle throw that first shot it be the death of Danger's dream, rest of Shawrelle shots dig the grave to dump it in.

Hymn sail into the ring and pin Shawrelle to the ropes where he hold on to him like a thief so I can come get Danger.

"How'd I do, Mist Scrap?"

I hug him to me. "You done great, Danger, you my man, you bad, you be next champion of the world."

Danger pull back. "No, I won't, Mist Scrap," he say. He smile his little smile, his bloody teeth look like neon shining in his mouth. "I shoulda knowed."

"Here, baby, let me hep you," I say, start to take off his gloves.

"I can do her, just untie the knots."

He want to clean up alone, but he need help. He come out front again once Hymn stop the blood with adrenaline and close the cuts on the boy's eyes, stuck the swollen edges of split skin together with butterflies. Danger's face go all lumpy with blue knots deep to the bone and one eye swole shut and he walk stoop over from Shawrelle body shots what separate his ribs.

Shawrelle strut, all proud with himself with his lips tight together all righteous. "Flippy Deedee Orbit be ready for the Hit Man now."

"Come on back to Scrap's room," Hymn say to Danger. "Lay down while I go get ice for my ice bag."

Danger say, "I would, Mist Hymn, and I sure thank you for all you done, but I'm fixin to go on back home to Bolivar right now."

Danger smile at me again, shake Hymn's hand and mine, and then he empty his pockets on a bench near the ring, thirty-two crumpled dollars, a piece of string, and some change that roll on the floor. Gym bum stand on a penny.

"Bye," say Danger. Simple as that.

"Here, son, take your money," say Hymn, he afraid Danger be paying him for training.

Danger say, "Goin home, Mist Hymn. Cain't go home I still got money."

He walk out on his own and gym bums scramble for the money, but now Shawrelle race over from the big bag and knock everybody back, ten-ounce gloves still on his hands.

"It mine!" he shout. "I whupped that white boy's ass and it mine!"

"No good," say Hymn. He grab up the bills in a tight ball and hold it in his right hand.

"I won it!" scream Shawrelle. "It be mine!"

"Boy, I said no good."

"Boy! You call me boy? You call me boy?"

"I don't call you Roy."

"That money by right be mine, old man!" Shawrelle yelling and trying to grab the money with his gloves.

"I said no good."

And then Shawrelle bang Hymn on same side his bad eye on. Hymn stagger and one leg lift up off the ground, but he don't go down. Shawrelle try to hit him again same right-hand shot, but quick as light Hymn slip the punch. He rotate his left shoulder back and in a half crouch he put his weight over the left knee. Shawrelle eyes roll like a mule's, but he know there nothing he can do once Hymn get the angle. Hymn still be holding Danger money in his right hand when he shift his weight and hit Shawrelle with a left hook *yip!* to the liver that made him gut-sick and spread yellow all through him and he know what be next on the way. Hymn he double up the shot, come on back *yop!* with a hook to the jaw that snap Shawrelle's neck like a hanging knot and put the boy out close to five minutes.

Shawrelle lay there twitching like a fit. Everyone in the gym back away, think he be dead. Fool with his foot on the penny take it off. Hymn hand me Danger wad of money and walk away. Shawrelle new trainer with his mouth all open go for ice water in a bottle he dump on Shawrelle. When Shawrelle sputter up on a elbow, I look down on him like he a pile of dog mess.

I say, "Punk, get a job."

Shawrelle fall back, spit out a red tooth. Leg still be jerking.

I go over to Hymn. I say, "Shawrelle Berry go to sleep wif Curtis Hymn Odom every night the res' a his life."

"Somebody don't stab him."

"What I do Danger money?"

"Find him, give it back."

"What I can't find him?"

"Buy pussy with it, go fuck, I don't care." Hymn don't talk like that, not Hymn.

I run out for Danger but he gone. I check all around, but he disappear. Wait a couple days, he don't come back. I think of ways to spend the money—buy a shirt, spend it on pussy and all, but somehow I can't spend Danger money any way I try. I still got it in a coffee can behind my bed up my room waiting on the boy.

Not long after Shawrelle and Danger, Hope Street close down and Hymn open up at 108th and Broadway in South Central, about ninety blocks south from Hope Street Gym. Long-ass way for somebody like Danger. He ain't showed up, but you never can tell. If he do, I have all his money for him, have it all ready for old Dangerous Dillard Fightin Flippo Bam-Bam Barch, tell him he whip that Motor City Cobra Hit Man Tommy Hearns once Hearns stop ducking Danger and give him a title shot. Make old Danger feel good, get him hopping and pitty-pat jabbing again. And that Shawrelle Berry, he ever bring his common black ass in Hymn Gym try to put a hurt on my man Danger, I shoot the nigga.

Rope Burns

he winnah! In the blue cornah!" The tuxedoed ring announcer shouted into the microphone, his pounding voice echoing through the vast sports complex. "By knockout, at two-twenty of the third round! And the amateur fighter to represent the United States! In the Light-Heavyweight Division! At the 1992 Barcelona, Spain, Summer Olympics! Henry 'Puddin' Pye! Pye!"

Joseph Mary "Mac" McGee sailed across the ring to his fighter. Mac was Puddin's trainer, and he kissed the boy on both cheeks, the sweat as sweet to him as Puddin's name. He removed the kid's headgear and hoisted him halfway to the overhead lights. Puddin was all teeth and pumped veins after he scored the knockout. As he raised his gloved fists in victory, the yelling crowd cheered even louder. Puddin went to his groggy opponent, shook his hand, said, "Good fight, bro!" and then ran back to hug Mac. Their first goal, making it to the Olympics, had been achieved. Puddin would turn eighteen in May. He was six feet one and still growing. To make the 178-pound limit at the weigh-in, he'd trained down from 187. Mac marveled at the kid. He figured Puddin would be six-three or -four in two or three years and fighting at a perfect 225.

Puddin's mother, Willa, with his two younger brothers, Felcie and Velcie, were in the stands, had shouted themselves hoarse. Tears glistened in Willa's eyes. First she thanked God her baby man hadn't been hurt, then for his victory, and then she turned to the spectators around her. Her voice rose above the noise of the crowd.

"That my dream baby! That my angel child! That my Puddin!"

Puddin's postman father was in the ground. He'd been shot dead in 1985 while delivering mail in South Central Los Angeles, caught and killed in the drive-by crossfire between members of the rival Crips and Bloods. Puddin saw himself as the man in the family, the one responsible for his mother and his brothers. His next goal was the Gold Medal. Including Cubans, he'd already beaten the best in international competition, both in Europe and Latin America, and was considered a sure winner in Barcelona.

But there was much to learn in the sweet science, so from the beginning Mac taught the kid to think in the ring, to fight pretty. The pretty fighter was the man, and fighting pretty meant you were slick in the way you moved, the way you threw punches, and the way you slipped punches; that you had defense as well as offense; and that you outsmarted your opponent; that you moved while you punched, so that you kept your opponent off balance and missing and without thump in his punches. So the first thing Mac taught Puddin was that balance meant leverage; that leverage meant speed; that it was speed that meant power, because balance and leverage were behind the speed, not muscle.

But winning as an amateur also meant outsmarting biased judges, who would sometimes give a hometown decision to the fighter who was a favorite among the local amateur officials. It was lousy, but it was true, and much too often promising kids would go sour because of it and quit. It happened internationally, as well. The dirty judges at the Olympics held in Korea was a classic example.

Puddin was jobbed in his eighth, tenth, and eleventh fights, when judges took fights from him that were clearly his. A knockout ends all debate, but the use of padded headgear and big gloves makes knockouts in the amateurs tougher to get than in the pros, which were tough enough, even with the smaller gloves and no headgear. Rules requiring headgear and big gloves were established to protect amateur fighters, and Mac was for that, but like all rules, amateur rules could be broken by people in power. Mac was tempted to train Puddin strictly as a pro, because he would put a lot of opponents to sleep. But a pro style would go against Puddin according to amateur rules, because it was the number of landed punches that counted, not the damage done by those punches—unless there was a kayo.

But just a knockdown in the amateurs only counted for one punch, where in a pro fight it usually meant a two-point round, the difference sometimes between winning and losing. In the amateurs, judges usually penalized a kid who fought like a pro, arguing that he didn't throw enough punches. But a perfect amateur style could become a liability as well. Some great amateur fighters never went anywhere as pros because they couldn't make the switch in styles, couldn't "set" down on their punches.

So Mac trained Puddin both ways. The kid would use primarily his punishing jab and the straight right, punching for the most part to the head during the first two rounds, typical amateur stuff. If Mac was sure Puddin had won the first and second rounds on points, then he'd have him switch to his pro style, punching to the body as well to the head, throwing power hooks and uppercuts, straight right-hands to the sweet spot on the jaw, and go for the knockout.

"Remember, if you want to hit him in the body, you go to the head first, that's to get him to lift his hands up, right? If you want to go to the head, hurt the body first to get the hands down. Trick him. Boxing is a game of lies."

"Boxing a game of lies."

Puddin put opponents to sleep with shots to the jaw, but he also put them down with body shots to the short rib, the solar plexus, and the liver. There were other legal punches that were terrible as well. On his way up from the juniors, Puddin lost a few fights fair and square to more experienced fighters, but winning by kayo meant Puddin couldn't be robbed, even with a crooked judge. Going to the body also prepared Puddin for the pros.

Kidney shots, rabbit punches, and low blows were illegal, both in the pros and the amateurs. Mac figured a hook to the sciatic nerve in the cheek of the ass was the best dirty punch in the business, because refs seldom if ever called them, and most people didn't know you could cripple a fighter with shots to his ass. Mac had taught Puddin all the tricks because he would have to know how to fight dirty just as soon as the other guy started it, and some-one sometime surely would. But only then.

"You never start the shit, but when it happens, you do what you gotta do to get respect."

"Do what you gotta to get respec'." Puddin repeated aloud things that were important, and never forgot.

The kid's double-trouble style would aggravate the officials, but once the first two rounds were already on record by the start of the third, and since Puddin had broken none of the rules, there wasn't anything the judges could do to cancel out his lead. As Puddin Pye became an international amateur name, judges began to admire his work despite themselves, to sit back like everyone else to watch how pretty he was.

Watching him fight was like watching chess with pain. He instilled fear in his opponents like the young Mike Tyson did, except Puddin did it with class, did it the way Sugar Ray Robinson did it. When Puddin stepped up the pressure in the third round, opponents often went down within the first two minutes—not always from a kayo punch that put them on their face, but down in fear of a Puddin kayo, one that could leave them rattled for days.

With the Gold Medal in Barcelona, Puddin would have lawyers standing in line to back him. Promoters would be licking their chops. That was fine with Mac, who aimed to bring Puddin along slowly, maybe hang as a 195-pound cruiserweight for two years or so, no matter how much his backers wanted to move him up to heavy. Fill him out mentally and physically, get him the right kind of fights. Not stumblebums, but guys that would stretch Puddin, fighters with enough experience and grit to make him think, guys who wanted to win and could bang hard enough to teach him to keep his hands up. Guys who would make him put out fires.

"The other guy gets hit, right?"

"Right."

"Who's the predator?"

"I the predator!"

From the beginning, it's what Mac taught Puddin.

"Predator is the one that eats, understand? When a zebra kicks a lion in the face, the lion'll starve to death because his jaw is broke, right? Same with a wolf, he gets hurt he starves. Predator's deal is win without getting hurt, or at least not hurt so bad he can't eat what he takes down and go on. With fighters it's the same. See, if you take too bad a beating in order to beat your opponent, then you ain't gonna last long enough in the game to get anywhere. Or even if you do, you could end up walking on queer street and talking like you got a dead tongue. You understand?"

"Yeah."

Mac wanted to make sure. "Let's say he comes rushing on you, maybe lands a good shot. You don't buck him, you don't fight his toe-to-toe fight, get me? You slide to the side, pivot, move out of range, mess with his mind, turn him and make him miss, and when he's tired, and he will be tired because by now he's holding his breath as he strains to get to you, now you jump on him, now's when you pound on him like he's a nail."

"Uh-huh, like a nail, I hear what you sayin."

Mac's goal wasn't to turn the boy into an animal, just the opposite. The point was to give him power, the physical and mental power that would keep him from becoming an animal when pressure made him want to revert.

"Fighting *bulls*, right?" said Mac. "Braver than a mama *bear*. They'll charge a train if they get separated from their group. But brave ain't enough when the train wins, right? And tough ain't enough when you start taking so many shots that sooner or later you start to lose. Or your body quits, says that's it, ain't going for no more pain. It's skill, and legs and speed and brains that get you through. Boxing's a pure, clean thing up there in the ring. It's about will and respect, but it couldn't exist without the ref and the ropes, and the warrior's mind."

"Uh-*huh*!"

As Mac spoke, Puddin's shoulders were rolling imperceptibly, the nerves from his spine sending messages to his fingers and toes.

Mac said, "It's having the moves, and knowing how to think like a predator, and staying out of the other guy's pocket because you know how to breathe and he don't."

"Think like a predator," said Puddin.

"That's right."

"And breathe every time I throw a punch, every time I take that step," said Puddin.

"You got it, Toyota."

Mac McGee was a retired cop who'd fought as a kid in the Golden Gloves, had trained at the old Main Street Gym. He fought as a welterweight in the navy, became champ of the Pacific Fleet after he lied about his age in 1943 and signed up at seventeen. During the Battle of Leyte Gulf he won the Silver Star. He stayed in the navy for another hitch after World War II, but when he got married and finished out his time in 1951, he didn't sign over. The LAPD took him on his first application. A daughter was born in 1955, a second in '57. A son, Brendan Patrick, stillborn two years later, was buried beneath a Celtic cross, buried with his father's broken heart. After fifteen years on the force, rising to the rank of sergeant, Mac ruined a kneecap in a rolling firefight chasing bank robbers from Eagle Rock to San Pedro. Prior to that, he'd taught boxing to Mexican kids at the Boyle Heights police gym. He worked as a P.I. a few years after the kneecap, but his love of boxing took him back to the fight game full-time by 1968. Despite his knee, he could punch, he could always do that. And he could still slip punches better than most, still pivot off the front and back leg both, could turn you 180 degrees with a tap to the shoulder, a tug at the elbow.

But his retirement money wasn't enough to satisfy his wife, despite the periodic jolts of serious cash he made off the fights. Besides, she wasn't happy with all the time he spent away from home, and she couldn't relate to his friends, all of them cops or fight guys. One Sunday he returned home after three weeks from a 1971 Tokyo title fight. The lights were out and he found his house empty, a FOR SALE sign stuck in the frontyard grass. His wife had moved out with the kids, the furniture, the station wagon, his cherry '57 T-Bird, everything. She left a note, along with her lawyer's card, in his daughters' room.

> Have your lawyer call mine. Half the house money goes to me.
> I want alimony and child support. You always said boxing was
> your life, bastard. Now boxing is your wife.

Mac figured losing her was all part of growing up, but losing his two daughters nearly destroyed him. First he went on the sauce, but after a while whiskey stopped killing the pain and he needed something stronger. He passed on weed, because he didn't like the stink, and moved on to the other stuff, using anything he could score that would disconnect his mind from his heart. In his arm, up his nose. The irony of being a doper cop hit him in the face like a slab of hog liver. All his police life he'd fought against enemies of decency, had busted dealers like they were rotten eggs. Then he became the enemy of himself. Friends avoided him on the street. It was his daughters' love and his love for them that saved him finally, and now he'd been clean for fifteen years. Father Carey had been instrumental in bringing him back as well.

"How much money these backer mens give me, you suppose?" asked Puddin, scooping up rice and beans and salsa with a tortilla.

Mac and Puddin were eating, as they regularly did, at Señora Cabrera's seafood café, Mariscos Acapulco. She was a squat and square Mexican lady with a long, thick braid laced with bright ribbons down her back. She looked after Puddin as if he were her chick, made him special refried beans without lard to keep down the fat in his diet. Her grandfather had been the lightweight champion of the world during the forties, when you fought fifteen rounds for the title, when many a fight was won in the thirteenth, the fourteenth, and the fifteenth. On the wall above the cash register hung a twelve-by-eighteen tinted photograph of her grandfather, a handsome little guy, in his fighting togs. Next to it was an eight-by-ten glossy black-and-white of Puddin when he won the regionals that took him to the nationals. The señora was a widow. Her gardener husband and her thirteen-year-old son were killed when a drunk driver ran a red light and plowed into their pickup on Central Avenue. Neither her husband nor the drunk had insurance. She opened a little stand that grew into the Acapulco and made it possible for her to raise and send her twin daughters to nursing school. Both were in their early twenties and still lived with her. Both were nurses at Los Angeles County USC Medical Center. All lived in a little house a few blocks from the café. The señora had been robbed once, by Mexicans, who came through a window of her house. Now her windows, like the windows in many of the houses in the neighborhood, had steel bars. Now she kept her grandfather's .44 Mag *pistola* under her pillow. In two years she would be able to retire to her hometown, a village halfway down the west coast of Baja, Guerrero Negro, where whales frolicked and salt was made from the sea.

The spring air was clear of smog, and Mac and Puddin sat at the outdoor counter because the dining room was full. Latinos and blacks kept the place crowded. It was located just off the corner of Vernon and Compton on the southeast side of Los Angeles, a crossover area populated by blacks and Latinos. Though gang members sometimes congregated on the corner, there was an armed truce between them in and around the café. The señora never had fights in her place, or trouble with gangs or her black neighbors. She was too nice and the food was too good.

It was two weeks after Puddin's win at the nationals. He needed a rest, but soon it would be time to get back into the gym. To be in top shape for Barcelona, he needed to be in good shape when he got to the U.S. training camp in Colorado Springs. There he would be taken over and supervised by Olympic trainers. This was the part of their triumph that hurt, because Mac wouldn't be allowed to work with Puddin in camp, or to be in Puddin's corner in Spain. It was the way it was done. It was at this point that Olympic trainers, acting as front men for wealthy backers, sometimes stole fighters from the trainers who got the boys to the Olympics. But no matter what it cost, Mac would be sitting ringside for Puddin's fights, where he'd be shouting up instructions. It would be Mac's voice that Puddin heard over all others, and nobody could do a thing about it.

Mac thought about Puddin's use of the word *give*. "First of all, nobody gives you anything. Backers pay for the right and the privilege to represent you, understand? It's business. Forget *give*."

"Forget give," said Puddin.

"But either way, it's too soon to talk about money," said Mac, "and it ain't good to count your chickens before they peck their way outta the shell, right?"

"Right," said Puddin. "But how much?"

"The way you bang, and with you on your way to being a big heavyweight, you could get a downstroke of a hundred grand, maybe more, plus a minimum guarantee of a hundred thousand dollars for each of your first twenty fights, something like that, as long as you win all of them. You don't win, you get squat. Could be they pay more, who knows? But don't bank on it. If you win pretty, and if you keep on keeping on. Once you fight for and win the heavyweight title of the world, now you're talking ten million dollars a fight."

"First ten million go to my mama."

"But all this is conversation, because you got to win big in Barcelona."

"I win and I win pretty, like you say. And you be my trainer all the way, Mac. Whoever want me, they take you wit me or I don't sign up. Like my mama say, you my daddy in boxing."

There's a saying in boxing: Don't forget the people you meet on the way up, because they're the same ones you'll meet on the way down. To that Mac always added: First your legs go, and then your money, and then your friends.

But many a promising fighter would dump his trainer of five or six years for sweet talk about big money from a stranger. Sometimes it worked out. Often it did not, and then the fighter had no one. But Puddin didn't lie, and Mac knew Puddin wouldn't dump him. And neither would Puddin's mother, a beautiful six-foot, two-hundred-pound Hershey-colored lady with short natural hair, with lines and flat planes to her suffering proud face that made her look like the mother of Africa.

It was Willa who had come to Mac for help. He made monthly bulk-food donations to her parish, St. Columcille's, at Sixty-fourth and Main, where Mac had gone to grammar school. It was an Irish parish from the twenties through the forties, the blue-collar Micks digging ditches and working the tire and steel factories on the east side of Los Angeles. Or collecting garbage and working the slaughterhouses, anything during the Great Depression to feed their kids. What is now Chinatown is where the bust-out Irish working the railroads first lived. Then came the Italians and the Chinese. Boyle Heights, now Mexican, was Irish first, then followed by Jews. Now St. Columcille's served blacks and Latinos, most of them poor, and Mac would drop off sacks of beans, rice, flour, sugar. Cooking oil and laundry soap, and cases of apple and pineapple juice. And Famous Amos chocolate-chip cookies for the kids. Cases of hard candy at Christmas.

Being white, Mac now stood out in his old neighborhood. It was after one of his deliveries in 1990 that he was boxed in by three carloads of teenaged black boys. They were high on Olde English 800 malt liquor, yelling *honky* and *whitey* and *old man redneck muhfuh*. Most were laughing, and he figured they were just trying to scare him. When he gave them a peek of his .38 Police Special, they sped off. If they'd been hard-core gangbangers, Mac knew that a six-shot revolver wouldn't get the job done had they been out to kill him. Even if six rounds was enough, there was still the problem of being white and of getting out of the neighborhood alive. The next day he bought his nine-millimeter Glock 17, which he packed on the left side of his belly, inside his belt. As an ex-cop in good standing, he had a license to carry a concealed weapon, a CWP. But if someone got to him first, say from a distance or from behind, it wouldn't matter if he had a hand grenade. But the Glock was tits, and if he saw trouble coming, it gave him a total of eighteen hollow-point rounds to work with—seventeen in the clip, one in the chamber. He hoped he'd never have to use the gun, but if some fool of whatever color was coming to kill him, he'd pop a cap in his ass in a heartbeat. Let the courts sort it out.

Mac had been about to leave after one of his deliveries to St. Columcille's when Mrs. Pye approached him near the kitchen. "Mist McGee, sir, I don't mean to bother you none, but I got me a boy wantsa be a fighter awful bad."

"How old is he?"

"He fourteen, but he big."

"Ma'am, I don't train amateurs anymore."

It had taken all Willa's courage to ask, so she was stunned by Mac's answer. "Why not?" she had asked, hope draining from her eyes.

"Most boys aren't serious, and they drop out on you the first time they see their own blood. So it's mostly a waste of time," Mac had said, "and with my white hair, time isn't something I got a lot of. Besides, like in the pros, there's politics in the amateurs, and after all the work you put in, politics takes the fun out of it. In the pros, at least, there's money to be made."

"Don't know about politics, but my boy don't quit, uh-uh."

"Who told you about me being in the fights?"

"Father Carey did."

Mac exhaled. "What makes you think your boy wants to box?"

"He fightin all the time."

"Who with?"

"Gang boys."

"That doesn't mean he wants to be a fighter."

"It all he talk about, boxin. Follow the TV boxin like it fried chicken. But he don't know who to see to learn, not no one decent, leastways."

Mac was getting in deeper than he wanted. He saw Father Carey watching from across the parking lot. Damn priest. "Why does your boy get into fights?"

"Gang boys jump Henry because he don't want no truck wit no gangs." She had bitten her lip to steady her voice. "Please, Mist McGee."

"Call me Mac, okay?"

"All right, Mist Mac." It wasn't what Mac had meant, but it's what she called him from then on. And he called her Mrs. Pye.

"Look, I'd like to help, ma'am, really I would, but I've got too many fighters as it is, all pros."

"My boy gonna die on the streets, Mist Mac. You my hope. He a good boy. He a altar boy, work wit the priest in Latin, too."

"Jesus," Mac had said.

That's how it had begun.

At fourteen, Henry Pye was five feet ten and weighed 155 pounds. He was muscle and bone, and you couldn't grab fat on him with a vise grip. He had big hands and feet and no hips. His shoulders filled a doorway. He was neat and clean and had close-cropped hair. He was polite and well-spoken. His deep black eyes were soft, shaped like a deer's, and set in a head with contours so noble that Mac knew he had lucked into something regal the first time he met the boy.

Mac worked with him, pressed him hard, hurt him with work, but the boy had no quit in him. He hit the speed bag and jumped rope as if he'd been born to them, the relentless *wahp-wahp-wahp* of the speeding leather and the steady sizzle of the rope as it smacked the hard wood were signs the kid had the hand-eye coordination and the ability to instantly shift his weight that would be necessary when it came time to hang. Without them, no matter how strong you were, you were TV fodder.

Soon the kid was working the punch mitts so well that old-timers slapped their thighs. It was the speed and power he had in both hands that made people wince, fighters and spectators alike. And his moves—moves that most people and many fighters could never learn, moves that fight guys called slick and sweet and pretty, that got the kid his nickname. After nine fights in the juniors, people were already calling him Puddin, Puddin Pye. When he reached 180 pounds at seventeen, he and Mac had their third goal in mind, the heavyweight championship of the world. Including his wins at the nationals, Puddin had an amateur record of 81 and 7, with 42 knockouts, a kayo ratio virtually unheard of in the amateur ranks. He would have had more wins, but trainers wouldn't let their boys fight him.

Mac called him his baby boy, loved him like he still loved his own baby boy, Brendan Pat. But Mac showed Puddin no favoritism in the gym, and there was no jealousy among the other fighters in Mac's stable. The fighter who had a fight coming up sparred first and got the first work on the punch mitts. That was it. The others waited their turn. The one difference was Señora Cabrera's café.

Puddin's mother worked from eleven until eight in the evening. She was a cafeteria cook at Jefferson High School, which was near their house, and where Puddin was a B student.

"I try for all A, but after the gym sometime, I eat and go asleep."

Willa would prepare him a good breakfast, pack him a bag of fruit and healthy snacks to take to school. She also gave him lunch money, but she couldn't be there to fix supper when he came home from the gym hungry enough to eat the couch. Because Mac didn't want the kid eating junk food, he began taking him to the Acapulco for seafood. It was a favorite from his days as a cop, and located about a mile from where Willa worked at the school with her sister Daisy. Home was a few blocks away.

In order to get sparring for Puddin, Mac would usually have to take his kid to different gyms in and around Los Angeles. The nearest and most convenient for plain workouts was Sewing Machine. A mile from the Acapulco, it was located off Vernon just east of Alameda, built in the basement of a Puerto Rican clothing manufacturer who had his own stable of fighters. Sewing Machine was decorated like a Puerto Rican nightclub, but it was clean and a serious place to work, despite the blaring Caribbean music. Mac's problem with it, and why Puddin went there only if it was raining or if Mac was out of town, was that it only attracted Latino fighters weighing 140 pounds or less, which meant there was never any sparring for Puddin at Sewing Machine. When possible, to save himself time on the clogged freeways, Mac would send the kid home on public transportation, and Puddin would eat alone at Señora Cabrera's, devouring broiled or poached seafood, nothing fried. Shrimp and *totoaba* from the Sea of Cortéz, as much as Puddin wanted, and lean steak twice a week, or chicken and rice, Mexican-style; or *pozole* with chopped raw cabbage and hominy. The señora called him Pudeen, prepared things for the kid that weren't on the menu. One of the dishes on the menu was Seven Seas Soup, Puddin's favorite, a huge bowl that contained seven different seafoods. He saved the baby squid till last, rolled them in tortillas and drenched them in salsa. He was the only black that ate squid in her café, and Señora Cabrera loved him for it. She also loved him because he was hungry all the time, and she knew he loved her, knew by the way he smiled as big as the Nile when he came through her door; knew from the expression on his face when he smelled her cooking; knew from the way he'd give her a hug and say, "*Muchas grácias*, Señora Cabrera"; knew when he finished that he'd leave her a dollar tip, which was a lot to him; knew that after he was champion of the world he'd remember back and tell stories about the nice Mexican lady he once knew, about her shrimp *rancheros* or maybe the shrimp *á mojo de ajo* he had at her humble little café. She prayed for him every night.

One of her illegal Mexican customers once told her she loved the black boy more than she loved her own kind.

"You are right, *caballero*," she said, nodding with a smile at the photograph of Puddin on the wall next to her grandfather. "*Mi muñequito prieto*, my little dark doll, is a *boxeador*."

The illegal raised his chin and eyebrows in understanding and smiled back.

Señora Cabrera's was nine blocks from Puddin's house, which

was on East Forty-first Street, and Mac always had Puddin walk home from the Acapulco in order to work off his meal. Puddin would call Mac on Mac's cellular phone as soon as he got home, so Mac would know he was safe. Mac's deal with Señora Cabrera was that he'd give her two hundred dollars up front. When Puddin had eaten his way through that, she was to call him, and Mac would stop by that day or the next with another two hundred. Mac had also provided Willa and Puddin with cellular phones, so Puddin could call her immediately after a fight, regardless of where she was, when they were fighting out of town. Afterward, she and Daisy would have to walk around the block, couldn't wait to tell their friends. Mac told Willa to call him if she ever needed anything. Sometimes she'd call for a progress report on Puddin, but since she went to all of his local fights anyway, the calls didn't last long. Other than information, she never asked Mac for anything, except to pray for her boys.

"Damn!" said Cedric "Cannonball" Lee, speaking quietly to Mac. "You boy got a jab on him like hop on a flea."

Mac had worked with his pros at Hymn Gym at midday. Now it was afternoon, and he stood on the ring apron outside the ropes of Cannonball's Not Long Gym. Inside the ring, Puddin continued to fire jabs into the face of a thirty-year-old pro, a light-skinned brother named Malik "Chilly" Tubbs, who carried gang tattoos and would sometimes throw signs to passing cars. Tubbs's promising career had been interrupted for seven years due to his armed robbery of a Korean liquor store. Some said he was an O.G., an original gangster. Now he was trying for a comeback, and his two wives and their eight children cheered him on from the low bleachers on the far side of Not Long. Their presence only made Malik madder, his nose having turned raspberry red from punishment. When he tried to counter the jab with a looping right-hand, Puddin would pepper him with another double jab, knocking his head back even further, taking his balance and making it impossible to punch with power. As Malik became more and more frustrated, he depended less and less on defense. Instead, he began to fight dirty and to talk trash through his mouthpiece, hoping to jail-talk intimidate Puddin. But Puddin stepped up the pressure and cranked hooks to Malik's body that made his legs wobble. Malik was heavier than Puddin by eighteen pounds and had built an excellent cruiserweight record of 21-3-0 with 13 knockouts. He was now a full heavyweight; his gloves began to stray below Puddin's belt line and he tried to head-butt Puddin in the nose, but he was unable to connect solidly. Meanwhile, Puddin continued to kick ass.

Malik had a smart mouth on him by Cannonball's standards, all the time talking about how bad he was. Gave himself the name Chilly because he said he was so cold when he dispensed justice to any muhfuh who messed with him. Cannonball enjoyed seeing him get a boxing lesson, knowing it was better to get a spanking in the gym than an ass whipping under the lights. But he also understood that most gangster fighters didn't want to work hard, which is why they were gangsters in the first place, and why most quit the game early on. Cannonball had his doubts about Malik, who had been confident that he'd give Puddin a boxing lesson, Puddin being young, lighter in weight, and an amateur. But as Malik grew more exasperated, he also got tired, and it was Puddin who took Malik to school.

Cannonball chided him from outside the ropes. "You don't do you roadwork, you better believe you can't fight."

Mac had learned a ton from Cannonball through the years, often training fighters at the Not Long Gym after Cannonball bought it with money he made off a Filipino fighter he'd taken to the title in '72.

"Yeah, my baby flip boy done okay by me. Little guy still call me from Manila, say he got a whole gang of young pussy waiting for me over there, say he pay my plane. Heh!, what I'ma do wit young pussy?" Cannonball mused a moment, thinking back down the long tunnel of time he'd passed through. "He the boy give me Lena, my old Colt .45. Say Lena come off a dead Jap in the jungle." Cannonball smiled. "Lena tear *up* you ass, I'm *tellin* ya. Bes' of all, she ain't register, some boy mess wit the old man."

Mac made Cannonball for at least eighty. His eyes and speech were clear after 120 fights, maybe more, since Cannonball couldn't remember them all. He was still his fighting weight, but he had diabetes and three of his toes on one foot had been amputated.

Cannonball's deep black skin was wrinkled but soft like leather upholstery, and he had craggy hands and big forearms. His wrists were surprisingly thin, but Cannonball could crack, which is why he got his fearsome nickname, one that came from knocking opponents clean out of the ring. He always wore a frayed, snap-brim dark wool cap that he kept clean and brushed. Tough as he still was, frailty had come on him in the last few years, the cords showing in his neck, and sometimes he sat staring at his hands, or tracing broken knuckles with a bent finger.

He'd fought all over the world, knocking out nearly two thirds of his opponents, but he could never get a title shot—his dreaded power was such that managers of then-champs refused to fight him. He forgot where, but he'd begun to fight as a pro at sixteen somewhere back around 1928. He fought through the Great Depression, sometimes for food only. Being a Negro fighter back in those days, a deep-black one, one who could knock you out with either hand, hurt rather than helped his career. He had a lump the size of a peach pit sticking out under his right arm from an untreated broken rib, a few scars around his eyes, and not much of a nose. But he had no bitterness, and often laughed when he told stories about riding the rails from town to town in search of fights, and about fighting for his life in hobo jungles, where they wanted to make him a slave.

The Not Long was located at Sixty-eighth and Normandie

Avenue. It was between Gage and Florence in South Central L.A., a
few miles from Puddin's house—a gym like Hymn Gym, where
heavier fighters worked out. Not Long was originally called the
Normandie Gym. When Cannonball bought it, he named it Not
Long, which he took from Martin Luther King, Jr.'s speech in
Montgomery, Alabama, the one he gave after the long walk from
Selma in '65. King repeated *Not long*. Some of that speech, Can-
nonball never forgot.

> I know you are asking today, "How long will it take?" I come to
> say to you this afternoon however difficult the moment, how-
> ever frustrating the hour, it will not be long, because truth
> pressed to earth will rise again.
>
> How long? Not long, because no lie can live forever.
>
> How long? Not long, because you still reap what you sow.
>
> How long? Not long. Because the arm of the moral universe
> is long, but it bends toward justice.
>
> How long? Not long, because mine eyes have seen the glory of
> the coming of the Lord, trampling out the vintage where the
> grapes of wrath are stored. He has loosed the fateful lightning of
> his terrible swift sword. His truth is marching on.

Cannonball and Mac had often worked together, though they
never were official partners, and sometimes they worked with other
corners when the call came. The South was still de facto Jim Crow territory in the late sixties when Mac and Cannonball traveled to places
like Houston or even D.C. Whites would put up a stink sometimes, but
they'd shut up once they knew they were messing with members of
the fancy. Many would even settle down to praise Joe Louis, Henry
Armstrong, and Sugar Ray, for whom they had great respect and of
whom they were genuine fans. Once in New Orleans a young black
hipster with Dizzy Gillespie lip whiskers confronted Mac.

"You one them gray boys wish he a spade, a ofay boy lookin a
get soul."

"Say what?" said Mac, affecting a high-pitched black accent. "Sheeuh, man, I got enough problems jus' bein white."

Cannonball laughed so hard that the hipster also had to laugh, since everyone nearby was laughing, too. He shook hands with Mac.

"You cool, daddy, you be cool."

Malik got serious about fighting dirty shortly before the bell sounded to end the second round. Mac and Puddin first took the head butts and low blows as unintentional. But when Malik came out trying to crack Puddin's face with his elbows and drilling him with hooks to the kidney, Puddin looked over to Mac.

Mac said, "Stay loose, keep working your same seventy-five, eighty percent." He spread his hands. "And do what you gotta do."

"Yop," Cannonball said, nodding once.

Instead of going to Malik's ass, or kidneys, or to his eye with a thumb, Puddin began with right-hand leads to the head and hooks to the liver, punching and moving to the left, turning Malik to the point where he could see him telegraphing his low blows. Puddin began to taunt the pro.

"You thought you the wolf. You the dog, man. Lemme hear you whine."

"Punk, I tear you a new asshole!"

Cannonball watched carefully, winked to Mac across the ring. He liked to see some mean in a fighter, but now he was watching for whether Malik would lose his temper, a bad sign in the fight game, because fights are won with the mind, not raw fury. Cannonball or Mac could always call time before the sparring session ever got too far out of control, so neither was worried. Since that hadn't happened yet, Mac wanted to see if Puddin could handle pressure from a big pro fighting outside the Queensberry Rules. Puddin was doing fine by Mac, the only marks on him were the horizontal red streaks across his back, rope burns that Puddin got from slipping along the ropes out of Malik's reach. Some Nupercainal ointment would take out the sting.

Between rounds, Mac said, "Why you not rippin his nose with your laces?, or coming up under his chin with your head?, crack him in the nuts and then you say you're sorry? Pop him in the ass?"

"I'm scheming on the brother," said Puddin, "tellin him lies. See how he reach when he try to counter off my jab?, how he head go back when he try to get off wit the right hand?"

"Yeah, I see it."

"You watch what you baby boy do this nex round."

Malik continued to try to bully Puddin, grabbing him and holding, saying he was going to tear him up.

Puddin taunted him back, then bent his elbows backward. "You the one goin down, sucker. I whup you like a stepchild."

"You mama."

"You ain't got a mama, you got a strawberry," countered Puddin. A strawberry was what you picked off the street, a crack whore, one of the street girls and women who gave head for a poke on a stained glass pipe.

"This over, I'ma cut you ass, boy."

"Onyest thing you cut be you ugly face when you shave."

Malik's two families continued to cheer him, which only made things worse for his pride.

He stopped punching in the middle of the round, turned to Cannonball in his frustration, "I ain't jivin, man, I'ma cut this boy, you hear what I'm sayin?"

"You be sellin woof tickets, sheeuh," said Cannonball. "You so chilly, why you don't go on back and whup the boy?"

Malik plowed forward, throwing haymakers. Puddin pivoted and threw three jabs—two quick and one slow. As Malik turned, he saw the lazy third left as his chance to catch Puddin with his power right-hand. He hauled off to throw it, his chin going up as he reached. Puddin was waiting for him. He stepped to his left, evading Malik's right glove, then dropped his own right at half power straight into Malik's Adam's apple.

Malik's mouthpiece shot from his mouth as he tried to clutch his closed throat. He thought he was a dead man as he twitched and jerked to the canvas, and his popping eyes did his begging for him because his mouth couldn't talk.

Mac and Cannonball jumped into the ring. Cannonball held Malik's shoulders down as Mac inserted his thumbs along the inner rim of Malik's nostrils, spreading them wide. He spoke slowly and softly.

"Breathe through your nose, not your mouth, through your nose." Mac repeated it twice.

Malik overcame his panic because of Mac's quiet voice, and did what Mac instructed, the air getting into his lungs and oxygen on up to his fading brain. After several gulps of air, he began to cough and wheeze, pink spit drooling down his chin and neck. Cannonball got Malik's gloves and headgear off and untied the laces of his shoes. Soon Malik's throat relaxed enough for him to croak out a few words of admiration.

"You a bitch, man," Malik said, congratulating Puddin as he got to his feet. "I'ma try you shit on some fool stick up he chin like me."

Once it was over, as things usually were in the ring, it was all over, and Malik and Puddin shook hands, would be friendly rivals down the way now that the line of respect had been drawn.

In the dressing room Malik gingerly rubbed his neck. "I can't believe the way that little boy got on me. I mean he big and all, but you know what I'm sayin?, he still a boy."

"That little boy a man," said Cannonball.

"Amen t'dat."

Cannonball left Malik to check his gym equipment. Along the way, he reassured Malik's wives that their husband was all right. Mac had toweled Puddin down and was packing his gear bag. After sparring, he usually had Puddin finish with four rounds on the punch mitts, four on the speed bag, four on the rope, and four sets of thirty-rep sit-ups, each exercise working a different part of his eight-pack abs. Because of what happened with Malik, Mac cut the workout short.

Mac said, "How's your boy's throat?"

"He fine," Cannonball said. "Scared more'n hurt."

"Puddin could have hurt him."

"Don't I know it?" said Cannonball. "Malik, he start that shit, but I could see you boy take some off when he go to the neck. That Puddin, he somethin else, man, he make you a million dollars that boy, and I ain't talkin shit."

"You might be right."

Cannonball said, "Shit yeah, I'm right, and he not even white. Let's just hope he don't have to fuck everthang that walk, crawl, or stand at attention."

"Huh!" Mac said. "Not the way I tell him stories, like about L. C. Poiter. And not with his mama getting him in bed by nine-thirty, and then up with him at five-thirty to run."

"It good you got hep wit the boy."

Mac realized that Cannonball was asking for work. He knew he'd soon need a backup man he could depend on, in the gym and in the corner, someone who knew the mysteries of the game and would be there when blood was flowing. He'd thought of Cannonball as his first choice anyway, had already talked about him to Puddin.

Mac said, "Puddin's turning pro after the Games, whatever happens. You think you might have time to work with us?"

"Hell yeah."

"We'll make Not Long our home base, you want."

"Damn straight. I can get heavies in to work wit 'im for you, and Puddin be my draw. Before a fight, I can charge peoples fifty cent to watch him work."

Mac knew Cannonball mentioned the fifty cents because he wanted Mac to talk money. "Tell you what," said Mac. "Work with us in the gym and in the corner, you get ten percent off the top of my trainer's ten percent, which is ten percent off the top of what Puddin'll make."

"You make a million, what I get?"

"A hundred thousand."

Cannonball wanted to be sure. "Big bills or small?"

"Whatever blows your skirts up."

Cannonball nodded several times while looking at the hardwood floor. In little more than a whisper, he said, "No way I'ma die now."

It was 5:45 on Monday, April 27, 1992. Malik wanted some gitback, so they agreed to meet on Wednesday the 29th at four o'clock for more sparring. The next day, Tuesday, Puddin would work the mitts with Mac. He'd get a bus west on Vernon to Normandie. Mac would wait for him there, and drive him down Normandie to Not Long. Puddin would later take the bus home from Normandie and Vernon, but if it was raining, or if time was a problem, Mac would drive him to the señora's, where they'd both eat.

Either way, Mac would double back down Normandie past Not Long to Florence to avoid traffic. He'd head east from there to the nearby on-ramp, where he'd pick up the Harbor Freeway to Gardena, the poker town he lived in just south of L.A. This day, he would pass through the Normandie and Florence intersection at 6:45. From there it was another forty-five minutes before he got home. He liked Gardena because of its Japanese, Chinese and Korean restaurants.

It would be at Florence and Normandie, forty-nine hours and one minute later—6:46 P.M. on April 29, 1992—that white truck driver Reginald Denny would have his skull fractured in ninety-one places by Damian "Football" Williams, among others, bits of Denny's skull piercing his honky brain.

As Cannonball and Mac shook hands on their deal, a black woman built like a defensive back strutted through the door and began handing out leaflets to Malik's wives and other spectators as well—many of them old men who sat around all day telling lies and playing checkers on boards so old the red and black squares were difficult to make out. The woman glared at people as she handed them the white sheets. "Do you know who you are?" she demanded. "*Do you really know?*"

She was five feet eleven but looked taller because of her spike heels and her Billie Holiday pompadour. She weighed an easy 190, and like Billie, she wore a white gardenia. She was a red-brown color and had the keen features of an American Indian. Her long-sleeved, tight-fitting dark patterned dress had a slit up one side well above the knee. She had needle tracks on the backs of her hands and a dark scar slicing from her left eye down to her jaw. Four front teeth were missing, but both top eyeteeth were gold. She smelled funky, like roadkill on a muggy day.

Cannonball yelled at her. "You git, Ruby Thigpen!"

"I ain't doin *nothin*!"

"I tell you before, bitch, now git 'fore I whup you ashy butt, hyuh?"

"You, maybe, but not that pin dick white pile a dog mess you wit!"

Cannonball smacked his pocket, indicating that's where he carried something she wouldn't want to deal with, and started toward her. She threw her stack of leaflets at him and stomped out. Cannonball shook his head, despite himself.

"She don't look it now, but man, there was a time."

"What's wrong with her?" Mac asked. He didn't appreciate racist shit out of anyone and wasn't one to put up with it, but neither would he buck someone on it unless they got in his face. They did that, he got respect. "Who is she?"

"She a ho got religion, if that's what you call it. She Ruby Thigpen, man, you know, the bitch ruin L. C. Poiter before he lose he title shot. When L.C. money gone, Ruby gone. By the time it all come down, and L.C. have O.D., all L.C. want was that shit in he arm, and a white bitch suckin on he dick. Blow job worst thing happen to a black fighter, ruin he legs, 'specially when a white woman do it."

Puddin crossed to them, carrying his gym bag. He was showered and dressed neatly. "Thank you, Mr. Lee," he said.

"Look like we be workin together," said Cannonball, smiling shyly.

"Yeah. Mac told me, if you want."

"We work good," said Cannonball, stooping to pick up Ruby's leaflets. "See you Wednesday, four o'clock."

It was balmy as they left the gym. Several old-timers chatted with people from the neighborhood, old folks mostly. Children tore around the cars in the parking lot. Malik and his two wives were packing his gear into an old station wagon. When Mac and Puddin got to Mac's car, white leaflets had been placed under both windshield wipers. Mac was curious and began to read one.

DO YOU REALLY KNOW WHO YOU ARE?

DO YOU?

Puddin stowed his gear in the trunk of Mac's car. Several of the people outside the gym watched as Mac read, but he didn't notice. Puddin noticed, and crossed behind Mac.

On the back of the leaflet, it read:

THE PICTURE EVERYONE BELIEVES TO BE JESUS CHRIST

IS A LIE! THAT PERSONS NAME IS CAESAR BORGIA

(A HOMOSEXUAL).

IS THE BEAST THE SO-CALLED DEVIL OR SATAN? NO!

IT IS THE SO-CALLED WHITE MANS GOVERNMENT.

READ KING JAMES ORIGINAL VERSION BIBLE ONLY!
STUDY AND LEARN THE TRUTH!!!

FOR QUESTIONS, CONTACT THE SCHOOL OF THE TEMPLE OF THE TRUE ISRAELITE (JEWS). ASK FOR RANDOLF, JAYSON OR INDIO.

As Mac was about to read the phone number, the leaflet was ripped from his hand.

"This ain't for you kind!" spat Ruby Thigpen, tearing up the leaflet and stamping on it.

"Sorry," said Mac.

"You sorry, all right! Now you git on back outta here go where you belong!"

"You put it on my car."

"I don't know it a whitey car!"

"I'm sorry, all right?" said Mac, backing away.

"No, it ain't all right!" spat Ruby. She noticed Mac's stiff leg. "You a cripple old white man, ain't that right?"

"What if I am?"

Ruby puffed up even more, got braver as Mac retreated. Every eye outside the gym was on Mac. Folks didn't necessarily want to see him get hurt because he was white, but they were curious to see whether he'd stand up, being white in South Central, particularly since just the day before they'd seen what Ruby could do to a man with her razor. Some knew Mac and liked him, but none liked him well enough to step between Mac and Ruby. The rule was you rode your own beef, and they didn't want to get cut. Besides, they wanted to see how the old man would do against the big bulldagger ho.

Puddin started to move forward, but Mac told him to stay out of it.

Ruby said, "Old white man still givin order a black folk."

"Look," Mac said, "I told you I was sorry, right?"

"You so sorry, gimme you money, peckawood."

"Nooo, no. Not giving you my money."

Ruby spoke to the onlookers. Even the children were standing stock-still. "He say he not givin up he money, huh?" She turned to Mac. "How 'bout you give Rodney King some you money?"

"I got nothin to do with Rodney King."

"*Bull*shit you got nothin to do wit Rodney King. Like the lady politician say, Rodney King git no jus'us, whitey git no peace. It be Uzi time, muthuhfucka!"

Mac tried to get to the door of his car so he and Puddin could leave, but Ruby blocked him. "It on tape what happen a Rodney King, why they need a trial, tell me that?"

"You tell me."

"I tell you them po-lice go free after what they done a brothuh Rodney, they be a gang a white blood a pay."

Mac was madder than he wanted to be. "Yeah," he said, "and if they're found guilty, it's still going to be white blood running red, right?"

"'At's right, an' we do it by any mean necessary, sucker!" said Ruby, the esses hissing like a broken gas line.

"Right on, mama, but him gettin his black ass beat was the best thing that ever happened to Rodney King, right?"

The spectators sucked air on that one, took that line hard, started to think that Mac was indeed a no-good white muhfuh who deserved a ass whippin. But they just as quickly realized that Mac was standing up, was telling Ruby to kiss his gray boy ass—and that Mac was talking about how much big money Rodney King was sure to score down the line. That made them laugh out loud, and when they did, it was clear they were laughing at Ruby, too. Inside the gym, Cannonball heard the laughter, but he'd heard laughter before and he went back to his racing form. But for Ruby, laughter was worse than a beating, and she touched her hair.

"What you say, you muthuhfucka slave-tradin po-lice dick-suckin faggot piece a redneck dog shit? Huh? What you say, cracker? Fuck wit me ain't like fuckin wit Rodney King. I cut you muthuh-fucka white ass from you dick to you nose!"

Again Mac moved away, but as he did, Ruby started moving on long, quick strides straight at him.

"I say you gimme you cripple-ass money, peckawood, gimme that money, hyuh?, or I'ma take it!"

"Get back," said Mac, his words barely audible off his dry tongue.

"I git back, huh? Where I git back? Back a the bus?"

"I'm saying I don't need no more of your shit."

"Or what, honky? What you gonna do about it, huh? Look around you for some white skin'll hep you, fool." Intimidation had made Ruby a lot of money through the years, in jail and out, and had drained the fight out of most that she confronted. But it wasn't working on this old white man, which made it imperative that she save face in front of a black crowd, obligatory that she become even more vicious in her attack against what she had figured for easy takings. "Just 'cause you white and you got a swingin dick instead a woman cock, I suppose to kiss you pale ass?, that how it is, huh? Gimme you money, punk!" she said, pulling a straight razor from her pompadour, the silver blade pinging as it flashed free of its black handle.

"Be good with that, bitch, or I'll shove it down your nigger mouth!"

Nigger made Ruby slow down, wonder what kind of white man would talk that shit surrounded by a gang of brothers. *Nigger* and the razor made the gawks back away, some of them shouting. People from across the street ran over. Now there were twenty people looking on. Cannonball heard the noise and started for the door. Puddin positioned himself for a try at Ruby's razor hand. But she was too quick. She rushed with the razor, hacking with it in short little strokes. Ruby aimed at Mac's face, but he was able to block the first slice with his forearm, pivoting to his right off his front foot. His jacket sleeve and sweatshirt saved him from serious injury, though his arm began to bleed and blood seeped down to his hand. Ruby didn't want him dead, she wanted him cut so bad he'd remember her every time he saw his reflection: she wanted her face to be the last face his mind saw every night before he went to sleep.

Mac knew what she was up to, knew the jailhouse mentality, and wanted to flat shoot the bitch and be done with it, but he also knew that he was the only marshmallow in the chocolate factory. He knew Puddin would cover his back, but that made two against twenty, and he didn't want Puddin getting hurt.

"Cut that white muthuhfucka's ass, baby!" someone yelled. "Do it for Rodney!"

"Dass right, ice da punk!"

"Jesus a faggot white-man church!"

"Cut him, baby, do you thang!"

Ruby moved better than many fighters, despite the high heels. She stayed close to Mac, even though he slid off at angles to her and her popping razor. When Cannonball came through the door, he saw the blood running down Mac's hand. Cannonball wanted to distract Ruby, but he didn't want to get close to that razor.

"Ruby Thigpen, I told you git!" Cannonball shouted. "That old white man gonna tear *up* you process ass."

"Shut you mouf, nigga! He call me a nigga, 'n' he gonna pay!"

Cannonball called to Mac over the racket, "You want me a call the po-lice?"

Mac didn't want police cars jamming into the Not Long and waved off Cannonball's offer.

"Then put the bitch on the ground, man!"

Mac knew Cannonball was right, though he had hoped for things otherwise. So Mac moved out of Ruby's way again, then suddenly faked a stumble on the loose gravel. Ruby went for the fake, quickly closing the distance between them, and flicked out with the razor as Mac slid to his left. He pivoted and with his left hand he gave a little push to Ruby's razor elbow, taking her balance and causing her to lunge forward, her neck stretching like a sprinter at the finish line. The razor nicked the side of Mac's neck, but he didn't feel it, though blood began to work into his sweatshirt. Onlookers saw it; some of them sighed.

With his right hand Mac pulled the cocked Glock. He was careful to keep his finger off the trigger, but as he gripped the heavy black plastic handle tightly, he slipped behind Ruby and whacked her full force across the temple with the heavy metal barrel. People started whooping; some let off a high whine. Ruby's head felt full of lightning. Semiconscious, and with her balance gone, she pitched forward on her face and dropped the razor, her eyes blinking as if flashbulbs had popped her in a dark room. Mac planted the heel of his shoe on the blade of the razor, then pulled full force up on the handle against the hinge and broke the razor in two. He threw the blade up on the low roof of the gym and turned to Ruby, who poured blood from the side of her head and rolled over twice before she could get up.

He was relieved he'd been able to disarm her, because he'd been ready to shoot her in the head. When Ruby saw her own blood, all the fight went out of her. She started to howl and began running for the street, falling twice and ripping the skin on her knees and palms.

"You goin see! You wait, honky! We git jus'us, we burn you ass *up*!"

Her yelling aroused the onlookers even more, and slowly the circle began to shrink around Mac. Hands reached out, faces were like claws. Mac trained the Glock on them, his finger now on the trigger, blood running from his neck and dripping from his hand.

"I say the motherfucking common-ass handkerchief-head nigga bitch ho got off easy. Anybody disagree?" said Mac.

Malik hated seeing a white man beating on a black anything,

but he also knew that Mac had saved his ass, knew that Ruby had started the shit. "Whoa!" he yelled, moving the others back. "Everthang cool here!, everthang be cool!"

Cannonball yelled at the crowd to go back to their business and quickly got Mac inside the gym before any O.G.'s drove by.

Cannonball washed Mac's wounds with hydrogen peroxide and stopped the blood with pressure and adrenaline chloride 1:1000 mixed with alum, an illegal mixture he used to stop blood in the corner. Puddin looked on, fascinated by the inside colors of human flesh. The forearm was worse than the neck, but the neck bled more and it took Cannonball longer to stanch the neck blood than the arm. He closed both wounds with butterfly bandages that pulled the sliced meat together for quicker healing and to minimize scarring. He used sterile gauze and ring tape to cover the wounds, which he left dry, free from ointments and salves so scabs could immediately begin to form.

"You goin emergency?" Cannonball asked.

"Emergency'd bring in the black-and-whites."

Cannonball said, "You lucky to be alive, all that Rodney King shit goin down." He gave a little hoot. "But I like that little move you put on the bitch, baby, the one when you go to the elbow?"

"I tried to talk, and then the pig-shit Irish in me took over, and I just about shot everyone out there." He thought a moment and exhaled, squeezing down hard to purge himself of the residue gases and fumes of rage. "Listen, I want to apologize for calling the whore a handkerchief head and a nigger, okay?"

"Nigga what she know," said Cannonball, noticing Puddin's smile, noticing how much these two cared for each other. "Hey, you one lucky-ass white boy you don't get jump out there."

"I was one lucky-ass white boy to grab that razor, too."

"That Glock what save you ass," said Puddin. "Got all the niggas' attention."

Mac was surprised. "How come you know about Glocks?"

"Who don't know about Glock?"

. . .

The sun was setting and Mac was driving Puddin to the señora's for supper. The kid had earned it. Besides, the old man wanted a Mexican beer, a frosted Negra Modelo, dark and with a thick head and cold enough to hurt his eyes. Mac was exhausted. His cuts began to creep and sting.

"Tell you what," Mac said to Puddin. "I'm tired like I just went ten hard rounds."

Puddin smiled; he was proud of the way the old man stood up to the whore and backed down the crowd. "I say more like twenty."

"I'll be too stiff and sore to work tomorrow," said Mac, "so I'm taking off, okay?"

"What I do?"

"I want you to run in the morning and then again in the afternoon. That way we'll still be on schedule for Colorado Springs."

"On top of that," said Puddin, "I'll do wind sprints bof times."

It was the way champions thought. If Mac could have chosen a son, Puddin was it. He thought of his little boy and his daughters and gagged back a sob.

Traffic was light, and they made good time on streets that were usually crowded. Strangely, very few people were out, neither black nor Latino. The taco stands and the Chinese takeout joints were empty.

Mac was depressed. Not because he'd retaliated against Ruby with *nigger* for *honky* but because he feared that by jumping on Ruby with *nigger* that he might have damaged something in Puddin, destroyed the kid's trust. Mac was so tired he could hardly drive. Tomorrow would be a bitch.

"Look here," he said, "about that nigger business back there. It's important to me you know I don't feel that way about black folks, okay?, but that I had to get respect. That whore had to know I can talk that racist shit, too. Because if she thought I was a punk, she'da grown on me same as an opponent in the ring, and that bitch was big enough already." Mac glanced at the kid. "What you need to know is that my talk out there ain't what's in this mean old white man's heart."

Puddin said, "Mac, you don't know you my daddy?"

Mac swallowed hard. "So we're square, right?"

"Sheeuh, nigga's what that Ruby is, man. Some nasty-ass white bitch talk nigga shit a me, pull a razor?, I call her honky trash in a minute and I shoot the bitch myself."

"My baby boy."

"But my mama say, what it is makin everybody crazy, is all this Rodney King mess. Say it a field a land mines, say all peoples end up cripple they don't watch they step."

No doubt, thought Mac, but he also knew that there were people out there of every color who loved those land mines. The verdicts from the first Rodney King cop trial hadn't come in yet, but Mac thought about the charges every day. All of Los Angeles did. From the Valley to the Harbor, from the beaches to the mountains, the city was like a stretched womb, most people waiting silently, afraid of the monster that might be born. Black political rhetoric was ominous and loud.

"No justice, no peace," one black female politician repeatedly croaked into the cameras, the TV channels always ready to oblige her hate.

Since the beating incident, Mac had seen that blacks were essentially of one mind, saw that most demanded a guilty verdict for an unmerciful and unwarranted beating by white racist cops of a helpless black man already on the ground. Blacks and whites both disregarded the 7.8-mile Highway Patrol pursuit prior to the incident, with King driving at speeds of 110 to 115 miles an hour on the freeway, 85 on surface streets. Instead, people focused on what happened after the chase. When Mac first saw the tape, he did the same. Who could not have experienced dread on seeing the awfulness of the tape? But being an ex-cop, he also knew that what was shown on TV wasn't always the whole story. What troubled him most, once it was revealed at the trial, was that the tape shown by Los Angeles TV station KTLA had been edited down from eighty-one seconds to sixty-eight. KTLA's explanation for the thirteen-second cut was that ten of the first thirteen were blurry. KTLA could not satisfactorily explain why the previous three seconds of the tape had been cut. It was during those crucial three seconds that Rodney King charged the officer who landed the first of many blows, in each case using a side-handled metal police baton. It was primarily this officer that viewers saw delivering the majority of the blows struck by the cops on that surrealistic night, blows delivered in an attempt to get King into a felony prone position. According to LAPD regulations, head blows were illegal—unless a suspect attacked an officer.

What the tape didn't show was King's resistance to arrest, that he had, from the ground, flung officers off like pillows when they tried to swarm him, a technique developed by police precisely to do minimum harm to suspects resisting arrest.

The media was quick to report that fifty-six blows had been thrown, but what the public didn't know until the trial was that just over half the blows actually landed. Only three were power blows. Mac knew three power shots had to be true, otherwise there would have been significantly more damage to King than his fractured face and shinbone—he'd have been dead. As to blows to the head, only one could be verified, the first one, which was in response to King's attack.

The officers were accused of racist postarrest comments as well. But Mac had seen enough combat in the Pacific, on the streets, and in the ring to know that remarks made by victors as well as losers were generated by exhaustion and adrenaline overload, that jokes were attempts by the mind to relieve convulsed stomachs and twitching nerves and pissed pants. Hadn't he himself just said and done things to Ruby he would never think of doing under normal circumstances? Mac was nonetheless unconditionally opposed to the use of excessive force. But that didn't keep him from being furious with politicians, black and white, yammering for justice— justice being a code word for either white convictions or black violence.

None of this had affected Mac's relationship with his many black friends and acquaintances in the fight game, and despite the heightened racial tensions, he had been surprised by the absence of hostility he had experienced as he traveled daily through South Central Los Angeles prior to his incident with Ruby.

The Acapulco was nearly empty as Mac and Puddin entered. Always before, the señora would smile and wave them over, no matter how busy she was. Not this time. Four young male blacks, wearing oversized $400 leather team jackets and new $150 basketball shoes, stood talking quietly with her at the cash register. Mac had never seen them in the café before. He judged the oldest at twenty. The youngest, nicknamed Fridge, looked sixteen. The two others were eighteen or so. Each was at least six feet tall. Fridge was thin, maybe 160 pounds, same as the twenty-year-old. The other two were 200-pounders. Each had his baggy pants slung halfway down around his ass, six inches of underwear showing. Their jackets hung on them like outsized cocoons.

Aside from the four, the place was nearly empty; two tables were occupied with a total of five people, two of them black. Usually the place was full of people unashamedly stuffing themselves.

Instead of flashing her big smile, the señora glanced away. Dirty dishes hadn't been cleared from three tables, one of which had been used by a party of four. Empty tables with dirty dishes were never seen at the Acapulco. It was clear to Mac that something was wrong, and he guided Puddin to the rear of the café, where both could sit with their backs to the wall.

"How about some service?" Mac called out, acting like a stranger to the place.

The señora excused herself and crossed to Mac and Puddin. She took their order without looking at them. She went back to the counter, said something Mac couldn't hear, and turned to go to the kitchen. The oldest of the group stepped in front of Señora Cabrera, slightly raising a black cane with a brass duck's-head handle to block her way. Mac drew the Glock, kept it hidden between his knees, and waited.

The twenty-year-old leader pointed a finger at the señora. He whispered something, and then he and the others ambled out of the café as if they were leaving a church. Three of them ranged from dark to very dark in color. The leader was close to albino white, except that he had a slight coppery hue to his pockmarked skin. He had green eyes. He wore his kinky auburn hair in lumpy dreadlocks and was ugly as a scab. His Negroid features were misshapen, parts of his face lumpy and looking like they didn't belong. Mac made them all for criminals, but he also knew that the ugly brick-top would be so easy to finger in a lineup that he'd be spending most of his life in the joint.

Mac waited three minutes before he holstered the Glock. When there was no movement in the doorway, he and Puddin both went to the señora.

She was trembling, but her slanted Indian eyes flashed fury. "Bastard sons-of-shit whores," she said in Spanish. "I shit in their shameless mothers' milk."

"Did they hurt you?" asked Mac.

"No yet."

"Did they rob you?"

"No yet."

"They have a gun?"

"I don't see one. But the ugly one he say he got sonthing for me inside he cane."

"Did they say they would hurt you?"

"No quite. The young one come in my kitchen and rattle my knives. The redhead ugly say there is bad people have started hurting stores and I hab to pay him to protect me. He say they hab they four dinners free tonight for down payment of what I owe."

"What did you say?"

"I say I no espeak no Ingli. They say they don't believe."

Mac turned to Puddin. "You know them?"

"I know 'em."

With Puddin able to I.D. the punks, Mac knew that he could trace them, but aside from walking out on their tab, which would be hard to prove, no crime as such had yet been committed. Besides, as a cop he'd been called in to similar extortion situations, but there was nothing cops could do until the perps actually collected money or beat on people, and by then the victims were so scared they wouldn't testify. There was Puddin to protect as well, because if Mac called in cop friends to roust these small-time hoods, they would know that Puddin had identified them. Mac had wanted to shoot Ruby, but he wanted to vaporize the four punks who'd leaned on the señora. He told her to cancel his and Puddin's food order and to go ahead and close up, that he'd help. She insisted on serving them. Mac turned to Puddin.

"Who are these pukes?"

"Couple still in school, but all are runnin wit the 43 Stokkers, that a feeder gang for the Five Tray Gangsta Crips. "Air Jordan" what they call the ugly nigga."

"Call him air-what?"

"Air Jordan. You know, he try you for you new jacket and shoes you alone on the street, or you look easy. Stealin new Nike shoes what give him his name. Hit you upside you head and while you down, he use scissors to cut off the laces. You fight back, Air Jordan stab you dead and steal you stuff right off you bones."

"They ever mess with you?"

"They know they try me, I won't be the only nigga get stretched on satin. They mess wit Señora Cabrera, I stretch all they raggedy ass."

"You let me handle this, okay?"

Puddin shrugged, nodded, knew Mac was right.

Señora Cabrera served them steaming shrimp in a spicy tomato sauce with peppers, onions, and cilantro. She served the shrimp with rice and beans and corn tortillas. The remaining guests paid and left. Mac drank down a cold, dark Negra Modelo before he began to eat and ordered a second. The señora sat at their table while they ate.

"I work so har'," she said. "My girls work here before they go to nurse school, speak two language. No one neber rob my food."

"These guys been here before?" asked Mac.

"Firs' tine."

"Best be they last," said Puddin, finishing his meal. He thanked Señora Cabrera and said, "Want me a walk on home or stay wit you and help close up?"

"I'll help her, but I don't want you out there alone tonight," said Mac. He turned to the señora. "I'll drive him home. It's two minutes. I'll be back to help you close."

"No, I'n okay."

"I know you are, but I want to."

Mac and Puddin hadn't been gone a minute when Air Jordan and the others pushed past the señora as she tried to lock her door.

"We back for forty-two takeout tacos a go."

"I'm close."

"You open now," said Air Jordan. He threw a chair across the room and flicked off some of the lights. "Cook, bitch, make the shit to go."

"Cook what?"

"Somethin good for twenty people, what you think chili peppah?"

"What you wan'?"

"I don't give a fuck what!" shouted Air Jordan. "Make sure we like it, that all!"

Señora Cabrera went to the kitchen wanting to kill and wishing to God she had her .44. She went straight to her storeroom for rat poison instead. She'd dump it into these *rateros'* fish tacos. Mac came in before she could use it.

He didn't waste time. He crossed directly to Air Jordan, pulled a chair over from another table, and sat down at the gang's table. He looked Air Jordan dead in the eye and smiled a little smile that had no humor in it.

"Am I glad to see you, bro. You won't believe this shit, but there are some white boys coming into the neighborhood, ugly like rotten meat. They go around to small stores and threaten to fuck over the people, you know I'm sayin?, small store people like the señora here got to come up with their money, or else, you dig?, like these cockroaches want folks to turn over their hard-earned bread, hear I'm sayin'? I mean, how low-down can white trash be?, understan I mean?"

Air Jordan glared at Mac. He wanted to wipe the floor with this snotty-ass old white man talking his bullshit brother talk, but he didn't know what might be waiting outside, didn't know what the fuck this crazy old man might be packing. It was exactly what Mac wanted, wanted Air Jordan to focus on him and to forget Señora Cabrera. The other three looked to Air Jordan for the go-ahead to scatter this white man's ass. Air Jordan was tempted.

Instead, he said, "Man, I don't know what the fuck you talkin about."

"What I'm sayin," Mac said, "is if you four fine, upstanding brothers ever see these no-account white pieces a bat shit come in here, know I'm sayin?, I want you to jump on their asses, dig what I mean?, like waste them for me, understand? I'm here all the time, so I'll probably shoot the muhfuhs myself, but if you're here, you do it for me, hear I'm sayin? Now, if you're afraid a white boys, that's cool, just have the señora call me at Not Long Gym. I'll bring my fighters over and we'll hang these punks by the balls from meat hooks under a bridge, know I'm sayin? 'By any means necessary,' like Malcolm said, right? Hey!, Malcolm had red hair, too, just like you, baby, right on!, my brother."

Mac could see Air Jordan was ready to snap, saw the others with their hands inside their jackets. Mac's hand was near the Glock.

Air Jordan said, "What you doin this part of town, old man?, you don't know no better?"

"People call me Mac, retired LAPD. But since I train fighters around here, I figure it's my part of town, too."

"I fucked a fighter in the ass in jail one time," said Air Jordan.

"I been in the fight game most of my life, but nobody ever fucked me in the ass," said Mac. "Say, you ever thought of being a fighter instead of a butt fucker?"

"Too smart for that."

"I'm surprised, you looking so tough like you do, or whatever it is you do look like," said Mac, still smiling, his eyes hard as spider's.

Air Jordan sat back. At that point he knew what Mac wanted him to know, that the señora had told Mac about him; that Mac was the heat, since once a cop always a cop, and that meant he had friends who carried guns; that Mac wasn't afraid of him; that Mac knew how to track him. Air Jordan wasn't happy. This old man was costing him money, and worse, his partners might lose respect for him if he let the old honky give him chump change. Killing the old man, for now anyway, wasn't the answer, because he'd have to kill the señora, too. And kill that uppity-ass Puddin, who could be serious trouble. Now wasn't the time, anyway. His fingerprints were all the fuck over the place. But fire would solve that problem.

"You a funny old white man, you know that?"

"Hey, we both know how great it is being white, ain't that right?" said Mac. "Whaddaya say, we got a deal? You help me out on this, I'll buy you guys dinner. Hey! I'll feed the four of you right now just to show my word's good." Mac called to the señora. When she got to the table, Mac said, "These boys are hungry. Spare no expense. Why don't you bring them out a nice big platter a squid?"

"What squid?" said Air Jordan.

"It's good for you, man, make you strong," said Mac. "You know, baby squid, sort of purpley-colored with ten little legs, know I'm sayin?, something like a octopus. Some squid can grow to sixty or eighty feet, but they're a lot harder to get in the pan."

"Aw, man!" said Air Jordan, standing straight up. Now he knew Mac was crazy. "You talkin that shit!"

Mac said, "Naw! She's got some live snake in the back, too. You like snake? Be careful, a couple of them got loose on the floor the other day. Hey, there's one behind you!"

"Where?" said Air Jordan. He and the others looked fearfully around their feet, began stepping high, like chickens in a barnyard.

"Over there," said Mac, pointing to the cactus, the eagle, and the snake on a small Mexican flag on the counter. "You boys like snake? Tastes like chicken, they say; you guys like fried chicken, right? Fry some snake right up for you. You like your snake in one long piece with the head and rattlers still on, or you like it in chunks, pull the scaly skin off like cracklins?"

All four were knocking over chairs on their way out the door.

"What's wrong, you ain't hungry after all?" Mac called after them. "Hey! We still got a deal about those white boys, don't we? What's your phone number? I'll call you!"

Mac winked at Señora Cabrera. Mad as she was, she was laughing. But she hadn't forgotten about her *pistola*. From now on she'd carry it under her apron until the day she died.

Two days later, on Wednesday, April 29, at eleven-thirty in the morning, Mac began working with his pros at Hymn Gym, at 108th and Broadway. Hymn was at the southern end of South Central, west of Watts and 70 percent black, the rest Latino. Mac was still hurting, but the cuts were healing quickly and there was no infection. He closely watched after his fighters but only had them spar or work the big bag. It would be a while before he caught serious punches with the focus gloves. He was due to pick up Puddin at four o'clock, then head back to Not Long, where Puddin would work with Malik.

Clogging the entranceway to Hymn Gym were boxers, trainers, and locals who stood watching TV for news of the cop verdict in the Rodney King beating. The station kept running the clip of the edited tape, which had some of the viewers yelling at the screen. Some were drinking from half-pint bottles in brown paper bags. No one gave Mac any trouble, and he wondered if word was out on what had happened with Ruby. On the previous Thursday, the jury had begun seven days of deliberations after seven weeks of trial.

Mac passed through the group watching TV to refill a water bottle. It was one o'clock, and the TV reporter at the courthouse announced that the verdicts had been reached. They would be read in open court at three o'clock that afternoon. Mac finished with his last fighter at 2:35. By the time he got his gear together and washed up, it was 2:50. He waited with everyone else for the verdict, but when it hadn't come in by 3:05, he left the gym. He drove north on Broadway for the Century Boulevard on-ramp to the northbound Harbor Freeway. Unless there was a traffic jam, he'd be early to pick up Puddin, so he took his time. His was the only car moving on the street.

Because of the imminent verdicts, and the potential violence they represented, Mac had thought about canceling the workouts. But his fighters depended on him, Puddin in particular, now that he had to be in shape to leave for training camp. One of his pros, a Liberian flyweight, was to fight the main event at the Forum in Inglewood. Mac's Mexican featherweight, also a pro, was due for a fight in Vegas a week or so following that. Time was critical. Since it might be another week before the verdicts came in, Mac decided to go ahead and work rather than lose two, maybe three critical days out of fear.

Like most, Mac believed that guilty verdicts were sure to come down against the four accused cops. Like many, he also believed there would be trouble in the black community regardless of a conviction, which was one of the reasons he thought about canceling the workouts. The one o'clock announcement that the verdicts would be read at three concerned him, but he believed that he'd be finished at Not Long before any real violence could erupt. He also believed, mistakenly as it would turn out, that there would be a massive show of force by the police to quell any violence, which was what happened when he'd worked the Watts riots of 1965. Many blacks believed the same, and feared it, which is why some black politicians lobbied against a police presence in South Central. Other blacks wanted the police there because they knew that gangsters and mob rule would fill the void if they weren't.

As he headed for the freeway on-ramp, which was still several blocks away, his car clock showed 3:18. What Mac didn't know was that four not-guilty verdicts had been read at 3:15, and that the astonishing verdicts were based primarily on Mac's understanding of the tape—that King's attack on the police had resulted in his own private Hiroshima. Mac was nearing Century Boulevard and was about to turn on his radio when the first of two calls came in on his cellular phone.

The first was from Cannonball. "They not guilty."

"Holy shit."

"Where you at?" said Cannonball.

"On Broadway near Century."

"Damn!" said Cannonball. "You git you white ass gone all the fuck outta where you at. Go where it white and stay where it white. Brothuhs talkin shit so cold I'ma close down and git up on the roof wit Lena."

"My kid comes in, you take care of him, right?"

"Don't worry, that boy too smart a come here, you worry 'bout you," said Cannonball. "Sorry this shit come down, Mac."

"I'm with you," said Mac. "I'll be in touch soon's this mess is over, okay? And listen, thanks for thinking of me."

"Why wouldn't I?"

"I got to ask you," said Mac.

"Yeah."

"You think we'll ever get along?"

"Truth to tell, I don't see it," said Cannonball.

"Me neither."

"Mac?"

'Yeah."

"I ain't just talkin about colored and white," said Cannonball.

"I know what you're saying, my friend, I do."

Mac turned back, heavy in the chest. He took Grand Avenue heading south and picked up the freeway at Imperial. Along the way, black teenagers on a school bus began screaming at him.

Willa called next. "We just heard the news. You stay away, Mist Mac, you hyuh? Puddin 'n' me be fine. This over, then we go head on back and do like we always do."

The riots officially began at 4:17 P.M. on April 29, 1992. Not with Damian Football Williams and Reginald Denny at Florence and Normandie, but with five young black males who stole several bottles of "8-Ball," Olde English 800 malt liquor, from a liquor store at Florence and Dalton. When the Asian owner tried to stop them, one of the blacks smashed him in the head with one of the bottles.

"This for Rodney King!" he said.

The attack on Reginald Denny at 6:46 P.M. was what first shocked the world. But several others, male and female, were also beaten at Florence and Normandie—Latinos, Asians, and Caucasians. One Latino was beaten and had a car driven across his legs.

The perpetrators, though committing their crimes on live TV provided by hovering news helicopters, would subsequently receive minor sentences, including the dancing and prancing Football Williams.

The riots ended on the evening of May 4, 1992, but only after the National Guard was finally mobilized. Over five days, fifty-four people would die. Twenty-six were black. Fourteen were Latinos. Nine were Caucasian. Two were Asian. Three who died in fires were so disfigured that their race could not be determined. Emergency rooms treated 2,328 injured people. Eight hundred sixty-two structures were burned. Ruby Thigpen was torched when a Molotov cocktail she was throwing slipped from her hand, broke on the sidewalk at her feet, and lit her up. Property losses were in excess of $900 million. More Latinos than blacks were involved in the looting, but there were white looters as well. Señora Cabrera's Acapulco was vandalized by blacks and Latinos. Someone defecated on the rug, and feces was smeared across the photographs of the señora's grandfather and Puddin.

"Air Jordan," said Puddin.

"You think?" asked Señora Cabrera.

"Devil shit where he want."

The señora's phone bill for just April 29–31 would be nearly a thousand dollars, an endless list of calls having gone from the Acapulco to places like Mexico City, Lima, New Orleans, New York, Guadalajara, Boston, Houston, Caracas, Panama City, and Chicago.

The señora was ready to throw in the towel. After eighteen years serving the very people who had destroyed her business, she was ready to torch the place herself. But Mac and Puddin showed up on the fifth of May, *Cinco de Mayo*, to help her and cheer her. Willa gave Puddin permission to take off from school. He would run in the morning, then Mac would meet him at the Acapulco and work cleaning up until the afternoon. Then Puddin and Mac would head for Not Long, where Mac would work with his pros as well as

Puddin. He was so tired sometimes that he could barely hold his head up. So Cannonball would fill in for him, and suddenly Cannonball was like a pup, his movements young and springy as he made moves and called shots.

"Man, I be shiny like the bulldog on a new Mack truck."

Puddin sparred with Malik sometimes, sometimes with someone else, sometimes he just worked the mitts and bags. But he loved working with the old-timer, was like a sponge as he added Cannonball's tricks and slicks to Mac's. The days of spring were getting longer, so Mac, Puddin, and Cannonball would return to work at the señora's until dark, often longer. Afterward, Mac would treat them to Italian, Chinese, or Dutch Indonesian food. Cannonball was crazy for *sate sapi*, skewered pork with spicy peanut sauce, and side vegetables cooked with coconut milk.

"Man, this the way to greeze."

In four days the Acapulco was clean again, the broken windows replaced, and the señora was almost ready to reopen. Much of L.A.'s infrastructure had been destroyed in the riots, including mom-and-pop markets and cafés. Hungry people continually stuck their heads in to ask when they could get fish again.

"When I put in my iron bars," Señora Cabrera would answer, sometimes to the same people she knew had vandalized her.

Her doors and windows were standard, and the supplier had her sizes in stock. Once the iron bars were delivered, Mac and Puddin began to bolt them in. That took another two days.

"Now I'm the one in jail for obey the law," said Señora Cabrera, shaking her head.

The Acapulco filled up the first hour it reopened. Señora Cabrera's daughters took off from the hospital to help her the first two days. Except for the usual afternoon lull, the place stayed busy from eleven-thirty in the morning to nine at night. Puddin would return to help her close, then walk on home again.

■ ■ ■

Air Jordan loved the riots. He set seven fires and looted stores in South Central, Koreatown, and Hollywood. Using a stolen little stainless steel Walther .380, he shot a fireman in the face. But no matter how much fun he had destroying people and things, what still nagged at him was that old white man clowning him in that Spic café. So the real fun now would be the git-back on the old man, because no racist white man muhfuh born of a woman would dis him and skate.

Air Jordan spent much of his time plotting revenge. He had already staked out the Acapulco and knew Mac's car and when Mac and Puddin would be there. Getting even was important, but getting away with it was more important. Standing over some sucker and laughing down on him as his life flickered, he liked that. Then to get so close the chump can see your eyes, and knowing that the chump will take your face with him to the satin, Air Jordan liked that, too. But how to hurt the old white man to his heart was the game now—how to hurt him so bad he wanted to be dead but had to go on living with what you did to him, that was the kind of git-back that made your dick get hard, the kind that was better than getting your nut.

Blind the old fuck? Cripple him? Maybe just set him on fire and watch him dance? Air Jordan enjoyed watching Mac and Puddin sweating their asses off putting the taco joint back in business. He knew they knew who smeared the shit on the fighters' photos. As far as Air Jordan was concerned, he knew all he needed to know about Mac and Puddin.

Air Jordan and his homeys hung out in front of a liquor store at Hooper and Slauson. "Check it out," he said. "You know a punk routine, you know the punk, see what I'm sayin? Once you know the punk, he yours, understand what I mean?, he be like you bitch and that what you want, right? The little fighter now, he eat in taco town every night startin around six-thirty, seven o'clock. He come on the bus from Not Long, or he come wit the old white man in the car, and then they bof eat. Every night except Saturday and Sunday. Now the boy check in the café around three-thirty when he get his little bus a Not Long every day except Saturday. That when he get a bus at ten-thirty, come home from the gym one-thirty, two o'clock. Sunday no bus and the café close and the boy stay wit his mama."

Air Jordan had never seen Cannonball.

"Now that beaner lady, she live on Forty-fifth off Compton wit her two girls that are nurses somewhere. They help the old lady sometime, and the old lady got a wetback dishwasher come in at noon and leave at eight-thirty, quarter a nine. That old lady, now, she come in at nine in the morning and go out ten o'clock at night, maybe later. After nine at night is when we go in do our business wit the old bitch."

"How you know all this?" grinned Fridge, the sixteen-year-old. "You sumpin else."

"It my business to know it, what you think? An' the way I see it, the best way to play the old man is to play him by he chickenshit Olympic, ain't that right?"

"Wait, man, Olympic a brothuh," said Shareef, one of the two-hundred-pounders.

"Fuck a brothuh. We go kill the old man, we in shit because he white. No good. So we go through the Olympic brothuh to get to the old man, hear what I'm sayin?, because to the po-lice, Olympic just one more dead nigga in a ice box wit a paper tag tied on a toe."

"Air Jordan cold," said Fridge.

"Cold how you stay alive," said Air Jordan. "That why we make our move in two ways, not just one. We ruin that Olympic, see?, but we only lean on the old lady, know what I'm sayin? We want her alive because she the money machine, like check it out, I see a hundred a day from her to start, then I up it from there."

"Air Jordan be trippin," said Emil, the other two-hundred-pounder.

Air Jordan said, "All we need is five mom-and-pops. That five hundred a day. Time six, that three thousand a week, and fuck Nike."

Air Jordan's homeboys looked at him like he'd led them to the Promised Land.

"Air Jordan be trippin!"

"When we goin back for tacos?" said Fridge.

"Saturday morning at eleven be a good time, Olympic already long gone. The old lady'll have money from Friday night and even more from Saturday night comin out her pussy because she got no way to get to the bank, can you dig it? Talk to her in the morning, make her shit her drawers, then go back at night collect what ours."

"What if she call the po-lice?"

"So what? No witness. After I talk wit her, she give us her money because she love us."

"When we go after that uppity-ass Puddin Mr. Olympic?" asked Fridge, his eyes already dead at sixteen.

"We get the boy when the time right. First we get the money. Puddin hear about that, chump'll come to us."

Air Jordan staked out the Acapulco for two more days. He also took some photos of the señora's daughters with a Polaroid camera he grabbed from a Hollywood camera shop during the riots. The pictures came out just fine.

"I just got the call from Vegas about my featherweight, Enrique," said Mac. "Eight rounds preliminary at the Mirage."

Puddin was toweling off after his workout on Wednesday afternoon. His weight had dropped to 182, and Mac didn't want him down to 178 until a few days before his first fight in Barcelona, so he had him just work the mitts and the bags and do sit-ups.

"Cannonball and Enrique and I'll be driving up tomorrow morning."

"When you be back?"

"Saturday afternoon. No big thing. Not Long'll be closed, so I want you to go to Sewing Machine gym tomorrow, Friday, and Saturday. You gotta go in early, remember, because Saturday they close around one-thirty, two."

"They know I'm comin?"

"I just called over there. But just a light workout, okay? Run easy in the mornings like always, then shadowbox, do the rope and sit-ups. You're weight's good, so we don't have to sweat that, and so's your wind."

"When you say you be back?"

"Enrique fights Friday night, so we'll start back about nine Saturday morning."

"How long it take?"

"Six hours, give or take. Maybe a little longer because first we got to drop Enrique off in Carson."

"I see you Saturday night?"

"Yeah. I been promising Cannonball a steak dinner at the Pantry."

"Yeah!"

Air Jordan and his homeys had been up all night partying. At nine o'clock Saturday morning, they pistol-whipped a woman and hijacked her van in a market parking lot near Hawthorne Boulevard and Sepulveda in the South Bay. It was a part of town, going west toward the beach, that was upscale and 95 percent white, an area where new vehicles were plentiful. They struck at nine because morning traffic would be light and because Saturday cops would still be having coffee at their favorite donut shop. Once they were back in South Central, L.A. cops wouldn't be looking for a South Bay van. They switched license plates on the spot and drove leisurely away. Air Jordan put on a blond ponytail wig.

Fridge slouched down on a backseat. It had taken less than two minutes.

Shareef and Emil drove Jordan's car, a dark, nondescript '86 Ford, taking the four guns with them in case Air Jordan and Fridge got popped. Even so, Air Jordan wouldn't give up his cane. The two vehicles would travel by different routes and meet at a chop shop in Maywood, where they would receive five hundred dollars for their work. From there, the plan was to head to the Acapulco. But on the way, Air Jordan got hungry for breakfast—for some more crack cocaine, each little rock in its own small plastic bag. Because it was still early, it took them longer to score than they expected, but once they had lit up, they shared a small, tar-crusted glass pipe. Inhaling deeply, Air Jordan began to feel his invincible self again. So instead of driving directly to the chop shop, he decided to first go by the Acapulco, where he'd terrorize the señora, impress Fridge, and have some fun.

Fridge jingled like a set of keys. "Bitch give us shit, I make her piss in a glass and drink it."

"My man."

Air Jordan pulled off his wig at 11:05 A.M. He parked the stolen van near the dog-leg turn on Compton Avenue, which was only a short block north of the Acapulco. He parked there to be out of the señora's line of sight, and so he and Fridge could approach the Acapulco from the rear.

At six o'clock that same morning, Puddin hit the street running. He'd stretched and warmed up and did his run at an easy pace, going the three miles in just under thirty minutes. Returning home, he showered, drank some grapefruit juice, and went back to bed. He woke again at nine. Air Jordan was beating a woman senseless at the time. Puddin did some homework while Willa fixed him a breakfast of hot cereal, toast with honey, and nonfat milk. He took his time, since he would be working out at Sewing Machine instead of Not Long, and finished with a crisp apple at ten-thirty. Willa was staring out the kitchen window. Her other two sons were playing catch in the driveway, but she didn't notice them.

"Anything wrong, Mama?"

"What? Well, yes, there always somethin wrong. But they always somethin right, too, like us. I was thinkin about all the folks got hurt by the riots. But we so lucky havin each other we blessed by God. I was thinkin about you daddy, too, thinkin how he up there helpin us, thinkin about how proud he must be of us all, specially a you."

"He a good daddy, my daddy."

Willa turned away so her son couldn't see the tears.

Air Jordan and Fridge quietly moved along a side wall of the Acapulco, then swiftly toward the door. Air Jordan slowly turned the knob, but the door didn't open. He tried again, then yanked at the door, but it was locked tight. He saw Señora Cabrera inside as she ran to the phone. He broke the door glass with the brass duck-head handle of his cane, reached in, and unlocked the door. He and Fridge stormed through, knocking the señora down as she tried to dial 911. Air Jordan ripped the phone from the wall. His wrist was bleeding from breaking the glass.

"Bitch!, why you make me cut mysef?" he yelled into the señora's face, causing her to wince. "Why you make me do you like this?"

He yanked her to her feet by her braid and slapped her hard. He was whispering calmly to her as Puddin got his old bike from the garage.

Air Jordan said, "Bitch, this what it is. We been too nice a you, protectin you Mex ass and not chargin you our regular price, understand what I'm sayin?, not stoppin in for what we earn?, but that shit all over wit now. Now you gonna pay what you owe."

"I no espeak Ingli."

"Don't be jivin me, ho!" Air Jordan shouted. "I put a broom handle up you pussy and pull it out you mouf!"

"I got no monies."

"See, you talk good as me. But you got plenty a money, so don't try a bullshit."

"No monies."

"No? No monies? You sure?" asked Air Jordan, his words pumped with crack cocaine. "Because you don't come up wit a hundred dollar a day, we go see you pretty little nursey daughters, know what I'm sayin? Cora and Dora whatever the fuck they name."

"I no espeak."

Air Jordan yanked the braid. "You speaky all right, bitch. So we be back tonight after you make all you money, understand what I'm sayin?, and since you lie a me about talkin Merican, we goin pick up all the money you owe us for every day this whole week. That six hundred dollar, mama, case you don't know. Maybe we have you fry up some shrimp, too, and put out a plate a fries, drink some a you Mexicano beer."

"Yeah!" said Fridge. "Drink up a whole mess a Mexicano beer!"

"Please go, for the name of God."

"Not so fast, mama. Startin this Monday, we be comin in every day for our hundred dollar, so git use to it."

"I got no money," said Señora Cabrera, but she was thinking of how she'd poison these *hijos de la chingada madre* sons of the fucked mother when they came in to eat. She had the *pistola* under her apron, but Air Jordan was so close that she knew he'd take it from her before she could fire.

Puddin left his house thinking to first go by the Acapulco and then head for Sewing Machine. He wore high-top white boxing shoes and dark blue sweats. On his back, in big, red block letters trimmed in white, was USA. He carried his gym bag on his handlebars.

Air Jordan showed the señora the color Polaroids he'd taken of her daughters. They were wearing their white nurse's uniforms as they were leaving the señora's white house. The señora leaned against a table, her knees ready to fold.

"Got no money, huh? Then you better git you some, hyuh?, because you don't, I give Cora and Dora some babies what look like me. You want them have some babies look like *me?*, understand what I'm tellin you? Or maybe me and my homeboys we run a *train* on Cora-Dora, *choo-choo!*, understand what I'm sayin?"

The señora understood, the faces of her beloved María and Magdalena clear in her mind, but her mouth went so dry from fear that she couldn't answer. She hoped Air Jordan wanted to eat. She'd feed him rat poison right now. She knew she had the will to do it, she knew that, but she was so terrified for her daughters that she couldn't translate from Spanish to English and continued to stand there dumbly.

Air Jordan turned the handle of his duck-head cane and pulled. The shiny blade of a grooved sword slid free of the cane. He let her see twenty inches of steel, then shoved it back into the cane. He carefully placed the bill of the brass duck against her left nipple.

"Check it out, maybe I won't give Cora-Dora a baby," he said. "But you don't come up wit our money tonight and every night, maybe I just cut Cora-Dora titties off instead, hear what I'm sayin'?, have you fry up some nipple tacos."

"I gib you money now."

"See there?" Air Jordan said to Fridge. "Money talk and bull-shit walk, like the man say." He looked the señora in the eyes from up close. "Somethin else, and you better understand this most a all: you call the po-lice, huh?, you shoot off you Taco Bell mouf a them, understand?, we come back and set you and Cora-Dora on fire in you little house. You be roastin inside because we fix the iron bars on the doors so you can't get out, hear what I'm sayin?"

"I gib you money."

"Every day. Say it."

"Ebry day. I tell no one. I gib you my money now."

She turned to the cash register, opened it, and began pulling bills from the drawer.

Fridge said, "*Look* out," pointing to the door.

Puddin had just pulled up and was lowering his kickstand.

Air Jordan turned back to the señora. "Leave the money in the drawer and close it," he said. "Now."

Puddin walked in. He hadn't pieced together the parked van and Air Jordan and was surprised. "What you want here?" he said.

Air Jordan said, "What you doin in here this late, my brothuh? It Saturday, you suppose a be at the gym by now sweatin."

"What you want here?" Puddin said again.

"Come in for McDonal, what you think?"

The señora signaled Puddin to leave, but he ignored her.

"You in the wrong place at the wrong time," Puddin told Air Jordan.

Again, the señora signaled Puddin to leave, not only for herself and her daughters, but also to protect Puddin.

"Why you dis me, man?" said Air Jordan. "I never say you mama a ho, I never say you little brothuhs take it in the ass for a dolla and give you change." Air Jordan smiled, having just said what he said he never said.

Fridge chimed in. "Fuck wit Air Jordan you find you ass scatter around town like used dick sacks on Saturday night."

Puddin knocked him out with a straight right, then came back with a left hook and knocked out Air Jordan.

He turned to Señora Cabrera. "They hurt you?"

"No yet."

· Puddin dragged both gangbangers out by their collars. He

dropped Fridge on the sidewalk and dumped Air Jordan on top of him. He pulled Air Jordan's pants and shorts down around his ankles. He went back for the cane, stuck the duck's head in the crack of Air Jordan's ass, and waited.

Fridge woke first, saw Puddin, and ran north on Compton, disappearing around the dog-leg turn.

Air Jordan woke a moment later, remained there blinking for a few groggy seconds, and then realized his pants were down. Lying on the sidewalk, he jacked his pants up. It was then he noticed Puddin standing there.

"What the fuck you doin a me, man?"

"I helpin you white ass get a tan, muthuhfucka."

Air Jordan reached for the cane, thinking to pull the sword, but thought better of it when he felt the lump on his jaw and realized that his vision wasn't clear. He fumbled with his belt and wobbled to his feet and then followed after Fridge. Looking over his shoulder, he said, "This you last time. Remember what I say, muhfuh, remember it for the rest a you life."

Puddin said, "I remember you mama turnin tricks and suckin white dicks."

The señora stood in the doorway shaking her head. "Now things get worse," she said under her breath. She looked over to Puddin and said, "When does Señor Mac come back?"

"Today," said Puddin. "Not long."

"No long," repeated the señora.

"They playin you for money again?, they say they hurt you or somethin?"

"No," she said. She would tell Mac everything when he got back.

Puddin was on his bike again. Crossing Long Beach Avenue, he was halfway to Sewing Machine. East of Long Beach was all Latino. Cars in the area were driven by men in straw sombreros, the backseats full of kids all speaking Spanish. Air Jordan was on Puddin's mind. He wished he hadn't lost his temper. Fighters who lose their tempers lose the fight.

Mac checked his watch. 11:45 A.M. He'd just driven through Baker, California. He figured that Puddin was halfway through his workout. Cannonball and Enrique were both asleep, Cannonball on the passenger side of the front seat with Mac, Enrique in the back. Mac reached for his cellular phone and dialed Puddin's number. Ordinarily, he wouldn't disturb the kid, but Mac was still excited about Enrique's fight, about the way Enrique had won, and wanted to tell Puddin.

Puddin was still on the bike when his phone rang. He fished it from his equipment bag and answered. "Talk a me about long-leg girls and piles a money!"

"It's the old man," said Mac.

"Say, Pops!"

"You in the gym?"

"On my bike. Got a setback," said Puddin.

"Enrique won, beat a good fighter, knocked him *out* in the third!"

"Awright!"

"Promoter wants us back for Enrique's first ten-round fight," said Mac.

"Awright, Enrique!" shouted Puddin. "Where you at?"

"About halfway to L.A. Be back in three, maybe four hours after we take Enrique home and dump my stuff at my place. You hungry?"

"Always hungry."

Mac continued. "Then we stop by Cannonball's so he can dump his stuff. We'll pick you up at your place around five."

"I'll be ready."

"What set you back?" asked Mac.

"Air Jordan."

Mac didn't say anything.

"You still there?" asked Puddin.

"Is the señora all right? Are you?"

"Oh, yeah. But some shit go down."

"Yeah? What kind?"

Puddin said, "He come in wit that hot dog punk Fridge. Did somethin to the señora, I don't know what. And they talk some shit in my face."

"And?"

"I put em bof asleep."

"Aw, shit. A fighter's supposed to be cool."

"Talk about my mama, what I'm suppose a do?"

Mac said, "Maybe it's better you just go on home now and hang there all day. I'm picking you up anyway."

"I'm almost at Alameda."

"Okay," said Mac. "But be careful."

"Air Jordan know better than mess wit me."

"Yeah, well, call me as soon as you get back home, all right?"

"Sure," said Puddin. "You think it all right we take my mama and my brothers a eat, too?"

"Why not?"

Puddin sped up, riding across the tracks on Alameda Street, which was divided for a stretch north and south of Vernon by railroad tracks. On either side of the tracks, traffic moved in both directions on the poorly paved roads. When a train passed through, traffic backed up and drivers cursed. Latino street vendors loved the train and did a brisk business with cursing drivers, selling chilled coconut meat, half flats of strawberries, ripe papayas, and slices of watermelon. Crossing Alameda, Puddin rode flat out the rest of the way to the gym.

Just before noon, he swung into the driveway of the 150-by-

250-foot bleached asphalt parking area going so fast that he almost collided with an exiting truck. Still at full speed, he crossed to the rear of the parking lot. He pulled up to a high chain-link fence next to the gym entrance and chained his bike to a metal pole supporting the gate. Going through the gate, he saw several Latino fighters who were already leaving, their gym bags heavy with sweated-out clothes, soaked equipment, and wet towels. They shook Puddin's hand and wished him luck in Barcelona. It made Puddin feel good that people he didn't know knew who he was.

What he didn't know was that Air Jordan and Fridge had followed him in the stolen van, had watched him chain his bike to the fence from the driveway on Vernon Avenue. Air Jordan met Fridge's cold eyes. Both nodded. Air Jordan smiled ever so slightly. They smoked another rock as Air Jordan drove carefully to the chop shop, which was only ten minutes away. Shareef and Emil were asleep in his car as he and Fridge delivered the van and collected. When Air Jordan woke them, Shareef said, "What the fuck happen y'all face?"

Emil said, "Shit, man, you look like you been fuckin wit a bear."

"That right, a big-ass Olympic bear. You ready go huntin?"

"Do Michael Jordan fly through the air?"

Air Jordan tucked his Walther inside his belt, Fridge did the same with a Beretta .40-caliber. The two-hundred-pounders had 357 Smith & Wesson revolvers with six-inch barrels that made the stainless steel weapons look a foot and a half long. When all four drove back to Sewing Machine in Air Jordan's '86 Ford, Puddin's bike was still chained to the fence. They lit up another rock.

"Just remember," said Air Jordan. "The punk mine."

The gym was located in a manufacturing complex two blocks east of Alameda on Vernon Avenue. It was at the rear of one of the newer buildings; many of the grimy old brick sweatshops and poured-concrete warehouses had broken windows and were boarded up. Connected to the west side of Sewing Machine's building was an empty loading dock several hundred feet long that during the week would be full. The large parking and loading area between the gym and the deserted buildings was used for a soccer field by Latino employees at lunchtime. Kids often used it on Saturdays and Sundays.

Air Jordan backed his car into the loading dock near the front of the lot, which was close to the driveway leading onto Vernon. He told Shareef and Emil to station themselves in doorways of two abandoned warehouses. Fridge was to hide behind some rusted-out trucks near the gym entrance until Puddin got on his bike. Once he started to ride, all four would converge on him from different angles.

"Then what?" said Fridge.

"Then mama start a cry and old man want a die."

Air Jordan waited like a cat in front of a mouse hole. A dozen or more fighters and trainers left the gym. Puddin wasn't among them because he was the last to finish working out. The remaining few left while he showered. He rolled his gym clothes and boxing shoes in a towel and put them in his gym bag with his wallet and phone. His blue sweats would keep him warm as he rode home. He was hungry, but put it out of his mind as he pulled on low-top gym shoes. Just before he left, the owner of Sewing Machine congratulated him for his spot on the Olympic team.

"You gonna win, ain'tcha?"

"Damn straight I'ma win."

"Good man," said the owner. "Do me a favor?" He handed Puddin a lock. "Lock the gate for me out back? I'll close up and go out the front door."

The temperature was in the low eighties, cool compared with the gym. Puddin closed and locked the gate. He unchained his bike from the fence, set his gym bag on the handlebars, and started slowly for home. He didn't notice anything at first, except that a dark car pulled out of the loading dock near the street. Then behind him he heard someone whistle. He turned and saw Fridge walking toward him. When he looked back the other way he saw Emil and Shareef, each walking quickly toward him from opposite sides of the parking lot. He started to ride for the street, pumping hard. But the dark car moved quickly to block him, and Puddin saw that Air Jordan was driving. Puddin made a run for it, pedaling as fast as he could toward the space between Air Jordan and Shareef, but they closed the distance, again blocking his way. He turned around and rode back toward the rear of the lot but realized that the only exit back there was the locked gate. He swung around, again racing past Fridge. He aimed for another space, this time between Air Jordan and Emil, but they were too quick for him and he retreated, this time riding in a circle within the shrinking space controlled by the approaching gangbangers.

"Say, dick sack," said Fridge. "It Saturday-night scatter time."

Puddin rode straight at him, swinging his gym bag as a weapon. Fridge pulled his gun and Puddin veered off.

Air Jordan grabbed his cane, set the brake in his car, and got out yelling. "Put you shit away, fool. It daytime!"

Fridge yelled back. "He fuck wit me, I stop that shit *now!*"

"You start that shit, all them beaner drivin by see us!"

"They see us now!"

"No good. What the beaner see now a gang a niggas playin basketball on a playground."

Puddin saw that he couldn't escape on the bike, so he got off and set the kickstand. He held on to his bag and backed away, hoping to get an angle and break through. He wanted to wade into them, but he knew that wouldn't work. If he could break through, he knew he could outrun them all to the street. Once there, he'd be gone, running full-bore against the flow of cars on first one, then the other side of Alameda until he lost them in traffic or between a building someplace. They wouldn't use their guns in plain sight, not in heavy traffic. The trick was to get Air Jordan to lead, so he could counter. He wasn't afraid of these crooks, he was afraid of losing, because he knew what that meant.

Air Jordan danced toward him, tapped his cane on the asphalt several times, then danced back. "You goin jump, froggy, huh? you goin jump?"

Fridge darted in, then back out. Then Emil and Shareef did the same, closing the circle by another two feet. Puddin knew that if he could break free, he'd zigzag, run low to the ground, and hope they'd miss him if they decided to fire their weapons. It wasn't much, but he'd seen victims of gang attacks and didn't want to join them in the ground.

Air Jordan rushed in with his cane again, tapping it near Puddin's feet and trying to get him to grab for it. If he did, Puddin knew they'd be on him like wild dogs.

"Boy," said Air Jordan, "that old man, he you daddy?"

"Who wanta know?"

"You brothuh want," said Air Jordan, trying to distract Puddin with words because he didn't want any more being knocked out again. "He ain't you daddy, what you doin wit him?"

"He my friend," said Puddin, stalling for time.

Air Jordan feinted with his cane, drew back. "No white piece a shit a friend of a brothuh. When a brothuh a friend of a white man, he ain't no brothuh no more, he a traitor to he race."

Still hanging on to his gym bag, Puddin moved around behind his bike. "Then check it out. I say Mac my daddy."

"Say he got a white man for a daddy!" shouted Emil, who began to hoot.

"That right, same as Air Jordan," said Puddin, taunting Air Jordan where he knew it hurt most. He next used Air Jordan's own words against him. "What wrong, green-eye froggy, huh?, you ain't goin a jump froggy, huh?, you four-to-one ain't enough for you chickenshit white froggy ass?"

"You a honky-lover nigga," Air Jordan taunted back.

"That right," said Puddin, "same as you mama."

"Ohhh," said Fridge, "dick sack be talkin trash!"

Air Jordan did a stutter step, going in a little closer each time, trying to get Puddin off balance and moving him further back in the lot. Puddin could see that the other three were waiting on Air Jordan, so he knew to go for Air Jordan first and hope to take the fight out of the others when their leader went down. But he had to bide his time, wait for either Air Jordan or one of the others to commit themselves. The circling dance continued.

"Fuck this," said Emil, walking in, punching.

Puddin threw the gym bag, forcing Emil to lift his hands to protect his face, and then Puddin dropped him in agony, nailing him full force with a straight right to the kidney and a left hook to the face that broke his nose. Emil went down, doubled into a tight ball. He was grunting with pain, and blood rolled from his nose and down along his cheek.

The others started to close in. Puddin swung his bike by its rear wheel and whacked Fridge in the face with the front tire. It knocked him down, but he wasn't hurt, and he rolled off to one side. Puddin threw the bike at Air Jordan, the handlebars opening a deep cut on the side of Air Jordan's head and knocking him to his knees.

"Git him!" Air Jordan screamed. "Git him!"

Puddin pivoted to his right and connected with a hook to the solar plexus that dropped Shareef flat, made him think he was dying. But Puddin tripped over his bike when Air Jordan threw it in front of him. Puddin rolled, found his feet, and then took three running steps toward Vernon Avenue as he rose. He thought he'd broken free. He straight-armed Air Jordan, but Fridge tackled him from behind. It didn't hurt, but it slowed him down enough for Air Jordan to kick him in the eye. The pain knocked him down again, but he kept trying for the street. Air Jordan shoved him off balance, then swung his cane at Puddin's head. Puddin slid under it, but the duck's bill ripped a hole in the side of his neck.

Puddin landed a glancing right to Fridge's face, knocking him down again, then dropped Emil with double hooks to the body that cracked three ribs and made him yelp like a dog. Puddin jumped on his bike thinking he now had room to make it, but Air Jordan jammed his ebony cane in the spokes of the front wheel and Puddin went over the handlebars, striking his head full force on the ground. Half conscious, he still tried to get up, but Air Jordan pulled the sword from the cane and ran him through just below the ribs.

The blade pierced a kidney and the stomach, and Puddin went down face-first, gasping. Air Jordan hopped across him and shoved the sword into his back, the blade going through the A of USA. The sword split a rib and pierced a lung. Blood from the puncture sprayed from Puddin's nose and spurted from his mouth, bubbled out of his back with each gasp. Puddin swayed to his feet, felt himself going out, and fell again. He clamped his mouth tight shut, trying to keep back his blood, but he coughed and red erupted from his nose and mouth again. He gagged on the blood, which made it gush from him all the more. He wasn't dead yet, but he knew he had been killed. His body began to jerk and shudder from shock and loss of blood, his heart pumping out of control.

"Shoot the nigga," said Fridge. "Git it over wit, shit!"

"No good," said Air Jordan, holding a hand to his bloody head as he extracted the sword. He got down close to Puddin's eyes. "Punk be dyin on he own blood, can you dig it?, but he still got time a think about me before he check on out."

Shareef said, "Air Jordan be trippin."

Air Jordan grabbed up Puddin's equipment bag, and all four ran for his car. Inside, Air Jordan rifled through the bag, finding the wallet, then the phone. He first covered his fingers with the towel so there wouldn't be fingerprints and then took three dollar bills from the wallet. He tossed the wallet and scattered the contents of the bag on the ground but kept Puddin's phone.

"But the po-lice see that wallet, they know who he is."

"That what we want," said Air Jordan, holding a rag to his head.

Knowing Puddin was dying back at the rear of the lot, they drove slowly to the driveway at Vernon Avenue, blaring rap music from the car radio echoing between the buildings. They entered traffic as if nothing had happened, and none of the other drivers noticed them.

Puddin gagged on his blood. He tried to rise again but couldn't; he tried to pull himself over to Vernon but couldn't.

"*Confiteor Deo Omnipoténti,*" he said, the Latin gurgling in his throat. "I confess to Almighty God."

He couldn't finish because blood choked the channel of his throat and he couldn't breathe. He coughed to clear it, then got to one elbow, dipped two fingers in his blood, and fell back. He forced himself up again, and using his blood for ink, printed the letter *A* ten inches high on the light-gray asphalt. Consuming the last of his life, he dipped his fingers into his blood again, this time printing a ten-inch *J* next to the *A* . . . *AJ.* He coughed a great spray of blood across himself, then slid back down, the earth spinning off and away from under him.

Henry Puddin Pye cooked in the sun for an hour and a half. It wasn't long before flies found him, began crawling up his nose. Ants walked across his vacant eyes. At three-thirty that same afternoon, a group of Mexican children eight and ten years old found him, were shocked and intrigued by what they saw. The oldest ran to the gas station on Vernon and Alameda and told the Iranian owner what was there. He dialed 911.

Earlier in the day Mac had stopped in San Bernardino to feed Enrique and Cannonball. Now it was 4:15 P.M. and he had hoped to drop off Enrique and leave, but he and Cannonball had to stay for a bottle of cold Bohemia with Enrique's family, ecstatic over his win. As Mac and Cannonball swung from the 405 to the 110 Freeway that would take them to Mac's place in Gardena, Mac was concerned that Puddin hadn't called him. Air Jordan was on Mac's mind, so he dialed Puddin's number. It was answered on the first ring.

"Yeah," said Air Jordan.

"Who's this?" Mac asked.

"Who you think?"

"Is this Puddin's number?"

"Puddin who?"

"Puddin the fighter." Mac by then recognized the voice, and his head arched back in pain.

Air Jordan heard the worry in Mac's voice, smiled, and hung up. He flicked the phone to off and smiled again. A white strawberry from Memphis was sucking him off.

Mac called back. A recorded message informed him that his party was away from the phone.

Mac immediately called Señora Cabrera. "You seen Puddin this afternoon?"

"Only this morning."

"Air Jordan was in there again, right?"

"Pudeen make hin leave."

"What did Jordan say to you?"

"He want money or he hurt my girls."

"I'll be there as soon as I can."

What Mac couldn't know at the time was that the police arrived four minutes after the 911 call. They reported the murder to the desk sergeant by radio, and he contacted the coroner's office. While the coroner's investigation proceeded, several members of the crew saw the letters *AJ* but at the time couldn't make a connection. Once finished, they transported Puddin's body to the morgue and contacted Willa.

"The coroner wonders if you could please come down? We need you to identify someone?"

"Identify who?" whispered Willa, dread fluttering through her.

"We believe his name is Henry Pye."

"What he look like?"

"He can best be described as being a male African-American, as being eighteen years of age, as being six feet one inch in height, as weighing one hundred eighty pounds, and as having short, black curly hair."

Father Carey drove Willa, her two boys, and her sister Daisy to the morgue. Willa and Father Carey were ushered to a chilled glass cubicle with one small overhead light that lit the top end of a metal gurney. On it lay a body covered in white. Beside it was a stainless steel chair. The attendant pulled back the sheet, and Willa let out a low moan. She kissed Puddin's closed eyes and touched his lips. She sat down beside him and kissed the torn skin and broken knuckles of his hands.

"Wake up, baby, you my angel child, you my baby man." She looked up to Father Carey, still unable to accept what was before her. "Wake him up, Father, this my dream baby. This my angel child."

After speaking with the señora on the phone, Mac forgot about going home and drove straight for Not Long. He wanted to telephone Willa but was afraid.

When they pulled into Not Long's parking lot, Cannonball said, "Best call."

Mac dialed Willa's cellular number, knowing that she always carried the phone with her. A man's voice answered.

"Who's this?" Mac demanded.

"This is Father Carey."

"This is Mac McGee, Father. Is Willa all right?"

"I'm about to drive her home."

"Where are you?"

"It's Puddin. We're leaving the morgue now."

Mac shouted. "What are you doin in the goddamned morgue?"

"I'm sorry to tell you. It's Puddin."

"He can't be dead! How can Puddin be dead, for Christ's sake? How could God let that happen? Why not take me?"

"Ah, Mac, if I knew that, I'd be God himself, wouldn't I now?"

"How did Puddin die?"

"Someone did it."

"Where?"

"In a parking lot. Some gym on Vernon."

"Sewing Machine?"

"That was it."

"How?"

"Some kind of sharp instrument. Maybe a sword."

Cannonball watched Mac, then lightly touched his shoulder.

Mac said, "I'll see you at Willa's, Father."

The priest said, "Mac?"

"Yeah?" said Mac. His chest had caved in.

"Don't do anything, understand me?"

"What's to do, Father? A hundred percent of nothin's nothin."

They first drove to the Acapulco. It was busy, but the señora came straight to them, worry in her face.

"Where Pudeen?"

"Puddin's—" Mac couldn't say it.

"He passed," said Cannonball.

"He die for me," said the señora, reaching for the gold Virgin of Guadalupe medal at her neck. "Where it happen?"

"At Sewing Machine, they say. Other side of Alameda," said Mac.

"It was the ugly."

"I think so, too. But I got no proof."

"I should hab poison hin the firs night."

It was still light as Cannonball pulled into the parking area next to Sewing Machine. Broken red bicycle-reflector glass and wads of yellow police tape at the rear of the lot drew them to where Puddin was murdered. When they got out of the car, they saw the rusty dried blood. Mac went down on his knees, then down on his face. "My baby boy." He wanted to die.

Cannonball knelt beside him, patted him. "Puddin a good boy, Mac, he all right now, he fine where he at now."

Mac got to his feet and stumbled around the wash of bloodied asphalt. He passed near the *AJ* Puddin had left, but the angle was wrong and he didn't see what it was.

But Cannonball saw it and knew what Puddin had left them. "Muthuhfucka," said Cannonball, pointing. His heart felt like it turned sideways in him. "We got proof now."

Mac saw it and his blood pounded through him like a madman racing down a tile hall. Parts of him flooded, other parts went dry. He covered his mouth to stifle a howl and forced himself to remain on his feet. He squeezed out the words, "Let the good times fuckin roll."

Cannonball drove to Willa's, but the house was dark. "C'mon back the gym, res' a minute. When she home, we come on back."

At Not Long, Cannonball brought out a half-empty bottle of Manischewitz concord-grape sacramental wine. He filled two jelly glasses.

"This my Manisherry I drink sometimes I be down."

The two old men each drank a glass of the powerful sweet wine, then a second. Neither felt the alcohol. Mac shuddered, then lost control and wept. Cannonball sat silently in the darkness, his woolen blue cap low over his eyes.

Mac wiped his face. It was after eight. He called Willa again and Father Carey answered.

"She's holding up, but it's sad to see."

"Should I come over?"

"Daisy, the boys, and a houseful of friends are with her now. Willa asked if you could come by later so you two can talk alone. She's a mighty woman," said the old Irish priest.

"I'll come by after nine sometime."

Mac hung up and noticed that Cannonball grimaced. "What's the matter?" Mac asked.

"This Air Jordan boy, he know you car?"

"Might."

"We take my old pickup, you stay down low," said Cannonball, pulling on a faded khaki windbreaker. "But first lemme get Lena."

Cannonball and Mac cruised the streets around the Acapulco but had no luck finding Air Jordan. At 9:15 Mac gave up for that night.

"Let's go to Willa's," he said.

At 9:18 they slowly passed the Acapulco again. The last diners had gone, but the lights were still on inside as Mac and Cannonball looked over. A nondescript dark car was in a parking space. From it, Air Jordan and his homeys slid out. Three strutted for the door. Emil, the last, hugged his cracked ribs. Cannonball drove on. He passed the dog-leg turn going north on Compton, then made a U-turn up the block. Neither he nor Mac had said a word.

Cannonball pulled over to the curb. TV lights flickered against the drawn blinds of the little, boxy 1920s houses that lined the dark street. Barred windows added to the hurt.

Cannonball said, "You get out here, baby, I park up the block. Once I inside, you wait a lick and then come in right behind wit Mist Glock spittin fire."

"Yeah, but what if the señora gets hurt?"

"What if they in there hurtin her right now?"

Mac wanted to dance in their blood, but he knew that he could never shoot first unless it was clear someone's life was in danger. He wanted to kill more than he wanted to live, but still he didn't want anyone to get hurt—the Christian dilemma. But for the señora's sake and Cannonball's, he had to think things through. "What if we wait for them ouside? Citizen's arrest, take them in the dark, get them in their car?"

Cannonball understood. "But what if they see us outside? What happen they grab the lady?, split wit her?, see us and start shootin? What we do then? Naw, we got to be quick."

Mac tapped his cellular phone. "We could call the police."

"What the po-lice goin do but talk, huh? We the ones wit evidence."

"You're right, but I go in first," said Mac.

"No good," said Cannonball. "They know you, so that leave me. I go in first, play the fool. Now they thinkin about me and you come on in. If they packin, I turn Lena loose in they ass so deep they think they be sittin on whale dick."

"What if they've already drawn weapons?"

"They crazy, but cut on that old lady?, naw!"

"I'm talking about guns," said Mac.

"So what?, like Miles Davis say. This our one shot for Puddin, and maybe for cuttin loose the lady."

"All right," said Mac. "But be careful. Be old and look poor."

"I be so pitiful they think I dead," said Cannonball.

Mac got out of the truck and Cannonball pulled forward. As he drove, he took Lena from his belt at the middle of his back. Already cocked, the .45 had one round in the chamber, seven in the magazine. He tucked the weapon under his left armpit, clamped it in place with his arm, and covered it with his jacket.

Mac followed, walking briskly, the cocked black Glock in his hand and pressed against his dark pant leg. Up ahead, Cannonball was nearing the Acapulco, could hear the blaring Mexican music Air Jordan had turned up to intimidate the señora.

Inside, Air Jordan was waving his cane and screaming into the señora's face. "Bitch!, whatchu mean!, you don't pay me my money? You lookin at sudden death!"

"Kill me, I don't care, do it," said the señora, her Indian eyes black as obsidian. "You can't hurt me no more."

"I can't, huh? I cut your pussy off, make you eat it, cunt hair and all, I can do that, bitch!"

"I gib you no money, you kill Pudeen."

"Who say? How you know that?"

"I know," said the little Mexican lady. "And Señor Mac, he know. He kill you for me and for Pudeen."

"Who Mac?" Fridge demanded.

"Yeah," said Air Jordan. "He that old man in here talkin snakes and shit?"

"I talk to you no more."

Air Jordan jammed the barrel of his Walther into the señora's eyeball. Fireworks of pain flared in her face, but she didn't cry out.

"Gimme my money, I shoot you dead now!"

"Do it. But you die, too. Ebrybody die."

Emil clutched his cracked ribs, winced with every breath. "C'mon man, this gettin messy, let's forget it."

"Fuck messy. The bitch owe me too much, and she know me too much."

"Shit yeah," said Fridge, drawing his Beretta. "Bitch got a die she holdin back on our money, man!"

Fridge pushed the no-sale key on the register with the muzzle of his gun, and the empty cash drawer sprung open.

Seeing it, Air Jordan hit the señora in the head twice with the Walther, knocking her down. "Where my six hundred dollar?" He jerked her to her feet again and pulled her close so he could see her eyes when he shot her. He shoved the short, stainless steel barrel into her mouth.

Before Air Jordan could pull the trigger, Cannonball shuffled through the door. Air Jordan whirled, aiming the Walther at Cannonball's face. The señora gave no hint that she knew the shabby old man.

Air Jordan continued to shout, veins bulging in his dreadful face, crack cocaine toasting his brain. "Who you, muthuhfucka?, whatchu doin in here?"

"Oh, no, Lord have mercy, put that down, don't shoot! I not doin nothin brothuh man, I jus' a hongry ol' nigga come in a res', get me a fish taco."

"You get you black ass tore up you come flat-footin in like that!" shouted Air Jordan. "What the fuck you want?"

"Fish, dass it," said Cannonball. He stepped from one foot to the other, like the floor was hot. "But now I don't want nothin, no suh, I be gone!"

"Who you wit?"

"I all alone, jus' one po' old man not lookin fo' no trouble." Cannonball took his cap off, held it to his chest to cover any part of Lena that might be bulging. Still stepping, he turned the cap by its leather band in supplication. "You got no trouble wit me, man, I so po I don't shit."

"What these changes you be takin me through, fool?" said Air Jordan, his voice going into falsetto. "All peoples gotta shit!"

"Dass right, boss man, but I don't get a eat much, dass all I sayin. It all right I go now?"

"Hell, no, it ain't all right. What you see when you come in here?"

"Nothin, man, forget dat, I got me dis bad eye here, see?, so I don't never know what I see."

"You goin a see what I'ma do a this bitch, so you know what I do a you funky old ass you start flappin you lips."

"Yeah, right, you da man. I don't be talkin a nobody, no suh, like I say, man, I don't even shit."

"Man," said Fridge, his brain as toasted as Air Jordan's, "you sure you don't shit?"

"Only when I has to."

Cannonball had done his job, got all four gangbangers looking at him instead of at the door. But he hadn't expected that Fridge and Air Jordan would have needed guns to handle the señora. He hoped Mac would stay out so maybe they could take Air Jordan some other way, but the bell for the fight had rung, and he knew better.

Outside, Mac had come along the rear of the building and was watching from the shadows. One of the señora's eyes was swollen shut, and blood trickled down from her hair. Air Jordan and Fridge were waving their weapons as if they were directing a movie. Mac knew that if he went in firing, no matter how good he was, he'd be up against two dope-heads with drawn weapons, one of them still aimed at Cannonball.

There is a saying in the sweet science, that game of lies, You box a puncher and you punch a boxer. It wasn't much to go on, but Mac had to get the señora and Cannonball safely out of the Acapulco. So he decided to box, to stick and move, to take Air Jordan into the later rounds—to mind-fuck. As far as Mac was concerned, what happened to him no longer mattered, so he slipped the Glock next to his belly, and with his hands held high, he calmly walked through the door.

"Look who here!" said Air Jordan. "It Peter fuckin Rabbit!"

Fridge aimed his .40-caliber at Mac, while Shareef did the same with his .357. Air Jordan checked outside and, satisfied that Mac was alone, came back in smiling.

"Where you car?"

"Took a cab. Was on my way over to Puddin's house when I saw you boys inside. You know about Puddin, right?"

"Us boys, huh? Took a taxi, huh?"

Mac could see that Air Jordan didn't know whether to believe him. Mac could also see the damage Puddin had done to Air Jordan and the others, see the splashes of dried blood on their baggy pants, the spots on their new white shoes.

Air Jordan said, "What the taxi-company phone number?"

"No idea. I forgot to get gas, what with all that's been going on, and I ran out. I hailed a cruising cab."

"Jive ass, ain't no cabs cruisin these parts, you think I a fool?"

"I was in Beverly Hills."

"Beverly Hill, huh? Yeah, that make sense, uppity old cracker like you in the land a Lojack and Jew-boys in ponytails."

Cannonball tried for a better angle, began to shuffle to the door. "Maybe I jus' go on over Odessa Johnson's You Buy We Fry fo' my fish."

"You ain't goin shit, nigga," said Air Jordan. "You know this here pig?"

"Nooo, suh, uh-uh, I don't know no white folk."

"You sure, old man?"

"Where I live, how I'ma know white folks, sheeuh, man? I jus' a po' old nigga wit trouble my own, uh-uh, I jus' come in for my wife Lena, take a little somethin home."

"Sit down," said Air Jordan. "I want you to see this pig die squealin."

"It best you don't be killin no white folk, no suh."

"You don't hear him dissin me?"

"No, I don't hear nothin, and I don't see nothin, dass me."

"Let him go," said Mac. "And the lady, too. I'm the one you want, right?"

"All I know about you is we goin a fry some snake and you the snake, *boy*."

"Maybe you will, and maybe you won't." Mac grinned at him, upped the stakes again. "Either way, Puddin kicked the shit out of all four of you punks, right?"

"I say scatter all of 'em, Jor, shit," said Fridge. "Do it now before some Mexes come through the door nex."

Air Jordan glowered at Mac. "You just like that Puddin Pye punk, right?, you in the wrong place at the wrong time. Ain't that right, Fridge?, he in the wrong goddamn place at the wrong goddamn time."

"Bad luck what it is," said Fridge, starting to laugh, "but if these muhfuhs don't have bad luck, they won't have no luck at all."

He and Air Jordan slapped hands.

Mac said, "Looks to me like you're the one with no luck."

Air Jordan laughed, the hard cackle coming from high in his throat. "Listen at this."

"I'm serious," Mac said. "Just think, when you clown me, you could be clowning someone in your family."

Emil stifled a laugh, the pain in his ribs cutting through him. Air Jordan stared him down. Turning back to Mac, he placed Puddin's cellular phone on the table for Mac to see.

"You sure you want a be talkin this family shit wit me, honky muthuhfucka?"

"Hey, talk bad all you want about honkies," said Mac. "But when you talk bad about this honky, don't forget that you could be talkin bad to your own daddy, ain't that right? Yeah, I think I remember your mama, two-dollar ho, a colored bitch, right?, ugly, same as you."

Air Jordan moved the Walther slowly from his right hand to his left, then pulled the sword from his cane. "I'ma send you a hell the way I send you little chickenshit Olympic." Air Jordan spat in Mac's face, then suddenly began to swing the sword like a saber, chopping chunks of meat from Mac's face and arms when Mac tried to cover up. In the instant before Cannonball could draw Lena, the señora fired her *pistola* wildly at Air Jordan, missing with two rounds, but she blew his right ear off with the third. Fridge knocked the .44 from her hand to the floor. Just as Air Jordan stumbled and grabbed the right side of his head, Cannonball shot him twice in the groin, the .45 sending Air Jordan backward over a table and onto the floor, his gun lost under the furniture. Fridge shot the señora four times as she stooped for her gun, but before he could fire on Mac, Mac dropped him with three rounds to the chest, the pattern small as a woman's hand. Emil tried to run, but Mac blew the back of his head off. Shareef blinked uncontrollably through the smoke and unholy noise and started aimlessly to pull the trigger of his Magnum. Five shots missed. Cannonball dropped to the floor. Shareef squeezed off the sixth round as Cannonball caught him in the stomach and chest with two more from Lena that blew out most of his back. Cannonball kept pulling the trigger until Lena was empty, but Shareef's last round had caught Mac in the throat, the hollow point blowing away Mac's left carotid artery and breaking his neck. Mac fell like a shot bird, but he lived long enough to watch his blood form into a pool around his face.

Cannonball was choking on the smoke. He was stunned from the noise and the violence, and his ears felt full of dirt. He flexed his jaw, but his ears continued to hum, and the wild mariachi music came through elongated, sounded bent as it bounced off the hard walls. He crawled over to Mac, tried mouth-to-mouth resuscitation on him, but his breath bubbled uselessly out of Mac's torn windpipe. Cannonball closed Mac's eyes, gently touching them with his fingertips. He did the same for the señora, who sat crumpled against a wall, her red mouth hanging open.

As Cannonball slumped in near-collapse, he heard something behind him, and gunless, he turned in panic. Air Jordan pulled a chair across himself as he tried to rise, then fell back. Cannonball scuttled back for Mac's Glock.

Air Jordan went falsetto again, his voice a high whine. "You a crazy man you kill my dick it be shot clean off brothuhs ain't suppose a scatter a brothuh you don't know that?"

Cannonball said, "You ain't my brothuh. You a wrinkle on Michael Jackson nasty white dick."

"My color not my fault."

"Nothin never you fault."

"How could you do this a me, man?"

"It easy, nigga," said Cannonball, his black eyes invisible against his black skin. "You burn down my church."

Cannonball shot Air Jordan in the belly to make him scream. Then he shot him in the eye, the .45 taking most of his brain with it out the back of his skull.

Cannonball knew he had to quick get out of there, especially if someone had seen the shoot-out from the street and called the police. But first he collected his, Mac's, and the señora's guns and wrapped them in his jacket. Next, he covered his hand with a napkin and dialed 911. When the operator answered, he hung up and waited. The phone rang immediately, as Cannonball knew it would. He let it ring. A patrol car would be dispatched immediately. Cannonball knew he had two, maybe three minutes to disappear. He switched off the lights with his elbow, touched Mac one last time, and hurried to his truck. He was breathing deeply, but it didn't feel like he was getting any air.

He drove carefully back to the gym. He wanted a taste of his Manisherry, but he was so tired that he fell across his cot and went to sleep with his clothes on. He woke three hours later gasping for air and terrified, and he couldn't go back to sleep. He worried about Mac but was afraid to call and ask the police where he'd been taken. If they came around asking about Mac's car, he'd tell them that Mac had hailed a passing cab the night before. He tried to go back to sleep several times, but every time he closed his eyes, he relived the gunfight, blamed himself for not going through the door with Lena singing fire and lead from the git. To keep his mind from more somersaults, he cleaned and oiled all the guns. He polished Lena until she glowed.

Before sunrise, he wrapped Lena, the Glock, and the *pistola* separately in old newspapers. He secured them with adhesive tape from one of the rolls he used to wrap hands. He placed the three guns in the small gear bag he used when he worked local fights. At six o'clock he drove to Los Angeles Harbor in San Pedro. He took one of the first of the streamlined boats to Catalina Island, which was twenty-six miles off the coast and separated from the mainland by one of the deepest channels in the world.

He had the jimjams bad. The ninety-foot boat was less than a quarter full, but he felt hemmed-in. He also felt himself getting hostile and wanting to fight when people looked at him, and immediately he realized that his blood-sugar level had dropped critically low. He bought orange juice and a chocolate donut from the coffee bar and downed them so quickly that all he tasted was the sweet.

When he leveled off, he left the cabin and went to the stern of the boat, which cruised at better than thirty knots. The water was just a few feet beyond his reach. A young couple wearing USC sweatsuits and hiking boots embraced in the wind. When the boy tried to kiss her, the girl said she was cold and wanted a cappuccino with a chocolate-almond biscotto.

Cannonball noticed that the water shifted from green to a deep blue, and he looked up. He could see the mainland behind him and Catalina beyond. When he decided he'd gone halfway, he checked the cabin and saw that the passengers were either standing at the coffee bar or looking out the windows toward the island. Satisfied no one was watching him, he returned to the stern. He lifted the sports bag and reached in. He dropped Mac's gun into the water first, then the señora's. Both went down with a trail of bubbles behind them and were gone from sight immediately, despite their white wrappings.

Lena was Cannonball's baby, would be his last love, but he knew he had to let her go. He shook his head, then leaned over the rail as close to the water as he could. His fingers and toes were numb, and there was something wrong deep in his chest. His blue cap fell into the water, but he didn't care.

He opened his hand and let Lena drop into the water as gently as he could. He watched the package sink, but as it disappeared down, he had the feeling he was looking up. He coughed a gagging cough, a heart cough. *How long?* Cannonball thought, remembering the words of Martin.

He felt his knees going, and he settled to the wet deck. Slouched on his side, short of breath, he began to whisper slowly. *"One. Two. Three. Four. Five. Six."* At seven he reached up for the rail. He pulled hard. *"Seven. Eight."*

At the count of nine, Cannonball was on his feet.

"How long?" Cannonball said. "Not long."

Between Rounds:
An Acknowledgment

Special acknowledgment and gratitude go to my Wizard, Mr. Nat Sobel, of Sobel Weber Associates, who made a silk purse from a sow's ear.